Dragonsphere

The Fallen King Chronicles Book 1

RICHARD FIERCE

Cover design by Kuro Ishi.

ebook ISBN: 978-1-947329-02-7
Print ISBN-13: 978-1-427329-04-1

DEDICATION

To the few and the loyal; my fans.
Your support means the world to me.

CONTENTS

ACKNOWLEDGMENTS

This book was born in the nursery at City Church
Savannah in Savannah, Georgia while I was playing a game
with a young boy named Dorian. Many thanks to the boy
who helped inspire this story and had no idea what he was
doing. I miss you buddy!

-from the Book of Faith

INTRODUCTION

Year of the Divines 418

It was dark and cold. The distant sound of dripping water echoed throughout the narrow tunnel, part of a large system of interconnected passageways and caves deep in the Viss Mountains.

A hooded figure navigated his way through them hesitantly, pausing every few paces to run his fingers along the stone walls. He desperately wanted to light a torch, but he knew it was a foolish thought. If he brought light into that chamber …

The figure halted as he felt the familiar sigils on the wall. He had traveled through this cave many times now, yet it seemed he could never memorize his way to the central chamber within the mountain.

"I sense you." It was a sound unlike anything in his most insidious nightmares. "Come forth."

An intense fear overtook him. His breath came short and quick and he could feel his heart throbbing inside his chest. His hands began quivering so he clenched them into fists, hiding them within his robes. Closing his eyes momentarily, he forced a deep breath before stepping into the chamber.

Every rational thought told him to flee. A horrible feeling wriggled its way into his heart, melting his resolve like wax in a fire.

"You have carried out my instructions?"

The man crumbled to his knees. He could almost feel it hovering around him, able to see everything while he was as blind as a bat.

It was more of a demand than a question. The man could barely speak and meekly nodded his head. "I have arranged the bones in the cave as you said." Something colder than ice touched his shoulder, causing his entire arm to go numb. It could only be the touch of his unholy master.

"You have pleased me. I shall reward your obedience when all falls into place." It seemed to him that the words slithered across the cave like snakes, wrapping themselves around him.

"Yes … m-my … lord."

"They thought they destroyed me. But I cannot be destroyed … no, I am eternal. And now … I will unleash hell upon the land."

The man looked around futilely in the dark cave and could see nothing. But he could feel it. A shudder in the ground, a tremor in the walls. He could hear loose rocks clattering against each other as the rumbling grew stronger.

A wicked, cackling laughter erupted, making him flinch unexpectedly. Then silence. Suddenly there was a loud cracking sound, as if something were splitting open. He heard the roar echo out across the mountains, but he also heard the distinct sound of flapping wings.

An ancient and mighty creature had been awakened.

The man couldn't help but wonder: *what have I done?*

Death was coming. A dragon was coming.

"All of history bears false witness.
Truth is only known by those who were present."

-from the Book of Faith

CHAPTER 1

Year of the Divines 419

When rumors of a dragon attack reached Demetrius, he dismissed them almost immediately. Having lived in the port city of Radda his entire life, he had heard many wild stories from countless travelers. Everything ranging from giant squids in the open seas to horses with wings. Admittedly this *was* the first time he heard mention of a dragon, supposed giant mythical creatures that fed on the fear of people and could lay waste to entire cities.

"Rubbish," he said. "Children's tales told by parents to scare little ones into obedience."

"I believe it," the old sailor remarked enthusiastically. "Captain heard it 'imself. Says the whole city was burned to the ground and everyone killed."

"Then how did your captain hear of it?" Demetrius eyed his friend sternly. The man's face was covered in wrinkles and his hair bleached from constant sun. The man had been a sailor since he was not more than a boy and was prone to believe almost anything.

"What d'ya mean?" the sailor, Bannigan, asked.

"If everyone was killed, how did your captain hear this story? Who would have repeated it to him?"

The old man remained silent for a moment and scratched his prickly-haired chin. "It not be my place to question the Captain, silversmith."

Demetrius laughed heartily. "Nice cover up."

The sailor stomped his foot indignantly. "It ain't no cover up. I trust the Captain's word. How's business?" Bannigan changed the subject.

"Profitable, as always. The war with Oakvalor hasn't put a pinch in anyone's pockets yet. I hear some of my fellow smiths have been requested to appear before the king, as to why is anyone's guess."

"Maybe the king needs more weapons."

Demetrius shrugged his large shoulders. He wasn't in the business of making weapons, so it mattered little to him. His craft was typically sought after by the well-to-do, custom pieces that didn't come cheap. Some people had so much money they apparently didn't know what to do with it. He could work with any metal he put his hands on, but he preferred silver. It was very easy to bend and could be cast or hammered which allowed him to form almost anything with it; from teapots to statues.

The clanging of the bell tower echoed loudly across the city, signaling noon. The bell tower was originally built to alert the populace of emergencies. Its main use now was to indicate the time. Bannigan clapped Demetrius on the shoulder and bid him farewell. "That's my call," he said, trying to be heard over the noise. Demetrius' shop was situated near the docks for convenience and the daily clanging of the bell had eventually become a normal sound to him.

"Be safe," he called out as the old man left. Bannigan waved to acknowledge he heard him. Not that anyone couldn't.

Demetrius was a large man with a thunderous voice. At six and a half feet tall, he was a beast of a man, with muscles so large that he had to be custom fitted for his clothing. His hair was light brown and cut short to keep it out of his eyes, and to keep it from being singed. His skin was a deep bronze color as he preferred to be in the sun most of his time.

He watched his friend until he could no longer see him among the crowd. He heard his name a few stalls down and glanced to see who said it. He could see a member of the king's guard talking to one of the vendors. The vendor pointed towards where he was standing. What in the Divines would a soldier of the crown want with him? He watched the soldier approach.

"Demetrius?"

The big man eyed the soldier warily. "Yes?"

"The silversmith?" he asked with an air of impatience.

"Yes."

The soldier withdrew a scroll from his belt and handed it to Demetrius. "What's this?" he questioned. The soldier shook his head. "Not my business, sir. I am just the messenger. I believe His Highness requests your presence at the palace."

"What for?" Demetrius probed.

"Not my business." The soldier's impatience was evident by his short, almost rude, answers. "I must be on my way, sir." The soldier turned and headed back from the way he came. Demetrius stared at the scroll, unsure if he even wanted to open it. Everyone knew he didn't make weapons. Why would the king summon him if he was seeking smiths to make his armies more weapons?

He snapped the seal in half and opened the scroll. It

read:

To Demetrius the silversmith,

Greetings from the Esteemed Ruler of Talvaard, King Garun. Your presence is requested at the palace. Do not worry about your business. You will be well compensated. A carriage has been arranged to meet you outside the city of Radda at sundown. Do not be late.

King Garun

There was a fancy signature and the crest of the king, a phoenix bursting forth from a pile of ashes, at the bottom of the parchment. Demetrius sighed. He hated politics.

Dusk found him standing near the road at the outskirts of his hometown. He had closed up his shop early much to his disappointment. There was a certain beautiful woman who walked by his stall everyday around the same time, usually carrying fresh bread. He had only noticed her because he caught her staring at him as she passed by one day.

Her look was one of admiration. At least, that's how he took it. She had smiled embarrassedly and blushed. And so Demetrius made it a point in his day to watch her as she walked by and smile at her.

Closing early meant that he missed her. He was more than slightly frustrated by that, as he had finally worked up his nerve to actually speak to her. His hope was that she would let him get to know her and perhaps they would see where things went from there.

The carriage pulled up suddenly and Demetrius noticed that the sun was just sliding behind the mountains. "Well at least the king is punctual," he muttered beneath his breath. The door to the carriage swung open and a man dressed in plain clothes, probably a servant, stepped out. He motioned to the carriage and bowed low. "If you would, sir."

Demetrius dipped his head in thanks and climbed inside. A quiet whistle escaped his lips. The inside was adorned with all sorts of glittering shapes. He looked closely and recognized most of the precious stones. Diamonds and rubies comprised most of the decorations, but there were also a few sapphires and a couple stones he did not recognize. The fabric that made up the seats was comfortable and smooth to the touch. It was hard to tell whether the material was dark red or brown in the fading light.

Demetrius was impressed. He didn't expect to be brought to the palace in luxury. Granted he was known among the higher ups for his skills in crafting, but he was not of noble birth. And most, if not all of them, seemed to ignore the fact that he was much wealthier than most of them, anyway. The servant did not get back into the carriage, but instead shut the door and climbed into the seat with the driver.

He had a decent amount of time to think as the buggy headed toward Tarvaarin, the city built around the palace. It was a thirty minute trip to the palace by horse. After what seemed like hours to him, he felt a difference in the road. Instead of bouncing about on the dirt path, the ride smoothed out and he could tell they were now on the stone paved roads of the city.

The carriage came to an abrupt stop and the door swung open. The servant stood there and motioned for Demetrius to come out. He had gotten comfortable and it took him a minute to move. Why did the king want him to come so late in the evening hours, he wondered.

The servant led him through enormously tall double doors and into a massive circular room that was normally filled with nobles and commoners alike, usually bringing petitions and requests to the king or his advisors. The room was empty and their footsteps reverberated off the walls.

Demetrius looked admiringly up at the vaulted ceiling, rising sixty feet above him. Support pillars were spaced every ten feet, outlining the main walkway through the antechamber. "This is huge," he remarked to himself.

"Sir?" the servant looked back at him. Demetrius shook his head and the servant continued his hurried pace. A door in the middle of the far wall was flanked on either side by two giant alabaster statues of winged men standing at attention, their swords drawn and held up before them. Demetrius thought them an odd addition to the room. The walls were covered with portraits of regal looking men, whom he assumed were previous kings, and large brightly colored tapestries depicting scenes of long ago battles.

He began to wonder why he had never made a trip to the palace, if for no other reason than to say he had been there. The servant stopped before the door. "Wait here, sir," he said breathlessly before disappearing through the door. Demetrius looked down at the floor. Stone tiles, painted orange and yellow, ran the length of the entire room, forming a triangular pattern. The tiles outside the three-sided shape were bright red.

He assumed there was some sort of significance to the design, but it was lost on him. Demetrius looked back up and noticed the servant was staring at him. "His Highness will see you now." He held the door open and pointed down a long hallway. "It's the last door on the left at the end of the hall."

The big man nodded his head in thanks and walked to where he was directed. The hallway, large enough to comfortably hold two carriages side by side, was barely adorned at all. A guard stepped out from the shadows and startled him. "I didn't see you," he laughed nervously.

"That would be the point," the guard answered, his face hidden by the hood over his head. He patted Demetrius down for weapons and finding none, opened the door for him to enter. "Go to the center of the room and do not leave the circle."

"Circle? Why not?"

"Just don't."

Demetrius was starting to regret having made the trip. Then again, seeing how guarded the king was, he doubted he would have lived long had he refused to come. He walked to the middle of the room and noticed the circle design in the floor. He assumed that's where he was supposed to stand.

The guard shut the door and Demetrius was enveloped in darkness. He cleared his throat and the sound echoed eerily. Torches flared to life and revealed a large wooden chair with a man seated on it.

"Demetrius," the unknown man greeted. "I don't think we've had the pleasure of meeting before."

Demetrius wasn't sure if it was the king or not. And if it was, should he bow? He didn't answer. The man must have took his lack of response as hesitance. "You can speak freely."

Demetrius felt a little better that he could speak his mind. He wasn't one to bite his tongue. "What is this about? Why am I here? I am a very busy man, and I have lost half a day's time—"

The man in the chair stood up swiftly and Demetrius fell silent. "I can assure you, master smith, that we are all busy. Some busy with tasks more important than others." The man tossed a leather pouch onto the floor in front of him. "Consider this payment for your time."

Demetrius didn't dare move from the circle to see

what was inside, heeding the warning the guard had given him.

"Talvaard has a shadow cast over it, master smith. A shadow that threatens to consume us all."

Demetrius assumed the shadow was Oakvalor, the enemy kingdom that Talvaard had been at war with for as long as anyone could remember. "Then I must inform you, sir, that I am not a weapon smith. I make trinkets and items ordered for noble houses. I think you have erred in your selection of men to build your weapons of war."

"Do you think that I am ignorant of those in my kingdom?" the man asked, revealing that he was indeed the king. "I know what you are capable of, Demetrius, and I have not summoned you here to build weapons. At least, not in the sense that you are thinking."

"What do you mean?"

Several other torches lit up, as though by magic, and exposed King Garun in all his splendor. He was shorter than Demetrius by at least a foot. His hair was long and black, pulled back tight into a ponytail. His nose slanted down his face, reminding Demetrius of a bird's beak. His eyes were hazel and set deep in his head. The king was nothing special in terms of attractiveness. What he lacked in looks, however, was made up for in bearing.

His posture and demeanor exhibited a great deal of confidence and his general appearance was enhanced by his garments. His crown gleamed in the torchlight and gave the impression that it was made of silver. Demetrius knew it wasn't crafted of his favorite metal, but was instead made of something much more valuable: white gold.

It had three gems set in the front. A rare black diamond, twenty karats by Demetrius' estimate, in the middle, surrounded on either side by two green serendibite stones. It was a marvelous treasure. The king's shirt was turquoise and had a lustrous, dazzling sheen that only silk could give. His linen pants were a brilliant green color tucked into black leather boots. During the daylight hours, when dealing with matters of state, he would also wear a mantle that extended to the floor, joined at the neck and open down the front, that was emblazoned with the large phoenix crest on the back.

"I'm sure you have heard the rumors?"

"Of dragons, Your Highness?"

"Indeed. I can read the disbelief in your face. I know how you feel, as I too was of the same mind when word first reached me. I can assure you," the king's tone grew somber, "there is no myth to these tales."

Demetrius was dubious. "What in the name of the Divines are you talking about? Dragons? Winged creatures that fly and breath fire? You can't be serious, Your Highness."

The king's face remained solemn. "Had I not seen the creature for myself, I would be as doubtful as you, Demetrius. Unfortunately," he paused, gave a great sigh, and continued, "it is very real."

Demetrius was still in doubt, but he didn't further voice his suspicion. "What does all this have to do with me?"

"It is said that no one in Talvaard can work silver like you."

Demetrius had certainly earned a strong reputation for himself, but he was down to earth and didn't like to boast. "So I have heard," he replied, shrugging his large shoulders. "You still haven't answered the question."

The king closed the distance between him and Demetrius with a few quick steps. "I cannot reveal the details just yet, as I myself do not have them. All I know is that the skills of a silversmith are required, along with a few other details. Our ally," he used the word frostily, "does not have the privilege of metal smiths. And we lack what they have. So you see, master smith, you would be doing Talvaard a great duty."

"And if I refuse?" Demetrius asked, more out of curiosity than rebelliousness. A job for the king could prove to be very profitable.

Garun eyed him dangerously. "It would not be in your best interest ... but you have a week to consider it."

Demetrius felt goose bumps run up his back under the king's baleful look. "I am loyal to my country, Your Highness. I would never refuse an opportunity to serve the crown."

Garun smiled, the first Demetrius had seen on his face, apparently pleased with the answer. "My servant will escort you out and deliver you back to your home."

"When will you require my services?"

"You will know," the king answered.

- Demetrius, silversmith

CHAPTER 2

The ride back to Radda seemed shorter than the trip to the palace. Demetrius pondered the king's veiled threat and his offer. He wasn't sure what Garun even wanted him to forge. And then there was the fact that the king believed there truly was a dragon rampaging across the land. He briefly toyed with the idea that the king had been drinking a bit too much wine. He didn't know the man personally, but from all accounts he was a man of intelligence, calculating, and courageous. The fact that he seemed troubled and had asserted to have seen the beast did add weight to his claim.

Perhaps Oakvalor had unleashed some sort of beast loose on Talvaard? Something frightening enough to make people think it was a dragon. Demetrius didn't know. He didn't care either. A job for the crown could make him rich enough to stop working. He could buy a house in Talvaarin and spend his days relaxing or sail the Ocean and see the world. He smiled at the thought briefly before pushing those notions aside. He had to do the job first. And he wasn't even sure that he could.

The carriage stopped and the door opened. The servant didn't bother to motion him out of the cab as he was already moving towards the door before it opened. The man stopped Demetrius and handed him the leather pouch the king had tossed him. He had completely forgotten about it back in the palace.

"The king said I will know when he needs me. How will I know?" he asked the servant who, in reply, shrugged his shoulders. So much for an answer, he thought.

He made his way down the worn dirt path that led through the center of the port city he called home. While his shop was located near the docks, his house was in the center of the town, where the "better" houses were. Radda was home to many merchants and traders, as well as some nefarious characters. Since the port's expansion some eighty years ago, the small town had grown to become somewhat of a city. While they didn't have the paved stone roads of Talvaarin, they did have some of the best inns.

One such inn was the Crab, owned by a wealthy sailor who had made his fortune in the crab fishing industry. Crabs were considered a delicacy, especially among the nobles. Having made more money than he needed, the sailor had retired and opened the inn. Demetrius would come here to unwind from his work.

He preferred it over the other places. It was newer than the others, and so had less sketchy individuals to worry about. He paused outside the doorway, considered calling it a night. He decided to have one drink and he would be on his way. He entered the building to find it mostly empty with the exception of two patrons. The barmaid, a young girl no older than twenty, was delivering a tray of food to one of the customers. The other customer appeared to be a woman, but he couldn't see her face and didn't recognize her as anyone he knew in the dim light.

He found a seat at an empty table and ordered some wine when the barmaid asked what he'd like. Demetrius laid the leather bag on the table and opened the flap to peer inside. His eyes widened when he was that along with gold coins, there was also some precious stones similar to the ones he had seen in the carriage. If this was just for his trouble of closing for one afternoon, he could barely imagine how much the king would pay for the actual job.

He slid the bag into his lap and kept one hand on it. The young girl brought him his wine and he sank down into the chair. The chairs were covered in soft cushions, another reason he preferred the Crab. Demetrius sipped his wine slowly, enjoying the taste and the solitude. While he did appreciate his customers, he needed time away from people in general to keep a cheery attitude.

Demetrius was still young, at least he considered himself so. He was almost thirty and had never married. Not yet, anyway. His mother had died giving birth to him and his father, a poor thatcher, had always been distant from him. Demetrius assumed his father's lack of attention was the result of the man's superstitious beliefs. He had viewed his wife's death as a bad omen for the character of the child. Whatever sinful things the child would do in the future resulted in the mother's death. A sordid payment of sorts.

Demetrius didn't hold a grudge against his father. Besides, he had an entire town full of people who helped raise him. The previous ruler, King Verin, had expanded the kingdom's trade routes with established nations across the Ocean and financed the expansion of all the ports in the kingdom. Since Radda was so close to the palace, it received preferential treatment. The city flourished and grew rapidly, bringing in people from all cultures of the world.

It was one of those people who had made the city his home that took Demetrius in as his own. Childless and widowed, the man took pity on him and made Demetrius his apprentice in the silversmith trade. And the big man had a knack for it. Under his adoptive father's guidance, he became one of the best in the kingdom. His goods were highly sought after, especially by the well-to-do.

His thoughts were scattered as the female customer stood up to leave. Her face was revealed by the lanterns that hung from the ceiling and he realized it was the woman from the market. His heart skipped a beat and he felt his stomach drop. What was wrong with him?

He stood up and their eyes met. He couldn't take his eyes off her which made her face flush pink. She smiled shyly and went to leave.

"Wait," he said gently. She looked back at him with a nervous look on her face. "At least tell me your name, woman."

She seemed to hesitate, as if she would not answer. Demetrius waited, thinking perhaps he was too forward. He wanted to know who she was.

"Tomorrow."

His confused look spoke volumes. "Tomorrow? That's … different."

She shook her head and smiled. "I will tell you tomorrow."

"I won't be here. I have to deliver some items to a customer. I will be gone for two days."

"Then when you return," she responded bashfully.

"That seems so long from now," he said, downcast.

"You have gone this long without knowing my name. What is a few more days?"

When he arrived at his house and slumped into bed,

his thoughts were of the woman who seemed to have stolen his heart. He had finally heard her voice. And it was more beautiful than he imagined. As he drifted off to sleep, he was still smiling.

● ∞ ● ∞ ●

When the sun shining through the window woke him up, he groaned and rolled out of bed. His trip to Kish was at an end and he would be heading back home. He had not wanted to travel, but the customer had requested that Demetrius himself deliver the items. He tried to explain that he was a busy man, but his customer would not hear it.

Normally Demetrius would have merely declined the job, but the client offered triple the price for the trouble. He couldn't turn down the offer; it was a great deal of money. If there was one thing he loved more than his craft, it was money.

Besides that, the man was an ambassador to Treyfeth, a minor kingdom beginning to grow into a power to be reckoned with. Word was that he was cousin to the king, something that Demetrius considered more seriously now after having met the king two days ago. He certainly wouldn't want to offend a man who could have him thrown in the dungeon, or worse. All of the preparations were ready, the person he normally used had ensured all would be ready by dawn.

His client provided breakfast which he consumed quickly. He was impatient to see the beautiful woman again. Judging by their conversation at the inn, he sensed that what he was feeling for her was the same that she felt for him. He could hardly wait.

The journey took half a day, but it didn't seem to take that long as his thoughts were in the clouds. The city of Kish was located in the same direction as the

Abbey of the Divines, the home of the monks. It was further east than the abbey, so he did not get the opportunity to glimpse their stone walls. There was one road that led out of Radda. It was a straight road north leading to Talvaarin, then it broke east and west from there. Far to the west was the nation of Oakvalor. He had never been that far west, as there was nothing but a lonely road that winded over the dormant volcano and the mountains that surrounded it.

He had no reason to go there anyway. Talvaard and Oakvalor had been at war with each other for the past thousand years, maybe more. When asked, no one could answer how it all started. Time had a way of erasing things. As Demetrius continued heading south, he thought he could smell smoke in the air. "Odd," he muttered to himself, attempting to block the sun from his eyes to get a better look ahead. He was still about a mile away and with the sun setting in the south, he couldn't see much. A foreboding feeling began to gnaw at him.

Demetrius urged the two horses pulling his wagon to speed up. As he got closer, the smell of smoke became distinct. The terrain was all flat grasslands except right outside the city, where small rolling hills slowed his wagon down. He could hear noises now, and he was gripped with fear. He leapt off the wagon before the horses had completely stopped and ran to the top of the last hill.

Fire raged across the city. Shrill, high pitched screams of women and children invaded the air, mingling with the shouts of men who were trying desperately to put out the spreading destruction. The smoke rising from the buildings was dark and thick, billowing into the air and blotting out the fading sun; a mere sliver of dimming yellow light on the horizon as it was.

The smell of burnt wood, and possibly flesh,

reached him as a cool breeze blew in from the Ocean. The massive port city of Radda was now a charred wasteland. Demetrius dropped to his knees, overcome with emotion. This was his home from childbirth. The people he knew, the woman he had hoped to know, all burned up in the inferno. Tears stung his eyes as he thought of his father, too aged to have run for safely. He punched the ground, raising up dust and cutting his knuckles on rocks. He barely felt it. He punched again and again, wishing he would wake up from this horrible nightmare.

The soft nickering of a horse beside him seemed a strange and out of place sound. He looked up through tearful eyes to see a man dressed in soldiers clothes with the crest of the king displayed on the shoulder. His clothes were different from the soldier he had seen at the palace.

The man sat upon the horse, staring unfazed at the carnage. The man turned and looked down at him. Demetrius saw another emblem on the man's clothing, one he supposed was the symbol of a general.

"Where are the king's men?" Demetrius demanded, his voice breaking with grief.

The general turned his eyes back to the burning city. "Scattered throughout the kingdom dealing with similar situations." The man's voice was devoid of any genuine concern. Demetrius also looked back to the city. He wanted to rush down there and help, but he felt powerless and weak. He could only see a handful of people and they were trying to escape the flames, not put them out.

"It's time," the general said abruptly.

"Time for what?"

"To fulfill your obligation to the crown."

● ∞ ● ∞ ●

Demetrius rode in silence. He followed behind the general who didn't seem inclined to talk anyhow. He had fallen into a state of depressive calmness. He could feel tears sliding down his face but he didn't bother to wipe them away.

He wasn't aware that they had reached the castle until the general cleared his throat, breaking the silence. Demetrius looked up and saw the double doors that led into the palace. He looked over his shoulder, having some idea that maybe he would see his home, fine and undamaged as when he had left it. He saw only the ten foot stone wall that separated the palace from the city of Talvaarin.

He slid off the horse and followed the general to the door, who entrusted him to the servant whom he had dealt with on his first visit. The antechamber was filled with servants and soldiers alike, dashing here and there, at times almost running into one another. The entire palace was in chaos. Demetrius oddly found comfort in seeing many people eye him with frowning faces, the only way they knew how to express their condolences.

The servant led him through the doorway in the middle of the chamber with haste. "Where is the King?" the servant was demanding to those who passed them in the giant hall. Some shrugged, others didn't bother to answer at all.

Demetrius saw two women that appeared to be attendants, talking in hushed tones. As they passed by, he heard bits of their conversation and learned that Radda was only one of many cities across the kingdom that had burned to the ground. People were blaming Oakvalor and their king's wizard for the destruction.

While he still held reservations about Garun's story of a dragon, he didn't think there was any way Oakvalor's armies could burn so many cities without a single person seeing anything. The servant stopped at the end of the hall and glanced about. Demetrius wasn't sure what he was doing. A hooded guard stepped out of the shadows and the servant nodded back toward Demetrius. "His Highness has summoned the smith. Do not delay me!"

The soldier eyed Demetrius warily but did as the servant bade. He watched the soldier run his hand along the wall. Seeming to find what he was looking for, he removed a key from his belt and slid it into the wall. There was a soft click and the wall opened inward about two inches. Both the guard and the servant glanced around again.

"Come," the servant said, motioning Demetrius to follow him. He pushed the door and it opened silently. Once inside, the guard shut the door and Demetrius heard it lock. There were small lanterns every few feet, lighting what appeared to be another hallway. They walked straight ahead for about fifty feet before the servant turned to Demetrius. "I hope you aren't afraid of small spaces," he remarked as the floor in front of them slowly slid open, revealing stairs that wound downward.

"Where are we?" Demetrius asked. The servant stared at him intently before answering. "The palace that you see outside is only a small portion of the castle. The rest is hidden beneath the mountains."

"Wait," Demetrius grabbed hold of the servant's arm. "We're under ground?" he asked incredulously.

"Not yet," the servant smiled. He began to descend the stairs, then paused and looked sternly at Demetrius. "You didn't see any of this."

CHAPTER 3

Demetrius found himself feeling a little claustrophobic. The chamber he stood in was enormous in terms of open space, but the knowledge that he was deep underground gave him chills. The idea that more dirt and stone than he could imagine was being held up by a few wooden beams was distressing. The air was cool, but he was sweating so profusely his shirt was soaked. It clung to his skin and made him even more uncomfortable. The servant had left him alone in the room, and he was beginning to wonder what was taking so long.

The door swung open and the same general who had met him outside Radda strode in, followed by two guards leading a blindfolded man in flowing grey robes. Demetrius looked questioningly at the general. "This—" he waved towards the man, "—is Vallen. He will be working with you."

Demetrius' brows rose. "Who is he? A prisoner?"

The grey robed man let out a chuckle. The general was not impressed.

"He is King Manaem's wizard. We don't need the Oaks having anymore advantages over us; hence the blindfold."

That put Demetrius on his heels. His initial shock, and then anger, was apparent on his face. "I will not work with some fool from Oakvalor," he cried angrily. "Especially not a servant of their king! Is this some sort of joke? My home was destroyed and you come in here …" his large body was shaking with rage.

"Be calm, silversmith. The Oaks," he used the insulting slang term again, "are facing the same problems we are. King Garun has issued an unofficial treaty of peace with Manaem. Do this task so we can be rid of the vermin from our land."

Demetrius almost refused, but the look on the general's face reminded him of the deadly stare of the king. He hated the Oaks as much as anyone else in Talvaard, but he valued his life and nodded in resignation.

"Follow me."

The general led them through a maze of passages and into a chamber similar to the one they left. There was a furnace and an anvil, as well as all sorts of tools hanging on one of the walls. "I still don't know what I am supposed to forge," he commented to the general, who in turn said nothing. He instructed the guards to take the blindfold off the wizard and left Demetrius in the room with him.

Demetrius looked at the wizard. He was young, perhaps younger than himself. His robes looked to be made of velvet. The man's hair was long and platinum colored, hanging down past his shoulders. His eyes were slate blue and brought the waters of the Ocean to mind. He carried an ordinary looking staff made of wood, but it was not to help the wizard walk.

The smith had never met a wizard. Before he was born, sorcerers were a common sight. A few bad seeds, however, caused a great persecution to break out against anyone who practiced the craft. The soldiers were able to quell the violence, but it was too late. Those who had not been killed went into hiding or gave up the craft altogether. It was whispered that the church had a hand in the revolt, but the Abbot condemned such accusations. It was also whispered that some wizards had the ability to control others with the power of their minds.

If the rumors were true … Demetrius suddenly wondered if this man had that power. He looked questioningly at the wizard, who frowned and muttered something about stupidity.

"Well?" Vallen said impatiently.

"Well what?" Demetrius answered.

"Are you ready to get to work or are you going to stand there until the beast destroys both our lands?"

"The king hasn't told me what to forge," he reiterated.

"I'm telling you what to forge, you fool."

● ∞ ● ∞ ●

Demetrius was the best at what he did because he worked alone. No one told him what to make or how to make it. His clients asked for certain pieces, true, but they did not dictate to him how to accomplish it. And that was precisely the reason he wanted to strangle Vallen. The wizard had drawn up a very specific blueprint and he insisted every detail be followed.

With each hammer blow, he would hear Vallen mutter something about "too much force" or "this is the best smith they could find?" Demetrius glared at him on one such occasion.

"Do you want to do this?" Vallen returned his glare but didn't say another word.

Demetrius prided himself on attention to detail, which was one of the reasons his work was so highly sought after. But this … this was just a round, hollow sphere of silver unadorned in any way. He had to shape it in two separate pieces, each one the wizard inspected meticulously. With both pieces complete, Vallen had him heat the metal pieces up so that he could engrave some sort of symbols onto the inside.

When Vallen was finished, Demetrius melded the two together, ensuring it was a perfect seal. For all the specifics, it looked like something he may have crafted when he was an apprentice.

"It looks unfinished," he lamented, turning his gaze to Vallen. For the first time since they had met, Vallen was smiling.

"It's perfect." Vallen reached over to pick up the sphere. "You *are* crazy, you blasted Oak!" Demetrius smacked the wizard's hand away. "The heat of the metal will burn the skin right off your fingers!"

The wizard's smile quickly vanished and turned into a scowl. "Watch what *my* craft can do." Vallen snatched the sphere off the anvil and held it close to Demetrius' face. "Do you feel any heat?"

To his surprise, Demetrius didn't. If anything, the metal seemed to be radiating a coldness. "What is it?" he questioned.

"This, silversmith, is a weapon beyond imagining. And it is going to save our kingdoms."

"There comes a time when one must sacrifice for what he believes in. I believe in my king and my country. And so into the mouth of death I travel. For King and Country."

- a page in Vallen's journal

CHAPTER 4

The sphere having been forged and imbued with magic, Demetrius thought his task was done and expressed his desire to go back to Radda to help the survivors with the task of burying the dead and rebuilding.

"Out of the question," King Garun stated in a tone that allowed no room for debate.

"The task you required of me is complete," Demetrius returned irritably.

"On the contrary. The wizard requires your continued assistance. There is one last thing that the crown requires of you. You must escort Vallen to the dragon's dwelling and ensure the safety of the sphere when the wizard captures the beast."

"I am not a soldier, Your Highness. I couldn't possibly protect it better than your men of war."

They were in the same room he had first met the

king in, which was just as dark and mysterious in the daylight hours. Garun dismissed the servants who were attending him and drew close to Demetrius. "Let me be blunt with you, since you are not wise in the ways of politics. I do not expect the wizard to survive the encounter with the beast." Garun's hazel eyes seemed to pierce his soul.

"Do whatever you must to secure the sphere for Talvaard's interests." Demetrius was catching on to the king's subtle words. "What interests would those be?"

Garun frowned. He was not accustomed to being questioned. "Let us merely imagine that it may be of use to us one day in the future. In the event that a certain kingdom begins to grow too powerful ..." his words trailed off. He called his servants back into the room. "Take our guest to prepare for his journey," he instructed them.

"Where are we going?"

Garun smirked. "*You* are going to Kerosh Pass in the Viss Mountains. I will remind you of the importance of having that sphere brought back here."

"Why me?"

"Vallen trusts you now. Do not fail me," Garun warned.

The servants escorted Demetrius to a room located two doors down. He was given fresh clothes to change into, as well as a lightweight suite of chain mail. The wizard was also there, though he refused to take anything the servants offered to him. "I will not have it said I accepted anything without payment," was his excuse. Demetrius figured the real reason was because they were not made by Oakvalor hands.

"How does anyone know where this dragon lives?" Demetrius inquired, still having doubts that it even existed.

Vallen pointed to a large map that hung from the

wall. "The border between our kingdoms crosses through the mountains of Ward and Viss. Within those mountains is a cave the creature calls home. We cannot hope to use the sphere within his domain, so we must draw him out into the open. One of the mountains is level at the top. That is where we will make our stand."

Demetrius was uneasy by the way Vallen seemed to be talking about their future encounter. Assuming the dragon was real, it was unlikely that he would be of any actual help to the wizard. Demetrius sighed heavily and half listened as the wizard babbled on. It was going to be a long journey.

● ∞ ● ∞ ●

Demetrius scrambled up the cliffside, almost slipping on the jagged rocks several times. The wizard had convinced him to enter the cave alone while the wizard stayed at the top of the mountain. Demetrius initially didn't care as he still didn't believe there was a dragon. But seeing the massive creature inside the cave suddenly put a lot of things into perspective for the smith.

The beast had seen him and that immediately caused Demetrius to turn and run. No amount of money or threats from the king could make him stay and do anything. He reached the plateau, his only thoughts on escaping and running as fast as he could. Vallen stopped him in his tracks by letting fly a blast of lightning. "Stay focused. I cannot do this alone!"

He knew if he tried to flee that Vallen would kill him. The wizard might trust him, but that didn't make them enemies any less. The ground shook beneath his feet and he looked around frantically. A mighty roar of the dragon echoed off the mountain tops. Demetrius covered his ears, afraid he might go deaf from the sheer volume. The dragon shot up into the sky, a blur of red against the blue sky.

"How are we going to get the beast to land?" he yelled at Vallen.

Vallen withdrew the sphere from a leather bag strapped across his shoulders. "That is the good news. We don't need it to land. We just need it to fly overhead. It is a fire dragon, the deadliest of its kind. As in nature, fire can be extinguished by ice. The magic infused within the metal has a twofold purpose, the main being that it will keep the dragon's fire at bay. The other purpose is about to be tested."

Demetrius' face turned pale. "Tested? You don't know if your magic *works*? Divines save us!" Vallen ignored the smith's terror.

"This is not something that has been done before, but I know it will work. The magic will imprison the creature inside. I will distract the beast from there," he pointed to the edge of the plateau, "and you hold the sphere up in the air as the beast flies over." He handed the sphere to Demetrius.

"I thought this was going to kill the dragon?"

Vallen shook his head. "Dragon's cannot be killed. At least, not the way we can be killed." The sound of rushing wings filled the air, and Vallen sprinted to the edge of the mountain top.

"Where do I stand?" Demetrius shouted at the wizard.

Either Vallen didn't hear him or Demetrius didn't hear the answer. He threw himself to the ground as the massive dragon shot by. The dragon landed close to Vallen, dropping down onto an upraised platform of rock. Demetrius watched with panic as the beast spewed forth gouts of flame from its mouth.

He expected to see Vallen consumed in fire. A blue light flared to life and protected the wizard from the flames. The dragon went airborne again. The force of the wind from the dragon's wings seemed to be turned into a weapon and flung Vallen off the cliff.

Demetrius cried out and ran over to the edge, expecting the worst. He found Vallen holding onto the ledge. Using every last ounce of strength, he pulled the wizard back up.

Vallen's facial expression was all the thanks Demetrius needed. The dragon was circling high above them. "Get back over there, quickly." Demetrius held the sphere tightly and ran back to where he had been standing. Death seemed certain to him. The dragon shot downward, halting overhead and flying a complete circle.

There was a sudden eerie silence. Why couldn't he hear anything? He heard Vallen's voice inside his head.

If anything happens to me, keep the sphere safe! Do not let the safety of the world be jeopardized by the greed of men.

The dragon swooped over the plateau and Demetrius lifted the sphere high into the air as it passed above. The dragon jerked awkwardly in the air. All life seemed to leave the beast and it crashed with jarring force into the ground, rolling and tumbling toward Vallen.

The beast, and the wizard, disappeared over the cliff edge.

Do not fail!

Those three words echoed in his mind the rest of his life.

- From the writings of Denrie'Aluth
Former Abbot

CHAPTER 5

Year of the Divines 544

The Abbey of the Divines was an ancient structure, dating back almost a thousand years. The ruler of Talvaard at the time, King Beraiah, had converted to the worship of the Divines from the pagan religion that prevailed in the country. After his change of faith, he used the royal treasury to finance the construction of the monastery and issued a decree that all other religions were illegitimate.

The edict had angered the leaders of the major religions and instead of continuing their rituals in secret, they joined together and declared war on the king. What ensued came to be known as the Eradication. Beraiah hired mercenaries to track down and slaughter the rebels. It was a dark time in the kingdom of Talvaard as Beraiah enforced his new beliefs on everyone. Many of his top advisors resigned their positions, not wanting innocent blood on their hands.

Eventually the defiance from the rebellious people subsided and they converted to the new religion; or at the very least did not voice their opposition. As the years passed, and the Church of the Divines grew, the mercenary bands were replaced with loyalists, people devoted to the crown. Beraiah made them an official faction of the government and split them into two groups; his personal bodyguards and the *Retribution*.

The Retribution was a secretive sect that sought out those few who continued practicing the pagan religions and brought them to justice. They would be disbanded three hundred years later by the fourth great grandson of Beraiah, who believed them to be outdated and an unnecessary drain on the treasury.

Yet the Church of the Divines flourished in Talvaard despite its violent beginnings. The Abbey was the largest ever built, containing more than two hundred rooms. It was one story, made from the dark brown stone that could only be found on the Isle of Eio. Beraiah had spared no expense on the monastery, bringing in craftsmen and resources as far as the forested mountains of Eurista, half the world away.

No one was sure of the origin of the belief of the Divines, though it was rumored that Beraiah had indulged a missionary from some distant land and had been persuaded to abandon the traditional religion of his royal bloodline.

The monastery was massive in terms of square footage, larger even than the royal palace. It was situated outside the city of Talvaarin, the quarters of the palace and capitol of the kingdom for as long as anyone could remember. It was surrounded by an island of tall grassy plains with a single wagon-worn trail leading to it.

At one time it had been open to anyone for prayer services and other ceremonies, but the Abbot in command closed its doors to the public when Demetrius brought the sphere to them. He claimed it was in the "best interests and safety" of everyone in Talvaard. It did spark some outrage from the king, who demanded that he be allowed to visit anytime he pleased, reminding the Abbot that it was, after all, the crown who paid for their building.

In a show of good will, the Abbot offered to send monks to Talvaarin each week to hold a prayer service and meet the needs of the people in the palace, to which the king agreed.

Inside the monastery, the monks continued their teachings by allowing only first born males into their ranks, referring to them as being 'consecrated to the Divines'. They took oaths of celibacy, forgoing their natural desires to serve the Divines.

Calderon was one such monk. He had entered the monastery at the young age of six, two years younger than what the Abbot normally allowed. His parents, devout followers of the Divines, had arranged for their son to be the exception to the rule. Many speculations followed as to how they managed it, but no one could decipher fact from fiction.

Nine long years had passed since the day his parents had dropped him off. Calderon had not seen them since. He could barely remember what they looked like anymore. The pictures he had conjured up in his mind when he first arrived quickly faded, leaving him with only a few distinct memories of events from his early childhood. He could not remember much outside the walls of the monastery. The monks were forbidden to leave without approval from the Abbot and Calderon was no exception.

It was past noon now, close to the first hour of the afternoon and the Abbot was winding down his exhortation. The Abbot, leader of the monastery and the priesthood in Talvaard, would preach his sermons each day at noon, and though he was typically long winded, today's seemed like it would be shorter than normal.

Calderon bowed his head as they closed the service in prayer. He quietly whispered his own invocation and rose from the pew. He searched the room but didn't see Velkyn in the audience. While attendance was not mandatory, his childhood friend hardly missed the daily service. He could always confide in Velkyn without fear of judgment. The two had become instant friends his first day in the monastery. Calderon had initially been shunned and bullied by the older boys because of his controversial admittance.

Velkyn, however, had taken justice in his own hands and pummeled a few of them. The masters had then punished Velkyn. His friend took it in stride and they became inseparable, doing all of their daily routines together. Calderon left the chapel and traversed his way through the winding hallways, occasionally glancing into private prayer rooms dedicated to the various Divines.

There was only one reason why his friend would miss the Abbot's sermon.

● ∞ ● ∞ ●

Velkyn finished his prayer and kissed the foot of the copper statue depicting Virtue and rose to his feet. Tomorrow would be the culmination of all his recent efforts. He would need all the favor Virtue would give him. The statue stood on a round dais made of curved red bricks that lifted the statue almost a foot off the floor.

The statue was probably decades old, but the lacquer that covered the statue gave the reddish brown color a shiny complexion and made it appear new. Due to the fact that the metal turned green from oxidation, the monks had to import the protective lacquer from one of the islands on the coast and arrange periodical maintenance.

He pulled the hood of his robes over his head. "I always know where to find you," Calderon's familiar voice echoed in the chamber. Velkyn turned to face his friend. "That's because you know me." Calderon was almost the same height as himself, though slightly shorter. His head was shaved as was the custom for all of the monks in the monastery. Unlike himself, his friend had deep blue eyes whereas his were green. He was also the only one who knew about Calderon's disorder.

"Are you ready for the ceremony?" Velkyn smiled as he asked the question. He already knew the answer. Calderon was nervous. He knew his friend well, but he also could sense it in his spirit.

"My soul is ready, but my mind betrays me. I want this *so badly*," he raised his hand and clenched it into a fist with the last words. Calderon used his hands often when he talked. "I am afraid, though." Velkyn nodded in understanding. "I know. I have my own reservations about what lies ahead, but I trust that if I am not chosen, there is another path for me."

"My biggest concern is having my disorder discovered. Perhaps I am not meant to be the Musician. I do not feel right hiding the truth." Velkyn put his hand on Calderon's shoulder. "We all have secrets that we must bear. If you confess your weakness, you will never be the Musician. And they may even kick you out of the order. I believe you are making the right decision. Besides, you know my secret. I would surely be excommunicated for mine. I do not feel guilty. Neither should you."

Calderon's downcast expression brightened. "I suppose you are right."

"Have faith," Velkyn said empathetically. The two sat in silence for a moment before Calderon spoke. "I have never understood that phrase."

Velkyn's mind was wrapped up with his own thoughts. He looked at his friend confusedly. "What?"

"That phrase," Calderon repeated, waving his hands about as he talked. "Have faith. Faith is a Divine, so how do we 'have faith'? I've never understood it."

Velkyn contemplated the question. "That is the beauty and glory of her love. She gives of herself to us, filling us with her spirit so that we may not only believe she exists, but that we may be empowered to obey her commands. That is how we have faith." He smiled at Calderon's look of amazement.

"You are wise beyond your years, my friend. Perhaps one day you might be the Abbot."

Velkyn grimaced. "With all my heart I hope that not to be the case."

● ∞ ● ∞ ●

Velkyn was up long before he needed to be. He was too excited to sleep anyway, spending most of the night tossing and turning. Today was the ceremony that would decide his fate. He would be asked grueling theological questions about the sphere, as well as about its history. Then his strength would be tested in a battle with a master of hand to hand combat. Each candidate would be tested separately by different masters. Then the masters would convene and decide amongst themselves who would be the next Guardian.

The positions of Guardian and Musician were very

similar with the exception that one played music to keep the enchantment on the sphere active. The Guardian's role was to guard the door to the sphere, literally, their entire life.

The Guardian would only get three hours of sleep each day when the Musician came to play their music. The Guardian's position was essentially useless, as the only enemy of Talvaard was Oakvalor. The two nations were at war, but the Oaks also served the Divines and the church kept itself separated from the political agendas of their royal counterparts.

The Musician was the more important of the two positions. It was the Musician who played the music that kept the freezing enchantment on the sphere. All magic expired over time without any influence. Demetrius himself had given them the musical notes needed to keep the sphere's magic from degrading.

Velkyn left his room and headed to the chamber where he had prayed the previous day. The sun had not yet risen, so he did not expect anyone to be using the room. Even though he walked softly down the stone hallways, the echo of his footsteps seemed loud in the silence.

He entered the chamber and stood before the statue of his favored Divine. He wondered if the statue was an accurate depiction of the deity. How the sculptor knew what the deity looked like was beyond him.

What if all he was praying to was a giant piece of elaborate metal?

One of the doubts that always seemed to dwell in the back of his mind had escaped his mental barrier. He drove the thought away and sighed in frustration. How could he be so wise and have so much knowledge, yet have so many doubts about his own faith? He knelt down before the dais and bowed his head in prayer.

Virtue ... I have sought your favor already, but I

come before you again to pray for my friend. I know he is the best suited to be the Musician ... he has worked so hard to get to this point. If it is Your will, I pray that you would give him your favor as well.

Velkyn's mind began to wander. He thought of Nydel, his secret. Monks were forbidden to have relations, but he loved her. How could they justifiably ask him, or anyone else for that matter, to bury their desires and emotions? He refused to. She had been his closest friend before coming to the monastery on his eighth birthday.

He smiled at the thought of how she had snuck in to see him over the years, sometimes desecrating this very room with their romantic episodes. He didn't know how or when, but he would marry her one day. It may have been contradictory to be praying to the saint of Virtue considering his secret sin, but he didn't care.

His entire future rested on becoming the Guardian, and he would pray to whoever he needed to for success.

● ∞ ● ∞ ●

Velkyn had been drilled for the last hour on every deep subject based on the sphere. "Then Demetrius brought the sphere to the Brotherhood to keep it safe. Though our nations were at war then as they are now, they had banded together for the good of the world. The king of Oakvalor disagreed with King Garun's decision to keep the sphere here, but he ordered the bones of the beast to be brought to Oakvalor.

"Demetrius lived the rest of his life behind these very walls. The sphere is said to hold the soul of the fire dragon that brought massive destruction on both our kingdom, and Oakvalor's. Our order vowed to keep it protected and safe after the death of Demetrius."

"What if it doesn't contain anything at all?" the

master inquired.

"That's a difficult but excellent question. The only way to know the answer is to stop playing the music that keeps the enchantment on the sphere. The better question would be, is it worth the risk to find the answer to that question? I do not believe it is."

"What if you spend your entire existence keeping it safe, only to find out that you wasted your life?"

"That is where faith comes in. I believe it though I have no proof. My faith drives my actions. If in the end there is nothing to what we do, did we really waste our lives doing what we thought to be just? I do not think so."

Velkyn was having trouble reading the master's faces. Was he answering the questions correctly? He could only hope.

"You showed a proficient level of training in your defensive skills. What if a member of the Brotherhood, meaning someone other than the Musician, sought to enter the chamber of the sphere—what would you do?"

"I would strike them down. Everyone in the Brotherhood knows the rules, and any fellow monk who breaks them deserves what comes to them."

"Please remove yourself from the chamber while we await the other masters." Velkyn turned and left the room, feeling unsure of how he did. Had he been too forceful in his answers? Was his hand-to-hand skill up to standard? Despite what he could glean from the masters, all of these and many more doubts assailed him as he waited outside the chamber. His thoughts turned to Calderon and he wondered how his friend was faring in his tests.

"Let your will be done," he whispered quietly, to no Divine in particular.

● ∞ ● ∞ ●

Calderon stood waiting outside the chamber he would be tested in. He could hear music playing through the wooden door, though it was muffled. His final and most challenging test would be to play his music for the current Musician. Calderon had only seen the man in passing a few times. Both the Guardian and the Musician led lives of solitude, kept away from the general population of the monastery.

A full hour of perfect notes without a single mistake was required to pass the test. He had been playing his flute more and more each day in preparation, but he had yet to make it more than thirty minutes without having to stop. All he could do was hope for the best. The music coming through the door stopped abruptly. Calderon leaned against the door and put his ear to the polished wood, hoping to hear what was happening. He could hear voices, but nothing audible.

He quickly backed away from the door when he realized someone was opening it. He turned his gaze up at the ceiling and pretended to be paying grave attention to the ceiling. One of the candidates walked out of the chamber, his face flushed red with embarrassment telling Calderon all he needed to know.

"Calderon," an elderly voice called out from the doorway, "it's time."

Calderon's heart began to race. His hands were sweaty, too. As he started walking towards the door, he dropped his flute. It clanged to the floor loudly, the sound echoing down the hallway. "F-forgive me," he stuttered, kneeling down to pick it up. He felt a weight on his shoulder and looked up. The Musician's hand was on him.

"Don't be nervous," the old man encouraged, "just breath."

Calderon nodded silently and stood up. If he was

meant to be the Musician, everything would work out. All he could do was offer his best. As he entered the chamber, he noticed a single chair. The room was devoid of any other furniture. The only source of light was from a small window in the stone wall behind the chair.

The old man sat down in the chair and motioned Calderon to stand in front of him. "It is very important that you can endure physical strain. You will stand there while you play. Perhaps when you are my age, you will have the privilege of a chair."

Calderon wasn't sure in the dim light, but he thought he saw the old man smile. He breathed in deep, placed the flute to his lips, and began to play. He knew the song well, he had memorized it when he was young. He distinctly remembered when he knew he wanted to be the Musician. Everything now depended on this moment. He couldn't see anything with the light shining directly in his face. He closed his eyes to focus on the music.

The next thing he knew, the old man was standing in front of him. Had he fallen asleep? His felt his stomach lurch within him.

"You did well, Calderon." The old man smiled, then motioned to the door. Calderon followed the Musician's direction and left the chamber. His thoughts tumbled around in his mind as he made his way to his personal quarters. He was confused. What happened? He couldn't recollect anything.

● ∞ ● ∞ ●

Velkyn and Calderon had been summoned to the Abbot's chambers as the sun was setting. Both monks knew that because the smell of food was beginning to waft through the air. The monastery served two meals a day, always at sunrise and sunset. They both stood staring, entranced by the decorations that covered the walls. Tapestries, paintings, and other items practically hid every wall behind a multi-colored landscape of artistic beauty.

The desk, though made of wood, was plated in gold and silver. Red stones, possibly rubies, cast a reddish hue across the room in the candlelight. They were so awed by the wealth that surrounded them that they did not hear the Abbot ask them to sit down.

"You may be seated," the Abbot repeated after clearing his throat. Once they were seated, the Abbot stared intently at them from across his desk.

"These artifacts are beautiful," Calderon said quietly, feeling like he was in a holy place. The atmosphere of the room was hushed and serene. Speaking almost seemed sinful.

"Thank you. Most of these items the church has acquired through donations. The wealthy people of the city send them to us, not realizing we have no use for such things. Turning down their gifts would not be respectful, so we keep them here. I have called you both here for other business. The masters have made their decisions. While I do not completely agree with their ruling, it is not my place to challenge them. Tradition separates the duties of guarding the sphere from my duties as leader of the faith. With that being said, I must inform you both that only one of you have been chosen."

Velkyn shifted uncomfortably in his chair. Calderon didn't move.

"Velkyn, you have been chosen as the new Guardian. The previous Guardian, master Groves, passed away just this evening." Velkyn's face showed a mixture of joy and then confusion and finally, sorrow. "How …?"

"Age has taken its toll on his body. The Musician will not be far behind him. They do not live long after the choices are made, due in part to the fact that we do not choose candidates until we know the current protectors of the sphere are close to death. He died doing what he committed his life to; guarding the sphere. It was an honor to have known him." The Abbot paused before turning his gaze to Calderon.

"There was some debate about you," he said. "The Musician believes you are the right choice, but some of the masters who oversaw your other tests disagree. The majority voted to go with Sevrin. Were it in my control, I would honor the Musician's desire. But in this matter, the masters have majority power. I am sorry. You are dismissed."

The tranquility shattered like a mirror being tossed to the ground. Calderon sat in disbelief. Velkyn nudged him with his elbow and motioned with his head toward the door. Calderon stood up dazedly, and slowly made his way out into the hallway. Velkyn sighed softly. This was not part of the plan.

"I feel for him more than he knows," the Abbot said. "As for you, however, you must report immediately to your post. Under less saddening circumstances, you would work with the master until he left this world. I assume you know your duties?"

"Yes, I know them," Velkyn answered solemnly.

"You are also dismissed."

- from the Book of Faith

CHAPTER 6

Calderon paused outside the door to his room. How could they have chosen Sevrin over him? By all accounts, he had passed the other tests just fine. Maybe he had fallen asleep when he played his music? That wouldn't explain why the Musician wanted to choose him though. He could feel the tears welling up in his eyes. He didn't want to cry, but he couldn't help it.

He had worked for years to get here, but this was not the way he expected things to go. Perhaps he truly was not meant to be the Musician. He entered his room and hit his knees. He cried, and he prayed. And then he prayed some more. And cried some more. His tears were selfish, he knew. If the Divines had willed Sevrin to be the Musician, then he would have to accept that. But he didn't want to.

It was easier to be selfish. He should not allow himself to wallow in self pity. He was stronger than that. He sat there on his knees, the hot tears streaming down his face. He was unaware of the passage of time. No light shone through his window. He didn't bother lighting a candle. He slumped down onto the cold stone floor and just laid there and stared into the darkness of his room.

When he woke up, small shafts of light were shining through his window. He was still lying on his stomach and his neck was a little sore from facing the same direction all night. A knock on his door startled him. "Yes?" he called out, not sure why anyone was knocking in the first place. It wasn't time for the morning prayers.

"Calderon," the Abbot's familiar voice rang, "I need to speak with you."

Calderon pushed himself off the floor with a grunt. He didn't bother trying to smooth his disheveled look. He opened the door and was greeted by the Abbot, who had a disturbing look on his face. "Due to unforeseen circumstances, you are now the new Musician. You will report to master Donovan this evening for instruction."

"Master who?" he questioned, only half awake.

"The former Musician. His name is master Donovan. And don't forget your flute." The Abbot turned and left, his departure as quick as his arrival.

"What just happened?" Calderon whispered to himself. Unforeseen circumstances? What did that mean? And why did he have a dreaded feeling about being the new Musician? He should have been overjoyed.

He wasn't.

● ∞ ● ∞ ●

Calderon made his way quickly to Velkyn's room. He knocked several times, but his friend did not answer. Could he be guarding the sphere already? He wasn't sure, but decided to go by the sphere chamber to see.

As he walked down the hallway that led to the room that housed the sphere, he saw Velkyn standing outside the door. "Velkyn!" he shouted. "I've got to tell you something!" As he approached his friend, Velkyn began to run toward him. "It's the strangest thing—" he began to say, but then Velkyn slammed into him, knocking him to the ground.

Velkyn's fists were a blur of raw fury, striking him in his jaw, neck, and chest. It was all he could do to try and block his face. The intensity with which Velkyn struck left no doubt in his mind that he was indeed the right choice for Guardian. "I'm the new Musician," he screeched.

As quickly as Velkyn attacked, he stopped. "Oh thank Virtue," Velkyn gasped. "Why didn't you say so? I could have killed you!" Calderon could feel blood on his face, but he didn't know where it was from.

"How was I supposed to know you would attack a fellow monk within our own walls?"

Velkyn helped him to his feet. "Lesson learned. That is great news, my friend. What changed?" Calderon shrugged. "I'm not really sure. The Abbot came to my room and told me there were unforeseen circumstances."

"Like what?"

"I don't know. I'm going to ask master Donovan tonight."

"Who?"

"Master Donovan, he is … or was, the Musician."

"Somehow, I knew you would be chosen. I appreciate you coming to tell me, but you really shouldn't be here until you are supposed to play the music"

Calderon wiped his face with the sleeve of his robe. "I'm sorry. I didn't know."

"Don't worry about it. Go clean yourself up. Someone is bound to think you received a beating." Velkyn grinned at him.

● ∞ ● ∞ ●

The day didn't pass fast enough for Calderon. He went to the morning prayer ceremony, helped some of the newer monks with the cleaning tasks, and even spent some time in the library studying some old books about the sphere.

As the daylight began to fade and candles started to be lit, his anxiety about being the new Musician returned. He was uneasy about it, but he was also excited. Unfortunately for him, the uneasiness seemed to outweigh his joy. How could one live their entire life leading up to a single moment with anticipation, and then be so afraid of what would come next?

He met Donovan at the same chamber he played his music in. The old man was slightly shorter than him, about five feet tall. His head was shaved like all the other monks, but his wrinkles gave some hint to his age. He was one of those men who time had aged beyond years. His eyes were dark brown and seemed to pierce Calderon's very soul.

"Good evening," Donovan greeted.

Calderon returned the greeting and bowed his head to the old man. "The Abbot didn't mention the reason for the change. Do you know what happened?"

Donovan's face softened with what appeared to be sadness. "Sevrin, though not my first choice, did well. He played the music under my supervision and did everything the way he should have. Afterward, he fell ill. We assumed it was a minor thing, perhaps some bad meat. But he did not survive through the night. The poor boy died in his sleep."

Calderon frowned. "My heart breaks at this news. I have to confess something."

Donovan raised his eyebrows.

"I have worked and waited my whole life to be here, to be the Musician. But now that I am here and this is all happening, I am afraid. What if I mess up? What if I am not meant to be the Musician?"

Donovan did not answer immediately. "The Divines work their will out in ways that we do not understand. Their ways are not our ways. Their thoughts are not our thoughts. Yet everything works out in the end the way it was meant to. Sevrin's death is a part of their will, though how or why we will never know in this life. Fear is a natural response to the unknown. There is nothing wrong in being afraid. We all have fears; we are only men."

Donovan stared into Calderon's eyes with that piercing gaze. "The true test of a man is not whether he is afraid or not, it is how he responds. I will be here to teach you and guide you as long as the Divines see fit. And when death comes to me as it comes to us all, you will be ready."

Calderon had a puzzled look on his face. "Ready for what?"

"To be on your own, as the new Musician."

● ∞ ● ∞ ●

Calderon found being the Musician to be less overwhelming than he expected. There were two things that Donovan was very specific about. The time that he began the music, and how long he played.

"The enchantment that is bound within the metal of the sphere is old. It requires the music to be played daily to strengthen it. Every twenty four hours, to the minute, it must be played or else the enchantment will weaken."

"What happens if it weakens?" Calderon questioned.

"The soul of the dragon that is captured within is a fire dragon. The enchantment keeps the sphere cold, which ensures the beast is trapped inside. If the enchantment weakens, the temperature of the metal drops. And if that were to happen, the dragon would be able to escape. Were the dragon to roam this world again … it would be the end of things as we know it."

The old man knew more about the sphere than any of the books he had read in the library. He was older than any of the other monks, older even than the former Guardian. Calderon didn't like looking into the man's eyes. His piercing gaze made him uncomfortable.

"That is why you must never be late. The music must begin at the exact time, and it must be for a complete hour. If either of these guidelines are not kept, you endanger the entire world."

Calderon was silent in thought. "Why entrust something so important to the monastery? Why did the silversmith bring it to us? Why not destroy the dragon's soul instead of trapping it?"

Donovan shrugged his thin shoulders. "Why he chose to come here is a mystery. From what I have learned in all my years is that while a dragons body can be destroyed, its soul cannot. They are from a time and world beyond ours. There are tales of wizards from ancient times that had dealings with the beasts, but dragons are sly creatures and often betrayed the wizards. No one knows where they came from or how they came to be in our world."

"What if I fail?" Calderon asked, hesitating to ask such a dramatic question.

Donovan didn't answer. Instead, he led Calderon to

the chamber of the sphere. They relieved Velkyn and entered the room. This would be the fifth night that he played the music. Each night became less stressful. His sleeping disorder even seemed less active than he could ever remember.

He put the flute to his lips and began to play his music. Perhaps he had been wrong about his fears.

● ∞ ● ∞ ●

Velkyn had trained for years to make his mind more powerful than his body. Guarding a door that could be attacked for twenty one hours a day, with only three hours to rest was no easy feat. The first couple days hadn't been too difficult, but it was beginning to catch up to him. He desperately needed sleep. It was hard for him to keep his eyes open. They were beginning to water and his eyelids were so heavy. He managed to make it to his room and slump into his bed. Sleep overcame him almost immediately.

His eyes shot open. How long had he been out? It felt like he had slept for hours. Panic gripped him as the thought that he might have overslept entered his mind. He heard a noise and sat up quickly.

"It's been a week since I've seen you," a female voice echoed in the darkness. Velkyn turned toward the doorway, where he heard the voice.

"Nydel … when did you get in here?" Velkyn whispered. He felt her soft hand touch the left side of his face.

"Just now. Why haven't you come to see me?" she whispered back, leaning in close.

"I was chosen as the Guardian. I get relieved late in the evening."

She hopped into the bed and straddled him. "I'm so proud of you!" she said excitedly as she wrapped her arms around him.

"Sshh! Not so loud, woman. Someone might hear you. I have to get back to my post soon. I only get three hours away."

"I saw you from down the hall, you just got in here. You must be exhausted," she pouted. "You are probably too tired …" she said sensually. She pulled her shirt off and tossed it to the side.

Velkyn shook his head and pulled her face close to his. "Mm … I missed you."

● ∞ ● ∞ ●

Velkyn arrived back at his post just in time to meet Calderon and Donovan as they were leaving the chamber. Donovan didn't say anything but continued on his way. Calderon stopped. "You look exhausted."

Velkyn waited until he didn't see the old man anymore. "Nydel came to see me."

"Here?" Calderon asked incredulously.

Velkyn smirked. "She's amazing. I *will* make her my wife one day." Calderon could only raise his eyebrows in response. He knew that wouldn't be very likely, but he didn't want to point that out.

"Are you going to attend the coronation?" Velkyn asked Calderon, abruptly changing the subject.

"The entire monastery is attending." Calderon responded. "Donovan just told me about it. How did you find out? And are you the only one guarding it?"

Velkyn shrugged. "I honestly don't know. I would imagine the other candidates will be under my supervision to keep it safe. I hear the king of Oakvalor will be present. Who knows what they might have planned. And anything that concerns the sphere comes to me first. After the Abbot, of course."

Calderon waited in silence a few moments to make

sure Donovan was completely out of earshot. "I am playing the music by myself from now on. Donovan thinks his time is coming. I'm nervous about playing alone. What if—" Velkyn raised his hand to quiet his friend. "Trust in yourself, Calderon. You have too much fear about what might be, when you should live in what is. They were not wrong in choosing you. You'll be fine."

Calderon wasn't so sure of that.

● ∞ ● ∞ ●

It was hard for Calderon to believe it was time to play again. The days seemed to drown together. He had not seen Donovan at all since he played his music the night before. It was entirely possible he had passed during the night. Given the importance of the coronation, it was unlikely he would get the news of his mentor's death.

As he approached the sphere's chamber, a tingly feeling spread down his back. He reached down to rub the spot and the feeling went away, but he didn't feel right. He felt ... off. Shaking his head, he continued on and relieved Velkyn from his duty. He pushed the door open and entered the dimly lit chamber, pausing to let his eyes adjust.

It was almost time.

Calderon placed the flute to his lips and breathed in deep.

He opened his eyes and was looking up at the ceiling. A horrible feeling of dread washed over him. He had fallen asleep! Calderon struggled up to his feet and tried frantically to determine how much time had passed. He pulled the chamber door open just enough to look out. Velkyn was not back yet. Perhaps he had only dozed off for a short moment.

He pushed the door shut and began to play his

music like normal. As he played, he glanced around the room. The room was so dim, he wasn't sure how much time had passed, if any at all. Perhaps he had passed out and not fallen asleep? He wasn't sure. He eyed the sphere closely. It did not appear noticeably different, though he never really paid attention to what the sphere looked like. Calderon rested one hand on the sphere as he held a note on his flute.

It was cool to the touch, but he had only touched it once before. Was it always cool to the touch? He couldn't remember.

Calderon was so engrossed with the sphere he did not hear the door swing open. "Calderon," he heard Velkyn whisper. He spun around, startled by the sound. Velkyn stood in the doorway motioning him. "Your hour has passed, my friend. Come, your duty is complete for today. The sphere must be readied for the coronation tomorrow."

Calderon nodded, unsure of how long he had played his music anyway. He assumed he had played long enough to keep the enchantment strong. He left the chamber and stood in the hallway as Velkyn shut the door. "I will see you at the palace tomorrow. Do you suppose we will meet the new king?" Calderon asked as Velkyn took his post.

"If the Divines see fit to allow it," Velkyn responded. "You look pale. You should get some rest. Wait …" Velkyn's voice lowered. "you didn't fall asleep, did you?"

"No, I didn't." Calderon lied. "I just feel a little weak now. I will see you tomorrow at the coronation. It will be exciting to see what lies outside these walls."

As troubled as Calderon was about his sleeping disorder having roused its ugly head, he had little difficulty sleeping through the night. As the light of dawn shown through the small window of his room, he was readying himself to see the palace for the first time in his life.

"The single most appalling atrocity perpetrated on the world happened when a mysterious man made the king believe the Divines were real. The horrible truth is this: they are the product of make-believe by a man who crafted his own religion. Because of this, the true knowledge of the Creator of our world may be forever lost."

- Jasiel
Former priest

CHAPTER 7

The palace was buzzing with rumors. Prince Ranaan sifted through the conversations of the servants as they dashed about, whispering in not-so-quiet tones. He feigned ignorance and continued making his way through the vast hallways that led above ground and to the throne room. The servants were always full of gossip and sharing the latest intrigue, but today was different.

Today, there was talk of death.

Barely reaching five feet, Ranaan was not an intimidating figure. His hair was black and of medium length, usually tied in a pony-tail. His bangs hung down in sharp points and he was always pushing them aside. His eyes were an icy blue and stood out vividly when he wore his formal white uniform. The youngest of his father's two sons, he would not take the throne but instead would be allowed to do with his life as he chose.

He reached the hidden doorway that led to the section of the castle that was above ground. At the end of the hallway was two massive wooden doors. As he approached he was greeted by two guards, one at each side of the entrance. They bowed low at his arrival. They grunted as they pushed the doors open, bowing once more as Ranaan swept past them without acknowledgement. The audience room was an enormous circular chamber. It was usually filled with nobles, but today it was empty.

His father was seated on the throne, a large oak chair plated in gold and silver. His brother, the heir to the throne, stood attentively at his side.

"You called for me father?" His voice echoed in the empty chamber.

Dagmar, his brother, had a grave look on his face. "He can't speak, Ranaan. His condition has worsened. The healers said—" his voice cracked and he paused. The emotional turmoil was obvious. "They said he won't make it through the night."

Ranaan stood in silence, unsure how to take the news. He loved his father dearly, but the man was nearing ninety and time had not been kind to him. A disease of the mind had consumed him and he was no longer the man Ranaan remembered. It was a confusing mix of emotions. Sadness at the imminent death of his father, but relief that his suffering would soon be at an end.

Byramm, the royal chamberlain, made his presence known by coughing softly. "Your Highness's," he greeted solemnly. "You know what this means.."

Dagmar looked to Ranaan. "Do you object?"

"You know I don't," Ranaan replied, lowering

himself to one knee. "I support your reign as king." He lowered his head in homage.

Their father, in a rare show of normalcy, reached up weakly and pulled his crown off. He looked at Dagmar and mouthed something unintelligible. Dagmar hesitantly took hold of the crown. Lifting it up, he stared at the large black diamond in its center. He looked to Ranaan, then to the chamberlain, and lastly, his father.

The old king nodded his head slowly. Dagmar placed the crown on his own head.

"Long live the king," Ranaan said.

There was complete silence. Byramm waited a few moments to speak, not wanting to ruin the moment. "My Lord's, I do not wish to rush your mourning, but there are things that need to be done. We must announce the coronation and summon the monks from the Abbey to bring the sphere." Byramm eyed Dagmar critically. "And we must summon the tailor."

● ∞ ● ∞ ●

"There is one more thing, brother." The tailor was busy taking Dagmar's measurements, her hands a flurry of fingers and measuring tape.

Ranaan looked questioningly at his brother.

"I am announcing a truce with Oakvalor."

Ranaan's face turned incredulous. "What! There hasn't been peace since … since anyone can remember. At least, not a real peace. How in the Divines are you going to manage a truce?"

"Marriage."

The tailor produced a plush violet robe and placed it over Dagmar's shoulders. Using needles and some sort of sticky parchment, she marked out where she would need to make cuts in the material. "I am going to marry the princess of Oakvalor. It is going to be announced at the coronation."

Ranaan was at a loss for words. "It is what is best for the people of our kingdom. And theirs. Enough blood has been shed in a war that neither side can win. No one can even remember how it started or why. It is time to leave our feuds in the past and work toward a better future."

Ranaan looked at his brother in a new light. He seemed wiser somehow. "It makes sense to me, brother. I'm not sure how the people will accept it. War is all we know. I stand behind any decision you make. And I will stand behind this one. My heart says peace would be a nice change, but my mind doesn't know what peace is."

"My prayer and my hope is that we can change that." Dagmar looked at himself in the mirror. "Do I look like a king?" he asked jokingly. Ranaan chuckled softly. He had to wonder if Dagmar meant 'we' as in he and his bride to be, or together as brothers. He supposed it didn't matter so long as the people of the kingdom were happy.

"You look noble to me, but what do I know?"

● ∞ ● ∞ ●

"No, no, no! You will stand here," the chamberlain screeched, pointing to a specific stone on the floor. Raanan rolled his eyes at the old man. He reminded Raanan of his grandmother, wrinkly and decrepit. Between the heat and the old man's irritating voice, it was all he could do not to snap. "Why does it matter where we stand, Byramm?"

Byramm's face turned a deep crimson color. "It is tradition! Which you apparently lack any knowledge of. You are fortunate you're not a child anymore."

Raanan smirked at the chamberlain. "Careful, Byramm. I might break your hip."

"Please brother," Dagmar interjected, "we must get this right before evening. Two days from now is the coronation and we will have the entire kingdom watching. The less inexperienced we look, the better."

Raanan conceded the point and stood where the chamberlain directed. That old man had been a pain, usually quite literally, when he was younger. Anytime he made a mistake, Byramm was always there to deliver discipline. Now that he was in charge of himself, he could pick at the chamberlain all he pleased with no painful retaliation.

The next few hours were full of boredom for Raanan as the chamberlain laid out the course of events that would unfold leading up to the coronation. The monastery would bring the sphere out as a symbolic display of power, there would be a few speeches by the people who had helped raise the older prince, and once they were finished, he would be crowned the new king of Talvaard. The only thing that would be different from any other ceremony, at least according to Byramm, was the announcement of the marriage and treaty with Oakvalor.

"The general has tripled the guard in the event the people do not initially take to the idea. There will also be archers on the rooftops. We are not only protecting our new king, but also our new ally and his entourage."

"That should be plenty of protection," Dagmar said. "I've given King Elkanah permission to bring his bodyguard as well. We have made every preparation possible. Now we can only trust the Divines for the best."

● ∞ ● ∞ ●

The palace grounds were crowded with people who had come to see the crowning of the new king. Many of them had traveled hundreds of miles from all corners of the kingdom to glimpse the ceremony. The kings of Talvaard were known to live long and die of old age rather than of battle or disease, so the ceremony was a rare event.

Innumerable banners and flags of bright orange, yellow, and red lined the buildings and walkways leading up to the Palace Square. Why it was called a square, no one was certain. The stonework that laid out the area in front of the great wall which separated the actual palace and the Square was in the shape of a rectangle. Whoever had termed it a square, the description stuck.

Soldiers wearing ceremonial armor, emblazoned with the royal insignia of a phoenix bursting forth from a pile of ashes, stood guard along the streets to ensure order and keep the crowds from overwhelming the plaza where the sphere and the new king would be. Archers lined the rooftops with bows in hand, keeping careful watch. The entire population of the monastery, with the exception of the Guardian and those under his command, formed a large circle around a short pillar to the right of where the king would stand. Velkyn and the three former candidates for his position stood alert with their backs to the sphere, forming a protective square. An identical pillar to the left held the crown used only for coronations.

Prince Raanan peered down at the scene below from the window of the throne room. Dagmar would pace the room, then turn, and pace back. "Are you nervous, brother?" Raanan chided. "You act as though you have never stood before a crowd."

His brother ceased his march. "It is easy for you to be calm. You aren't the one who is accepting a crown that has many enemies. Not to mention the ire I may receive from the people of our kingdom with the announcement I make today. So yes, brother, I am nervous." Dagmar continued pacing back and forth.

Raanan shrugged and turned his gaze back to the scene outside. He could see the glint of the sphere through the veil that covered it. Enormous groups of children waved miniature flags with the royal crest. It seemed that the people were happy. The Square was a much different place the night before when they held the funeral. The same people who were excitedly waving flags and banners were also the same people who had cried and openly mourned the loss of their previous king.

Ranaan thought about how his father looked inside the casket. He had always viewed his father as tall and strong, wise and venerable. Seeing him shriveled and pale just lying in a box made him conscious of the reality of death. It was no respecter of people or their status.

Trumpets signaling the approach of King Elkanah momentarily drowned out the sound of the people talking and cheering. Raanan looked to see which direction the entourage was coming from and spotted them to the west. He could see about twenty men dressed in the colors of Oakvalor marching in front of a carriage.

"Brother," he said loudly, "our guests have arrived."

Dagmar seemed not to hear the news, so Raanan motioned the guards to escort the visiting king to the plaza. "Have you seen her?" Raanan asked aloud.

"Who?" Dagmar replied.

"Your future wife. Have you seen her?"

Dagmar still did not cease pacing the throne room. "No. Why do you ask?"

"What if she is ugly?" Raanan laughed, though his brother did not.

"I do not see how the beauty of my queen has

anything to do with bringing peace to our kingdoms."

"It doesn't." Raanan answered. "Though it would be humorous for you to go into the history books as a king who married a repulsive woman." That did cause Dagmar to stop his pacing and glare at him. "Come now, brother," Raanan left the window and embraced his sibling. "I only jest to lighten your heart."

"There will be plenty of time for you to jest after the ceremony," Dagmar said curtly. "Though … I do hope she isn't unsightly." He smiled at Raanan and continued his pacing.

One of the generals appeared in the doorway. "Your Highness," his deep voice echoed in the giant marble chamber, "The king and his daughter await you in the plaza."

Raanan removed the robe that lay on the throne and wrapped it around his brother's shoulders. "That's our queue."

● ∞ ● ∞ ●

Calderon could hear the Abbot arguing heatedly with someone in hushed tones. When he looked to see who, he was surprised to see Donovan. His spirits lifted when he saw his mentor, but when he realized his mentor was the one arguing with the Abbot, he got confused. He could only hear pieces of their conversation over the noise of the crowd.

"You must remove it," Donovan said.

"That will never happen. The coronation will begin any moment, and we will not insult our new king."

"Something is wrong … I feel … dangerous," Calderon strained to hear what Donovan was saying, but the crowd was getting louder. "It's not safe."

The sound of horns blaring overpowered every sound and shook the ground around them. "All hail

Prince Dagmar and Prince Raanan!" One of the heralds roared.

Calderon thought the crowd was loud before the princes arrived. The masses shoved forward and it was all the soldiers could do to hold them back. He could see a general barking out orders but couldn't make out the words. Then the two bothers entered the plaza, surrounded by a host of at least two dozen men armed to the teeth. He had not seen much outside the monastery and was overwhelmed by everything.

He looked to where Donovan had been but the old man was gone. The Abbot seemed unfazed by whatever his mentor had said. Velkyn looked calm and composed compared to the soldiers fighting to keep the crowds at bay.

It took almost twenty minutes to restore order and get the people to be silent enough for the ceremony to begin. Despite the chaos of the crowds, everything seemed well orchestrated as each person who had written a speech about the new king came forward and spoke about their memories of Dagmar as a child and various other stories about his character.

As soon as the chamberlain finished talking, an odd hush fell over the crowd. Calderon wasn't sure why everyone suddenly went quiet. It was probably the only moment of silence he had experienced since leaving the monastery that morning.

Byramm approached the pillar that held the crown and gently picked it up. He turned to Dagmar and lifted the crown into the air. "It is my esteemed honor to name you, Prince Dagmar, as the new king, by royal lineage, over the kingdom of Talvaard and its people." Placing the crown upon Dagmar's head, Byramm turned to the assembly. "I give you King Dagmar!"

A great shout filled the air, though the people did not try to surge forward this time. Calderon noticed

Prince Ranaan was staring at the sphere. The veil had been removed and it seemed so bright. Ranaan seemed to be entranced by the thing and oblivious to anything around him. The prince closed his eyes and opened his mouth in a scream that was lost in the sound of the thousands of people cheering.

Panic gripped Calderon as he wondered what was wrong with the prince. He was about to rush forward to help him but noticed that one of the soldiers came to his aid.

Raanan kept shaking his head and seemed unsteady on his feet. It seemed to Calderon that nobody had noticed the prince's odd behavior. Suddenly Raanan seemed fine. He stood straight and pushed the soldier away from him.

Calderon kept his eyes on the prince to see if anything else happened, but he seemed fine. Dagmar was trying to hush the crowd, and eventually Calderon turned his attention away from Raanan.

"I have an announcement," Dagmar yelled loudly to be heard as the noise of the people died down. "We have long been at war with our neighbors, and I am sure you are all wondering why the king of Oakvalor is here for my coronation. Today the nation of Talvaard and Oakvalor put our feuding past behind us. Today, my people, we forge a peace that not even our forefathers imagined. Today, I will marry the daughter of King Elkanah and seal a treaty of peace between our kingdoms!"

There was complete silence. Calderon eyed the crowd. Everyone just stood there, staring at their new king with wide eyes and in some cases, wide mouths. Then someone in the back started clapping. Then another followed suit. And another. And another, until everyone was clapping in approval of the union.

King Elkanah brought forth his daughter and the

people began cheering loudly again. To say the woman was beautiful was an understatement. Calderon was awed by her eyes. They were bright blue, and her white flowing dress made them seem all the brighter. Her hair was blonde and long, perhaps reaching the middle of her back.

The two kings embraced each other in a hug, and then Dagmar took the woman by her hand. "What's your name?" Dagmar asked embarrassedly.

"Nizana."

"It's as beautiful as you are," he complimented.

A great smile spread across her face, revealing her teeth which were just as white as her dress.

Despite the loudness and chaos of the crowd, Calderon was glad to have experienced this moment. "History in the making," he whispered to himself. He noticed Prince Raanan was hovering toward the back of the plaza, his behavior seeming odd again. And then …

Calderon watched in sheer horror as a scene more nightmarish than anything he could ever dream played out before his very eyes.

Ranaan shoved his brother to the ground from behind. Unsheathing a sword from the soldier who helped him, he thrust the blade into Nizana's abdomen. Blood spurt forth onto Ranaan's hands and onto the floor. There was a wild look in the prince's eyes as he jerked the blade free.

Dagmar stared in horror and confusion, unsure of what to do. King Elkanah pointed at Ranaan and ordered his bodyguard to seize the murderer. The crazed look on his face made the guards hesitate. Then in a quick fluid motion, he swung the blade in a giant arc and decapitated his brother.

Time seemed to cease for Calderon, but for everyone else, all hell broke loose. The Talvaard soldiers, unsure of what they should do, grouped protectively around Prince Ranaan. King Elkanah's bodyguards did likewise and began systematically moving him away from the Square to the carriage, pushing their way through the distraught crowd.

People were screaming and trampling each other to get away from the horrific sight. Calderon's attention snapped back to the direction of the sphere when he heard the familiar voice of his friend Velkyn shouting for the monks to shield the sphere with their bodies. The thunderous sound of magic boomed and lit up the square in a bluish-green light and King Elkanah's carriage, and his entourage, disappeared from sight.

"So there are wizards," Calderon whispered in disbelief. He felt a hand on his shoulder and looked up to see the Abbot. "Go with Velkyn and the others and take the sphere to safety." Calderon nodded and left the circle to join his friend. He noticed that the soldiers had moved Ranaan behind the stone wall of the palace.

"What in the name of the Divines just happened?" he yelled. Velkyn shook his head grimly. "I'm not sure, but it seems like a coupe just happened."

"A what?"

Velkyn pointed to the dead body of Dagmar. "An overthrow and seizure of the throne by a jealous brother. Come, we have to get the sphere back to the monastery."

● ∞ ● ∞ ●

The trip back was rushed and nothing like the trip earlier that morning. Calderon had been entranced by the beauty of the capital city and the surrounding countryside. Everything now seemed different. Velkyn personally carried the sphere and only allowed Calderon to walk near him.

"Why would the Prince kill King Elkanah's daughter, let alone his own brother?" one of the monks whispered to another.

"Why indeed?" Calderon looked questioningly to Velkyn.

"Your assumption is as good as mine," he replied, holding the sphere tightly to his chest. "Perhaps he wasn't happy with not being king."

Calderon's heart was heavy with grief. This was the only time he had left the monastery since he entered the sacred halls and it ended in bloodshed. A nagging thought in the back of his mind kept reminding him that the day wasn't over yet.

*"The Tunnel is an omen of the worst kind. Through much research
we have found that it is an omen that only appears in Oakvalor, and
within Oakvalor, only on the Five Islands."*

-Lord Aio's journal

CHAPTER 8

The sun was barely a sliver of dimming yellow light on
the horizon. The few clouds in the sky shone red in the
waning light of day above the low, forested hills of the
Red Island. If one were watching from the hills
overlooking the east or west parts of the valley at this
time, he would have seen a shadow slowly stretch over
to the south, creeping slowly down into the valley over
the vast patchwork of fields, orchards, and pastures. All
that could be seen of the Aiakh River was a dark ribbon,
glittering like a long snakelike diamond in the last rays
of the sunlight, winding its way north up the valley and
out through a tunnel under the hills.

One could see the campfires of the ruby and iron
miners being lit on the hillsides. The familiar sounds of
cattle, sheep, and goats being herded into their caves just
above the valley. The smell of dead fish that were daily

brought upstream for trade with the farmers came up from the valley, rising with the heat of the day. Occasionally, a warm, gentle breeze would blow from the valley up into the hills, the richness and aroma reminding the entire island of the impending harvest.

A horn sounded, heralding the coming of night. In response, the sound of a flute playing an ancient melody rose from one of the campfires. It was a beautiful song, composed ages before the migration of the first twelve tribes of the Aihi into the Five Islands of Oakvalor. Such a song is very difficult to describe, as one would not hear the likes of it elsewhere. If one listened closely, you could hear voices coming up out of the earth, singing their ancient chant to the sound of the flute. The branches of trees rustled in the gentle breeze, humming along with the music. All of nature seemed to sing the song of the flute. If the song had words, one could be sure that all of the men, women, and children on the Island would have sung its chorus on that peaceful night.

All was peaceful on the Red Island as the sun set on that late summer evening. One felt like celebrating with every breath, such was the richness of the pre-harvest air. All the children were sleeping soundly in their beds, while the mothers prepared nighttime meals for their husbands coming back from a long day of work in the fields, pastures, and orchards.

As soon as the sun had set, the moon in its full brightness rose from the southern horizon. Proceeding, guarding, and following it were thousands of bright stars, lighting up the heavens. The sun had gone to bed along with the children of the valley, and then had come the moon, escorted by her children, to continue the great dance across the sky.

If any man by this time still had a trouble, discomfort, or sense of foreboding on his mind, it would have soon been forgotten. For once, all troubled thoughts and worries could be put aside until the morning. For just a few hours of time, man's mind could be at peace. All of the Red Island sang with that flute song, and the hearts of mankind sang with it. For just a short period of time, in the face of eternity, all was at peace.

The aged prophet made his way up the lonely mountain path after his journey to and from the busy streets of the capital city, Aicatan. He and his disciple, Lord Imen, had traveled much during the previous week. After four days of treading the valley roads, a week of sleeping in the cramped rooms of the city inns and taverns, and many rigorous ceremonies and rites of passage, both master and—especially—pupil were glad to be returning to their peaceful homes on the mountain, and looking forward to a comfortable rest in their own beds.

The prophet, called Lord Aio, would have had little trouble hiding behind any medium sized tree trunk or small boulder without having to crouch low or stand sideways. His pupil, who was of average height and build, dwarfed him considerably. His scarred, withered arms told of many long death matches. What little muscle that could be found on his diminutive frame would have been hard enough to force any Cannibal to leave the morsel in frustration, claiming it in the primitive Cannibal tongue to be a peculiar type of stone. His brown, oven-baked face—but one of the many perils endured—was decorated by a long, unkempt and unwashed scarlet beard, framed on top by hair of similar color, length, fashion, and state. The dark eyes sinking deep into his face had not lost the fire of youth, but had been stoked with over a century of war and wisdom. His thin, cracked, dry lips almost matched his face in color.

His earthen-colored traveling cloak was covered with dust of a slightly lighter hue. His feet and ankles were so caked with dust, sticking to his skin from the sweat caused by wearing sandals for an extended period of time. The aroma of pipe-smoke mixed with the odors of sweat and old age emanated from his body.

They halted for a moment. The prophet inhaled deeply, feeling the warmth and richness of the air surge throughout his entire body, restoring some of his long lost youth.

"A fine evening, Lord Imen," he said.

"It is, Lord Aio," said Imen, attempting to catch his breath before the tireless prophet continued the seemingly endless march.

The Lord Aio nodded. "The Ai has shown us favor in giving us such an evening. One hundred and forty-three years ago this hour, the personified Ai, the Great Aio, appeared on this Island."

The young High Priest wiped the sweat off his forehead as he gazed out over the Island, looking over every twist in the river, every small campfire, every stone and tree, the moon and every small star, and every lighted window that was visible in the valley; hearing every miner's flute and every grazing beast that was raised in the valley; absorbing every breath of wind, the odor of fish and manure. All of this, the good and the evil, the agreeable and disagreeable, the pleasant and the unpleasant, had been made by the Ai. All living and non-living things were of the Ai.

In the past—he had been told—the Ai had spoken to mankind through visions, or through the clouds, and sometimes in a great, blinding white light. However, the Ai, for a short period of forty-eight years, came to the Five Islands in the form of a man. It was at that very hour, and on that Island, one hundred and forty-three years before, the Ai has chosen a place for his unannounced arrival. For a moment, Imen forgot all of his troubles, discomforts, fears, and even his exhaustion in that thought.

Following that brief pause, they continued their arduous climb up the narrow, steep, winding trail for what seemed to the pupil to be an hour (though it was probably a good deal less than half). It had always amazed Imen how the decrepit old mentor always managed to be a good three paces ahead of the young warrior, never tiring or seeming to need a rest, while the youthful student felt as if his legs would fall out from under him.

They came to a place where the ground leveled off, surrounded on all but one side by high rock formations. In the center of this area lay five large, flat stones arranged in a circle, all of them large enough for one to sit upon with space left over for a staff, cloak, or a sword. If one were to look over the side not surrounding the mountain, he would have seen a patchwork of fields and orchards spread from beneath him, allowing him to view almost the entire valley.

The Lord Aio suddenly stopped, staring into a space that had opened up in the side of the mountain during his absence. For what seemed like an eternity to Imen, he stared in amazement and terror at the opening, never once blinking or letting his gaze shift from the tunnel before him. If he had not been paralyzed by the sight, his body would have shuddered violently. The look of death shone in his eyes.

Imen, at the sight, felt a mountain of fear fall upon him. He had heard of this omen, its meaning, and its history, yet he had never seen it until now. He wished he could have run and hidden, or better yet, jumped off the cliff wall that fell below him into the valley. The Tunnel had again been opened.

"This cannot be happening," stated Imen, the shock evident in the shaking of his voice.

The words of Imen breaking him from his stupor, the Lord Aio shook the dust of the ground off his traveling cloak, muttering to himself in the ancient tongue of the Ai.

"The Tunnel has again been opened to us," he said to Imen, "and troubled—nay, far worse than troubled—times are to come. The East Wind grows bolder than ever; life eludes the West Wind; the fire grows cold. Sit upon this sacred stone, Lord Imen, and guard the Tunnel with your life. Let no one pass in or out unchallenged. I feel that an evil has come upon the Island. An evil I have not known for almost ..."

Wincing as if feeling pain from some terrible memory, the Lord Aio turned quickly and walked up the path to his hut. After his master was out of sight, Imen sat down with his sword drawn, his eyes searching, and his ears ever attentive.

He could feel the cold winds of danger and fear cut through him like a sword. The ancient melodies played by the miners, and the warm, peaceful atmosphere that had just a few minutes earlier dominated the entire Island was suddenly gone. He shivered a bit, even though the night was warm and the weather fair and despite wearing a traveling cloak.

Just a few minutes before, he thought only of a long, peaceful sleep. Now, he felt as if he had awakened to find himself living in one of his worst nightmares. Every rock looked as if to conceal a ghoul, a Cannibal, or an Orc behind it. Likewise, every tree was the dwelling place of evil spirits. Imen felt as though the Tunnel itself would swallow him. The smallest sound was an army of demons. Every few minutes, Imen would check behind the rock he sat on to assure himself that no danger lay hidden in its shadow.

What reason had he to fear? He had been hungry. He had been without necessities. He had suffered pain. He had been betrayed. He had seen war. He had seen defeat. He had seen death, and had even faced it a couple of times. He, more than the population of the Five Islands, would know what it meant to have troubles. But the Tunnel? Nay. Although the High Priest knew of troubles, the opening of the Tunnel meant troubles of the worst kind. Atrocities that had caused even the greatest warriors to cower and flee as children escaping some punishment for some seemingly great offense, tortures that had caused even the most devout Priests to publicly denounce the Ai and claim allegiance to the forces of evil. A living death within a living death, as the Lord Aio had described some of the wars he had fought in during the time of the opened Tunnel.

High Priest over the Red Island was he, and a proven warrior. High Priest *and* warrior. On this night, however, he felt more like the small child that has strayed from his mother in a place he does not know. Although the Lord Aio and the other four pupils were just a few minutes' walk up the mountain trail, well within earshot, he felt as though even his closest of friends had betrayed and deserted him in the thick of a battle.

The Tunnel had again been opened, and although he knew not what would happen, impending doom lurked behind the mask of that once peaceful evening.

- Father Ean

CHAPTER 9

At first glance, to say that he was an elderly person would have been the grossest of understatements. So numerous and deep were the wrinkles that creased his aged face, he was almost beyond recognition as a man. The darkened, earthen color of his face, the large forehead, the small, black deep-set probing eyes, the slightly pointed ears, a long, crooked hawk-like nose that looked as if someone had pulled on it too long, and a thin, slightly darkened pair of dehydrated lines he called lips did not help. The unmistakably human salt-white beard that hung from his protruding chin was the only thing that identified his human ancestry at this point in his life.

Beginning at the top of his head, coming down to the side in both directions forming an arc, his head was adorned with thin, dirty white hair of moderate length resting upon his shoulders. For the most part, this was

76

unkempt and in it, one could find the remains of dead insects, traces of spider's webs, leaves, twigs, and almost any other type of small objects that can rest in one's hair. On very special occasions, he would wash it, comb through it with his eleven gnarled fingers (their appearance more like claws), and thread an intricate pattern of vines, leaves, and wildflowers into it. He had not had such as occasion of celebration in over ninety years. The greasy quality of his hair, as well as the dirt and filth that had claimed his head as a permanent habitat were quite conspicuous.

His tall, bony frame was clothed (if at all) in the leaves of the oak tree, woven together in a complex pattern by a myriad of pine needles. He would have two sheets of this covering, one in front, the other in back, connected on the sides and top by long, thick blades of grass or even the vines from his extensive vineyard.

Regardless of what ages he had seen come and go, he had towered above even the tallest of men from each race. Although not carrying a single drop of giant's blood in his veins, he appeared as one with a tall wisp of a body, strong arms of immense length that one would think they could stretch to the ends of the world, claw-like fingers, and the thin, stick-like legs and feet that could have been mistaken for roots taking into account the leaves and twigs in his hair and the leaves that covered his body.

On this particular morning, he sat at the edge of the lush, green forest on the Island of Cerel, his eyes peering down into the bustling commerce and life that was characteristic of any bay in the dominion of the Five Islands. Well hidden from view, a sighting of him by one of the people in the town below would have upset the whole of the Five Islands. It had been centuries since any man had ever seen him, much less spoken to him. Even to the Council of High Priests, he was merely a legend, a story told among the more youthful circles sitting around the campfires. There had not been need for an appearance for a very long time, and he felt no desire to appear.

He had begun to feel the pangs of old age settle in about one hundred years before. From shortly after the founding of Oakvalor as a nation, he had forsaken the path of the rest of men and chose to serve the Ai, to look after and tend Oakvalor. On choosing this, his body and functions had changed dramatically. He had become one with the earth, his body aging ever so slowly. However, as all men did at some point in their lives, he would have to die. He did not expect to admire the bay from his camouflaged position again.

Looking down upon the bay at the brightly colored ships, the acreage of canvas used for sails, the fathoms of rope and netting, the crates, the sailors and vendors, the merchants, and the many people there to see what goods were to be had after market day, he could not help thinking about how much things had changed, yet how little the Aihi themselves had changed. The race had been much the same when he had been a part of it, caring only for its immediate pleasures, at most, thinking of how to build a strong financial foundation for the next generation. The Aihi had not changed.

He had changed, however. He had at one time been as those he viewed from afar, seeking pleasures that he knew would satisfy him only a short while. Perhaps it was the long centuries of his work that had caused the change, or the knowledge he had accumulated during that time. Perhaps it was from having seen the history of Oakvalor. Maybe his longevity. It could have been all four reasons, or even others unsurmised. "The answer will be known but to the Ai," he thought. "Perhaps I shall be informed after my death."

Having seen millions of people, empires, races, and

even ages come to life, bloom, and then whither one would expect him to be an authority on death. This was the farthest thing from the truth. Although he had seen death in all different manners (even having caused it on occasion), his extensive knowledge ceased its long reach when it came to this concept. He had spent his entire life helping things to live and grow, giving life to the plants and animals of Oakvalor and the Five Islands. What lay beyond the moment of the body's death, not even he could foresee.

For the first few centuries of his work, he had feared death more than pain, hunger, or fire. Having seen the ages rise and fall, having witnessed most of Oakvalor's history— the extremes of evil and good—he no longer feared death. And despite his lack of knowledge on the subject he would have welcomed it at any time.

He sighed. To be even as blissful in the ignorance of these people once again! He had seen too much, had lived too long. He longed to purge himself of his body, to finally join with the Ai.

A hand came to rest upon his shoulder. "A fine bit of handiwork, brother."

Without turning, the old man nodded. "The work of my master, the Ai."

"It would have been destroyed by these creatures we let populate it without your help."

"Perhaps," he pondered. "Perhaps. It will not be long now, however, before I must select for myself one who will carry on my work. I have not much longer as the gardener of Oakvalor. I wish to live no longer. I beckon death. It draws nearer, as we speak."

"Nearer, brother. It has been many a century since I said those exact words. How correct was the wise man that said, 'The parting of oneself from one's body brings momentary pain, but ever after, blissful rest.'"

The old man closed his eyes and nodded. "Blissful rest. When I undertook the task of tending Oakvalor, I was young and restless. Perhaps a touch of foolhardy."

"Foolhardy!" interrupted the other speaker. "It becomes you less to speak of it as such. Curious, maybe, as is the nature of all men, but foolhardy? Nay."

"Curiosity then!" continued the old man. "And overflowing of it was my cup. I had seen nothing of the world's horizons surrounding the Five Islands. I was young, even to the standard of the time. Did I care for the life of the farmer, the herdsman, or the miner? Nay, I was the explorer. Before I had reached the age of thirty-three, I knew everything there was to know about the Five Islands. The mountains, the valleys, the mines. It was I who first discovered the Tunnel."

"No small feat," commented the speaker.

"At the time, no," said the old man. "But of what purpose did it serve my lust for wandering? Did it satisfy? Nay. It only increased my appetite for more."

"That I remember," said the speaker. "Our father would not allow us to take one of the boats any farther than a mile past the outer coasts."

"They would not have lasted half that distance," said the old man, laughing. "That much knowledge I have gained from my work."

"That you have. You have tended not only father's nets, our uncle's fields, but you have gardened a nation. You have seen everything that was worth seeing, as well as everything that was not worth seeing. If a new field was ploughed, you knew of it before the man's neighbor heard a sound of the plough animal. If a new pocket of rubies was struck, you knew of its worth in countless ways before the miner recognized the stone. If furnaces beneath Oakvalor have displayed their glories through the tops of the mountains, you welcomed the spectacle while most creatures in fear would run for cover. Many great empires have risen, their numbers far beyond even my reckoning, only to become no more than the soil in which a child's garden in planted. You have even seen the Great Lord Aio face to face, a thing that even I cannot boast. It was destiny that called you from our mother's womb."

"Yes, it would seem that I would be the most fitted to the task. However, it is because I have seen the good, the evil, the land, the mines, the mountains, the empires, and a great deal of the history of Oakvalor that I wish to die. There are no more mountains to climb, forests to probe, valleys in which to run. My lust has been sated and has become distasteful to me. I am tired, brother. I wish no more to explore the new. I can but revel in the memory of the old."

"Perhaps it is not that you are tired of the new, but that you tire of that which you know. An eternity would scarce suffice the time necessary to explore completely even one room in the House of the Ai. Think on it. You have lived long in Oakvalor, long so that even the marvels of this place are common and wearisome. Your desire to explore and discover has not yet been sated, but has merely soured in the absence of novelty. The House of the Ai? You need not worry about running out of worlds to explore. It is more than even your mind can comprehend. Even I, the long-dead mortal fisherman who wished for nothing more than his boat and nets, have developed a taste for exploring."

"You make me feel as the youth I once was, many ages past. The energy, vigor, strength, and unfettered curiosity that our father would whip me for! To have that again! To explore and to discover again! You tempt me, brother, to follow you back this very moment!"

"And as much as you deserve," said his brother, "I would relish in the company of my now much older brother again. You have served well. You have, however, but one more task before your time."

The old man turned and smiled. "A word from the Ai. Such as I have not heard since the beginning of my changed life, and from you, who have not walked Oakvalor for many a thousand years. I live only to serve. Speak on, brother."

"This task will require all of your abilities, and perhaps cause you to discover a few others. You have heard of the advance of Orlek."

The old man spit on the ground in response. "He was a good pupil. He could have served alongside me, maybe even succeeded me. A much earlier death for myself. His is the dominion where even I will not dare to tend. The reek of such evil I cannot bear."

"That he could have succeeded you," said the messenger. "I have only this for you: You are to do whatever you can to assist the new Lord Aio and his followers. However, you are not to make an appearance unless it is completely necessary."

The old man sighed. "I do not have any love for man. Only the Ai. Neither do I love death or peddling it. The only appearance I wish to make is before the Ai himself in His own House. However, I will do what my master has asked. Now, for the sign of your master."

"You were never able to give up the traditions considered old even in our time," said the messenger, laughing from the memory that had been unearthed after millennia of burial.

"I trust you," said the old man. "You are my brother, you are my blood. However, the law is the law, and the law is still in effect. I will not be caught neglecting it. If it was practiced for the message of a mere tribal leader in our day, should we not use the same if not greater precaution for the Ai?"

"You are a true servant of the Ai, brother. Your sign. Look behind you."

The old man slowly turned, a grin mixed of shock and joy forming on his face at what he saw, and their numbers. That which he had not seen in Oakvalor for many centuries. He turned to the messenger. The man had left as he had come, silently and unnoticed.

"Farewell, my brother," he said. "Our day of reunion shall not await me much longer. I shall met you once more, this time in the House of the Ai." The old man turned to his new—or old—friends. "Greetings, cousins," he said, embracing each of their scaled necks. "It has been a long time."

One of them shot a wisp of smoke out of his nostril in affection. "Much time indeed, Father Ean."

"Too much time," said another. "The Serpentauri have been long in waiting for the day we should return to Oakvalor and avenge ourselves."

"Your time has come, my cousin. It has come," said Father Ean. "A pity you did not come to me these hundred years. I am old, and my powers are not what they used to be."

The first of the Serpentauri to speak reared on his hind legs, bellowing in a long column of fire and smoke. "You have not to fear of such, lord, nor to dwell on an imagined weakness. I am Kelros, Chieftain of the Serpentauri that live, descended from our ancestor's of Orlek's golden age. You have as many of us as live to stand behind you."

Father Ean nodded. "Although I would have you stomach your fire until your time to fight has come, I accept your pledge. The battle we fight will not be anything as simple as the one which was fought those generations past. Our enemy has grown strong and all the more bitter in ninety-five years. He has remained alive all this time, an advantage over yourselves."

"We remember. Although the Aihi might let such things slip their memories, the Serpentauri never forget.

We have had just as long as Orlek to remember, perhaps longer. Should we die in battle, better that we die a thousand deaths than back down against an enemy of more advantage, though our race should live to rule Oakvalor."

The old man nodded. "You might think it stupid of me when I ask, but where has been the dwelling place of the Serpentauri these centuries past? I had noticed a drain on the magic that gives life to Oakvalor, but had always thought it to be the festering hole in which Orlek lies."

Kelros laughed. "You were probably correct in the assumption that the dominion of our old friend Orlek is responsible for the drain on magic, although I suppose that we just might have been responsible for a small portion of the loss. The race of the Serpentauri somewhat ... died out ... after the fall of the age of Orlek, at least, that is, disappeared from the Five Islands."

Father Ean nodded in remembrance, allowing the chief to continue. "There is a land to the East, far beyond the limits of the maps and charts used even today. You have been there, I presume?"

"That I have, and know it well," said Father Ean. "Continue."

"A large number of our people set off to the east in whatever boats we could find that had not been destroyed in the battles in an effort to escape the wrath of Orlek should the outcome of the war have been favorable to the orcs. We sailed east with the hope of finding some haven of safety for our race. The boats, built by men for men, did not accommodate us well and had not been built to withstand such a voyage, the length of which our ancestors could not surmise. Many boats fell apart, the occupants drowning. Those vessels that survived the journey were seriously leaking and had become dangerously waterlogged by the time land had been sighted. We were unable to travel further, and the land was to our liking, so we settled there."

The Serpentaur's tongue flicked out across his nose. "Why you had not discovered our presence is a mystery. Perhaps we were guarded by some strange magic."

"Perhaps we were," said the second Serpentaur.

"A fantastic story of perseverance, cousins," said Father Ean. "I still do not see how even one of those boats could have lasted such a journey. I am surprised that our harbors held anything seaworthy after that battle."

"Unbelievable it is, even to us," stated Kelros, smoke slowly trickling up from out of his large mouth. "Even more a mystery, however, is the tale of our return."

Father Ean rested his chin on the top of his staff. "Please tell me this as well."

The Serpentauri began to mumble among themselves, until one said, "We do not remember, Father Ean. We fell asleep this past night. When we awoke, we were sitting here, in this forest. A man approached us, telling us to remain here in silence until you should come to us. You were sitting on that rock when the same man came and spoke to you."

A fourth Serpentaur stepped forward. "Now that we have told you our history, what are our plans? When, Father Ean, do we begin?"

Father Ean laughed. "You must be patient, and not show yourselves until the proper time. The old Great High Priest has been killed, and no doubt his body has been discovered and is being buried this day. The new Great High Priest has yet to be given the Red Sword, the new Council of High Priests to be ordained. We must wait until the battle has begun. I swear to you by all that I was, am, and will become and all that we labor towards that you shall have your revenge."

"Then may the Ai hasten the start of the battle," said Kelros, "and may I live to see the victory, or die amidst the lifeless bodies of my enemies. Victory or my death, for I shall not back down, even if I am the last of the Aihi forces standing. Life for myself on the victory of the Ai and his people. My blood is fairly wagered."

A fifth spoke up. "What are we to do for now, Father Ean?"

The rest of the Serpentauri mumbled in agreement with the question. "He is right," stated Kelros, "for we cannot hide ourselves in this place much longer."

Again, a general agreement from the group. Father Ean sat down again, looking out over the bay. "We have before us a few choices. I could disguise you all as common animals …"

"And be captured and hunted by men. Or eaten by the animals of the forest?" interrupted the second one.

Father Ean continued, ignoring the remark. "The Tunnel entrance has been opened. I suppose that just this arm of the Tunnel would be sufficient to conceal you. A bit dark, though."

"The Priests of this island, at least while our race walked Oakvalor, have guarded the entrance to an opened Tunnel most heavily, letting no man, woman, orc or any other thinking creature enter. Even disguised, we would be destroyed. I say we stay to the places on the Island that are traveled little, such as the Deep Woods," said Kelros.

Father Ean pondered the option a moment. "True. However, there are some, mostly youthful adventure seekers, that still enter the Deep Woods. What would you do if one of these were to discover you? Roast him alive? Nay. The Five Islands will need that hand of the sword before our time is through."

One of the younger of the Serpentauri walked over

to Father Ean, nudging him on the shoulder with his snake-like nose. "The choice is difficult. I, for one, would not lead my people to their deaths, nor wish to cause a friendly hand the same affliction. On this Island, there are not many choices available. We do not know of the habits of these people so changed from the stories handed down through the generations. We can only make a decision and hope it to be the best. You, Father Ean, know this land and its people. You have seen the changes of this race even before our people made alliance with them. You were born as one of these people. We let you decide for us, Father Ean."

Father Ean paused for a few seconds, then grinned. "The Ai's pardon on the poor pupil in green armor that watches the entrance of the Tunnel this night."

Ideas of what was to happen already forming in their minds, the rest of the Serpentauri began to laugh, almost losing control of their fire all at once. After a bit they calmed down, waiting for the sun to bid Oakvalor goodnight. Clouds lined the horizon. The stars would dance behind the billowy curtains that night, almost no light being left for the Tunnel guard to see by. A small amount of magic would be sure to get them past the guard unnoticed in the dark of night. They had but to wait.

"You cannot have a proud and chivalrous spirit if your conduct is mean and paltry; for whatever a man's actions are, such must be his spirit."

- Byramm, chamberlain

CHAPTER 10

Prince Ranaan's attendants would not come near him. No one would except for the chamberlain. Byramm stood in the royal audience chamber, trying desperately to sort through the actions of the young prince. Why would he kill his own brother? And worse, why would he give more reason for Oakvalor to continue the war with them? Prince Ranaan strode into the chamber and sat upon the throne that had long been his father's.

"My Prince," Byramm began. Ranaan looked to him and held his hand up, silencing the chamberlain. "Am I not king?" he asked. "Yes, my lord, but there is the ceremony to make it official. Plans must be made to—"

"I am king," Ranaan interrupted, his tone ending the argument. "I do not need a ceremony to make it so. Call for my generals." Byramm shifted uncomfortably. "My lord?" Ranaan motioned for Byamm to come near. "My brother thought to unite our kingdoms in peace through marriage. There can never be peace. Elkanah sought only to subvert our kingdom through his daughter. My brother was weak to think there could ever be peace."

Byramm shook his head. "You do not believe that." Ranaan glared at the chamberlain. "Do not presume to tell me what I believe. I will not suffer fools. Now call for my generals."

Byramm left the chamber to do as he was bid. Something was amiss. He had raised both Ranaan and his brother from birth and knew that this was not Ranaan's character. Something wasn't right, and he was going to find out what.

Soon after, the men who had faithfully served Ranaan's father as the leaders of the kingdom's military had gathered before the throne. "I demand your loyalty as my father did," Ranaan said, standing tall and straight before the group of generals. Some of them began whispering. One of the men, Lord Sius, stepped forward. "Your father did not demand our loyalty, he earned it by fighting beside us. You haven't even wielded a sword."

Ranaan smirked at the brash general. "I thought you might say that. Hear me out before you make your decision." Sius conferred with the others, then nodded to Ranaan. "We will listen."

The dragon's spirit that had possessed the prince could feel the man's own spirit battling against its will. The dragon easily pushed the man's spirit aside, but could feel him still, trying to fight. This man was persistent. The creature only needed the body long enough to get his own back. "We have long been at war with Oakvalor. My brother thought wrongly to join us with our enemies. That would never do. No, we must drive our enemies out."

"Out?" asked Sius.

"We must drive them out of their own land. We must recall all of the troops and march against Oakvalor.

We will drive them out before the might of our armies. My armies."

The look on Sius's face revealed his incredulity. "We cannot simply call them back. Especially not the men who protect our western borders. And even if we could, it would take weeks just to get them here. It would take months to mobilize them all. Add to that the set up of provision lines, ensuring we have enough water for the troops and the animals … it is not as easily done as you would think, young Ranaan."

"*King* Ranaan, and do not forget my title again, Sius. Either you will carry out my orders or I will appoint someone who will. Someone more loyal to the crown." Ranaan smirked at the general. Lord Sius knew to who Ranaan was referring. A talented young upstart who had earned his way into the dungeon through some disreputable acts. "When do you want to march?" Sius questioned.

"Immediately," Ranaan answered tersely. "My lord," Sius began. Ranaan interrupted him. "You will take the troops still stationed here at the castle immediately, and those recalled will follow. Consider them reinforcements."

"I refuse," Sius said defiantly. He crossed his arms over his chest to accentuate his point. A few of the other generals followed his example. Ranaan's smile left his face quickly and he stared at Sius for long moments. "It wasn't a request." Sius didn't answer, but kept his posture of insolence. Ranaan nodded his head and several heavily armed men stepped out from either side of the throne. "Take them to the dungeon," Ranaan said. "And release Maverick and bring him to me." The guards grabbed Sius and the few men who stood with him and led them out with their weapons drawn.

"As for the rest of you, I am honored by your loyalty," Ranaan smiled again, but it was not out of joy.

"Ready the men and march first thing in the morning. I will have Byramm send out the recall orders without delay. I want a report every two days. As soon as you cross into Oakvalor and reach Palindrom, inform me at once. I will ride to meet you. I would watch the city burn to the ground."

The generals nodded their accord and left the audience chamber. "The dungeon, my king?" Byramm asked hesitantly. "We cannot afford men who will not obey the crown to be running about Talvaard. It is for the safety of the kingdom. Now go and issue a recall of all soldiers. They are to report to the castle. If I have already left for Palindrom, they are to march straightaway to meet the armies there. Oakvalor will fall within the week."

Byramm wasn't so sure about that last statement. Talvaard had long been at a disadvantage due to the fact that Oakvalor had wizards among their cities. Oakvalor might fall, but at what price? Byramm determined that he would follow the king's command. Perhaps he would expound on the orders. Yes, he decided. He would add a few things to ensure there was no miscommunication. He walked with a surety to his step that he had not had since the days of Ranaan's father.

Ranaan finished the remaining affairs of state and retired to his personal chambers. He gazed out one of the windows. It had been too long since he flew above the clouds. The dragon, Cordathvellonth, yearned for his body. He had been promised mountains of gold if he would terrorize Talvaard. Yet that blasted orc Orlek had deceived him. Orlek promised that no wizard had the power to come against him, and yet one had crafted a spell strong enough to wrench his spirit from his body. Blast that wizard! He had killed the wizard in the end, true, but he had spent the last hundred something years trapped in a cold ball of silver.

And so he would raze Palindrom to ensure that would not happen again. He had hoped the king of Oakvalor would have used his bones to decorate the royal carriage. Then he could have resurrected his body and assumed his true form. Instead, Cordath had learned that some fool had the idea to use his bones as decoration for one of Oakvalor's war machines. Now he had to live inside this wretched human until he could find a way to get near his bones. Perhaps when his newly acquired armies marched into Oakvalor, they would bring forth their war machine. Cordath smiled at that. Yes, he could feign retreat and goad Oakvalor into pursuit. And at the right moment, he would fuse his spirit with his body once more. Then he would slaughter every man, woman, and child as retribution for his imprisonment. Cordath felt Ranaan's spirit shudder under his thoughts. Cordath flashed some of his memories at Ranaan, visions of entire cities burned to the ground, mutilated bodies by the hundreds that littered desolate landscapes.

Cordath took pleasure in Ranaan's torment. Orlek had summoned him to this world, but when Cordath was finished with his fiery rage, this world would be nothing. And after he had destroyed everything, he would go back to his own realm. The following morning, when the armies of Talvaard began their march, Cordath knew he was one step closer to annihilating this pathetic world.

CHAPTER 11

Imen mourned the tragic circumstances that found him the temporary leader of the four other pupils. First, the reopening of the Tunnel, and then the death of their beloved master, murdered within the walls of his own hut; a symbol drawn on his back in blood.

The Lord Aio had been murdered the night of their return from Aicatan, the night they had discovered the opened Tunnel. A quick glance at the inside of the hut, the burn marks and gashes made in the walls and on the furniture, the scattered papers, the books, writing materials and weapons tossed carelessly around the room, and the shredded clothing told of a great struggle. The body of the Lord Aio was found in the center of the hut, facedown, a symbol carved into his bare back. Only one thing could have caused the incident to go unnoticed to the group of five pupils, considering all the noise that must have been made by such a struggle: magic. A strong, evil magic.

Certainly, with the unexplained murder of the Lord Aio, the young High Priest would rise to yet a new level of leadership and seniority, having pupils of his own, each one listening intently to every sound that would come out of his mouth as if it had come from the Ai himself. He would continue in his priesthood, most likely as the High Priest on one of the four other islands. Although his power would not be of a political nature, his influence would stretch even into the Great Cabinet. He would have power over the beliefs of hundreds, perhaps thousands, of gullible people. If he said that milk came from horses, all the milkmaids on the Island he presided over would attempt to milk their horses. He would have the ability—which he would never exercise—to corrupt his position and deceive the people for his own gain. All however, without the Lord Aio to guide him.

Imen doubted himself. He was being thrust into a position of leadership that he did not feel himself capable of holding, in a time when one would need such self-confidence more than any other. Imen wished that he could have died with the Lord Aio, or perhaps even in his stead. He had always wished to be the great leader, the great warrior, the Great High Priest. At this time he did not wish for any political influence or moral power. As his dream became more of a reality, losing its sheen, as the burdens gained weight, he felt an increasing desire to give it all to anyone. Even to Erasan, the pupil maladroit. Having raised himself on the streets of the city, the fourth year pupil was afraid of very little. At least he would have accepted any type of challenge such as this with the enthusiasm and determination to conquer an army of orcs.

Even more than his desire to delegate his responsibility elsewhere, he wished that he could have had the Lord Aio to guide him in his new role. He had expected him to be there with him when he had been appointed High Priest over the Red Island, just a few days earlier. Now, to be placed even higher in the hierarchy of High Priests, he had no one familiar to guide him as the storm approached.

The body of the Lord Aio had been taken care and disposed of according to the ancient customs of the Aihi. So as not to discourage the people of the Five Islands in letting them know that one of the greatest warriors and priests in their history had not merely died, but had been murdered, the occasion went unannounced outside of the small group of Priests, Priestesses, and pupils. Nonetheless, there was much weeping as the earthen mound covered the lifeless form.

The aged prophet had been the beloved master to many for over a century, and of the five pupils, to Lord Imen the longest. As a child, Imen had seen much of the High Priest, usually from a distance, and had thought him to be a small, harmless yet frightening old man. As he departed his youth for a life in the service of the Ai, the harmless old man gradually grew larger in the pupil's eyes, the essence of wisdom and strength. The two had fought together during Imen's early days as a pupil and as a warrior-priest, each saving the other's life many times during battle. Over the years following the wars, the Lord Aio had become somewhat of a father to Imen. As Imen prepared the body, performed the rites of burial, and led the group in songs of mourning, he found his grief of a greatness that would not allow the tears to form. The whole of the ceremony had found new meaning for him, the High Priest finally understanding the importance of the ceremonies of burial and the honoring of the dead. The Lord Aio had died, the part of

Imen that lived life seemingly dying with him, disappearing with the full shovel of earth on the burial mound.

The dawn of the eighth day after his death marked the end of the week of mourning. A messenger, the pupil Erasen, was sent to summon the Lady Melar, High Priestess of the Island of Ban, in order that she should take her place as the Great High Priestess.

Although the others did not recognize—much less understand—the symbol cut into the Lord Aio's back, Imen understood it altogether too well. Immediately after Erasen's departure for the Island of Ban, Imen had sent the Lady Moren to Aicatan to warn the Great Cabinet to mobilize all available military units from the various armies of the Five Islands. It was for the same reason that Imen had sent the Lord Forgotten Man to warn all who remained faithful to the Ai on the Island to either take up arms and prepare for battle, or to take up their things and flee to the mountain.

It had been three days since the three messengers had gone out from the mountain. Only Imen and Las remained. Imen spent most of his time looking over the valley from the Clearing of the Five Stones, near the Tunnel entrance. Las worked at preparing the huts for the new Great High Priestess and whoever else might be moving in or out, busying herself with every task imaginable, accomplishing very little for the amount of effort invested.

At dusk on the third day, Las had run out of tasks to complete, while Imen continued to look out over the valley. It was on that evening the young Priestess chose to interrupt the thoughts of her senior.

She sat on the stone nearest the right of the High Priest.

"Sitting all day, looking over the valley will not bring him back or cause our three messengers to return more quickly, you know."

Imen's gaze ahead did not falter. "As busying oneself with futile tasks does not cause time to alter its course for the faster?"

She laughed, probably for the first time in the eleven days that had passed since the return of Imen and the late Lord Aio. "You are starting to sound more and more like the Lord Aio."

Imen turned his head toward her, raising an eyebrow. "Am I?" he asked.

Las nodded. "You are also starting to act like he used to. Why do you sit and stare at the valley all the time as he did?"

Imen returned his gaze to the valley as he pondered the question. "I used to ask myself the same question of the Lord Aio for the six years in which I studied and trained for the priesthood, and in my ten years as a priest. I believe now that I understand somewhat. For one, when sitting here, I am not taxing an ever-limited supply of energy on pointless errands and labors."

They both laughed at this.

After a few moments, Imen went on explaining. "Having put mourning for the loss of the Lord Aio behind me, I have been thinking these past three days. Thinking about the recent twist in what will be the history of our people that has put me in this temporary position of authority. Thinking about what will happen to us all. Thinking about the death of the Lord Aio, his murder, the hut, the body, and the …"

He stopped himself short, his composure normal, and his eyes telling of unfathomable torture. He shook it off, yet not before Las noticed something.

"The symbol in the Lord Aio's back?" she asked of him. "It was the one thing that you could not take your eyes off of while investigating the hut."

Imen quickly turned to her, the pain in his eyes

returning with a deeper ferocity. It took him a full minute to quell the inner disturbance. As it subsided again, the fire died within his eyes. He cleared his throat and spoke.

"You are quite observant. I tried my best to hide my reaction to the symbol. I see that you have been wondering as to its meaning."

"When he died you became our leader, for the time being. I would imagine the others observing you just as closely, as well as wondering about that symbol."

Imen smiled. "For reasons that have not been forgotten with the death of Lord Aio, this is something that has been kept within the confines of the High Priest Council ever since Lord Aio became the Great High Priest. It is probably better if you do know. You are to be a High Priestess someday, and judging by recent events, you will not have to wait long. These things have already begun to pass. I see no reason why you should not be informed."

He stood, taking his staff, drawing the symbol in the dirt.

"Many years ago, the Great High Priest Dazu called Aio, while on his deathbed, made a prophecy which is recorded in song. He spoke of the returning of evil into the Five Islands. An evil so great it annihilated the Serpentauri, and all but destroyed our people."

"Orlek!" Las gasped in a fearful recognition.

"That is correct," said Imen as he continued. "Our deceased master, Daio called Aio, was present as the successor took the position of Great High Priest. Since his death, the song has been taught to all who are to become High Priest and High Priestesses. I myself have known this song for scarcely a month. However, considering all the events foretold are taking place as we speak, I believe that now is the proper time to be teaching you."

Las positioned herself into an upright posture, listening attentively, as Imen destroyed the symbol with his foot and, singing, began to draw another one with his staff. A line to draw the horizon; a small circle depicts a moon. A banner abreast the bright sun to hail the impending doom.

There was a moment of silence as both High Priest and Priestess took in the full meaning of what had just been sung. It seemed as if all life had frozen for a short moment after he finished. Nothing stirred, not bird, not beast, not fish, not man, not woman, not child. The wind seemed to stop blowing. The river seemed to stop its steady flow toward the sea. The sun seemed to hold its position, giving off the waning light of day for just a few moments longer.

Imen broke the silence. "Tell me, Las: what do you know of our history concerning Orlek?"

Las looked up at the darkening sky, searching her memory. "I admit my knowledge concerning this is limited," she said, somewhat sheepishly. "Just what I learned in the school as a child."

Imen frowned. "Very well, then. Much of this you will have heard before, but at least some should be new to you. To properly tell this story, it must be started from the beginning. Over two thousand years ago, before the Great Ai, before the twelve tribes of the Aihi had united to form the Republic, there lived on the Five Islands the cave-dwelling orcs, the legendary fire-breathing Serpentauri, and the Cannibals, as well as the Aihi.

"The four groups battled amongst themselves, no race seeming to gain any sort of advantage, each struggling futilely for mere survival. This went on for five hundred years. The twelve tribes had been reduced to no more than twelve small families. the Orcs, a small band of paranoid, dangerous cave dwellers. The Serpentauri had taken to isolation in the area on the coast of the Red Island where we have built Aicatan, and the Cannibals eating leaves, insects, animals—and, occasionally, themselves—in the hills.

"Out of desperation, the Twelve Tribes of the Aihi united and chose from among themselves a leader who would travel to the caves, the coast, and the hills to speak to the other three races about peace. This representative's name was Daio, now called Daio the Uniter. After many man-to-man struggles and death matches with members of each race, he finally united the Aihi, Serpentauri, and the Orcs under one central government, controlled by a council consisting of a representative from each race. The Cannibals continued to live in their primitive state in the hills, not willing—and perhaps too primitive—to join with others.

"For the next thousand years, the three races prospered working together. The Orcs mined the hills, the Aihi farmed the valley and raised cattle and sheep, along with helping to mine the hills and fish the rivers and the sea. The Serpentauri took part in every activity, using their breath of fire and their great strength to help till the fields, herd livestock, and carry loads of product. Commerce developed between the Five Islands and the mainland of Oakvalor, which resulted in the king of Oakvalor buying the Five Islands. Each race became more adept in magic and science. Every once in a while, a band of Cannibals would enter the valley or raid a mine, killing a few Orcs or men.

"Toward the end of that thousand years, an Orc by the name of Orlek was elected to the Council as representative of the Orcs. Of the races, Aihi included, he surpassed all in knowledge and power.

"For many years he led his race and the whole of the Five Islands in becoming the strongest and wealthiest civilization. Through his discoveries, magic had peaked to a point that has not since been bested. No other nation would have challenged the Five Islands in any move it made. Even the king paid tribute to the Islands. A citizen was considered poor if he did not have at least ten slaves and double his weight in gold and rubies. Orlek became a symbol of pride for the Five Islands."

At this point, Las spoke up. "If I remember something about this period of history, Orlek began to delve very deep into the magical arts. From my understanding, he was on the verge of discovering the secret to all magic and power."

Imen spat on the ground. "Yes, I suppose you could say that. Could one also say that he was about to benefit the three races and, eventually, the entire world with this last secret? That because of overwork and exhaustion he went mad, all but destroying the Five Islands?"

Las looked down. "That is what they said, what I was taught at …"

Imen spat on the ground again. "*School?*" he finished for her, the contempt in his voice unconcealed. "You would be best not to accept as fact anything you have learned about our history in school. I call them not teachers. Agents of Orlek would be more appropriate."

Las gave him a nod partly indicating agreement, partly indicating her impatience for an explanation. Imen continued with the story.

"It is true, that Lord Orlek came close to the discovery of this great and terrible secret. It might even have been that his original intentions were to use it for the good of the Five Islands. However good his intentions, he was not able to control his knowledge. In the end, the knowledge and magic controlled him.

"For many years, he remained mostly in the solitude of his tower, allowing only a few select orcs to see him, and not too often at that. When he did come out, it was only for a mandatory session of the Council. Even in those sessions, he was not of much help to the

Council or the Five Islands, usually deferring any important decisions or economic matters to the other two members, taking on only small responsibilities concerning magic, none of which he ever fulfilled.

"All the while, he had been using his chief advisors, all Orcs, to spread sentiment against the Aihi and the Serpentauri among the Orcs, teaching them certain depths of the magical arts as favors for those who were successful, usually torturing to death those who were not.

"The Five Islands were losing their power in the world. Those nations who had once paid us tribute ceased to do so, using that money instead to build their armies and wage war against one another. The stronger nations even maneuvered their armies to positions in which they could easily attack the Five Islands, resulting in the endless war with Talvaard. With an Orc population unwilling to do anything with or for the other races, our armies began to dwindle. Ruby production all but stopped and our treasury was steadily growing smaller.

"It came time for the Council members of the other two races to confront him. He was either to find some way to prevent the Five Islands from an almost inevitable fall, bring them back to their former glory, or to abdicate his position, letting another Orc be elected in his place."

"I don't imagine he was all that pleased," said Las.

"You are correct in your understatement of his emotions. He was infuriated. The moment he was given that ultimatum, he drew his sword and beheaded the Aihi Councilman. He managed to kill the Serpentauri member as well, but not without his left arm being burned so badly that it completely fell off his body.

"Within the hour, the entire Orc army he had been building on the Red Island had been mobilized and had begun marching to occupy Aicatan, led by the magically empowered Orcs. The mass of bodies was so great, it completely covered the valley floor. It was evident that much innocent blood would be spilled before the end.

"The other inhabitants of the Five Islands were not without advantage, however. Aicatan, although it lacked natural defenses, employed every able body male citizen into its army, as well as keeping large reserves from the other Islands. The Orcs within the city were easily done away with at no loss to the city guard."

Las interrupted his telling of the story again. "Having heard that, what little I know is starting to make sense to me. I believe—correct me if I am wrong at any point—that after the death of the two council members, a civil war broke out. The Orcs and their vast numbers against the Aihi and Serpentauri, A good deal of the Serpentauri and men in the hills and the valley were killed within minutes of Orlek taking control of the Council building, outnumbered and caught off guard. A few managed to escape to the cities, giving warning to the people, allowing them to make what preparations that could be made."

Imen nodded. "So far, you are correct. Please continue."

"The combined efforts of the Aihi and what remained of the Serpentauri were able to repel the Orc attacks on Aicatan for some time," she continued. "They had the Council building surrounded, but because Orlek gave them little trouble, they were content to keep him prisoner, concentrating most of their strength on the city walls.

"When it started to seem that the Aihi-Serpentaur forces would prove victorious, Orlek began his attack from within. Buildings went up in flame for no apparent reason. The group of men surrounding and guarding the Council building suddenly found themselves naked, armed with flowers. It was then that the city began to concentrate its efforts on the Council building, allowing most of their outer defenses to disappear altogether.

"At this point, Orlek put up a magic field around the building to shield himself from his attackers. Then the Orc militia began its invasion of the city. What few handfuls of men that had been left to the walls had already been eliminated with the next attack, and those that fought to get to Orlek were being cut down from behind. Despite all their desperate efforts, the main body of the army turned to fight the Orcs. The Orc lined advanced, destroying everything in its path, drawing nearer to the Council building and their dark Lord Orlek.

"The use of magic was not limited to Orlek and his minions, however. A few men still practiced it at a powerful level, though none as powerful as Orlek. It was through their combined efforts that they were able to break down the magic defenses of the Orc King. Although they died from their overuse of magic, the inner forces stormed into the Council building and threw Orlek out of a high window onto the ground, where everyone near was able to hear the snap of bones and see his lifeblood drain from his body.

"Having seen their leader supposedly dead, and feeling the absence of his magic, the Orcs took to a madness, most of them killing whatever they could find, including themselves. The rest fleeing the Five Islands to the mainland of Oakvalor."

Imen laughed. "Very good. I give you far too little credit for the time spent studying history in school."

Las shrugged. "Knowledge of the past has its advantages. For the most part I knew all of that history, save the corruption of Orlek. The schools and libraries never fail in failing to teach in a precise, consistent, and accurate manner concerning that. They claim not to know the cause, yet believe that it could be excused as a madness from overwork."

"Interesting how that information never falters in its absence from the minds of the people. Very well. In continuing, our people had another four hundred years of peace and prosperity. All of the Orcs had fled to the Vish mountains in Oakvalor and the Serpentauri died off after Orlek's death. What remained of men on the Five Islands began their attempt at rebuilding into what they were in the 'Golden Age'. The sciences and magics, however, were ignored in the stead of more primitive ways of life and development. It was science and magic that had brought them to the depth at which they were, and the Aihi did not wish to experience such again.

"For a time, the people followed the Ai with every twitch of their muscles. Quickly, however, through corrupt priests, they forgot about the Ai, reducing him to a legend that their parents would tell them in front of the hearth, or the name that the teachers and priests used in frightening followers into obedience.

"A little over a hundred and forty-three years ago, there appeared a young child, who was called Aio. Although very few people would believe it at the time, he was the Ai, put in human flesh. At first, only twelve men believed. Among these were the Great High Priest Dazu, called Aio, and his successor Daio, called Aio, who was the last living man to have spoken with the Great Lord Aio. Over ten years, they united the priests of the Five Islands, commenced reform among the priests and schools, and brought a large portion of the people back to a following of the Ai.

"Aio had many enemies, however, among some of the middle and lower levels of the priesthood as well as in the Cabinet. His actions had cost many of them their political power, as well as their control over the people. Many corrupt priests had had their cloaks shredded because of this man who claimed to be the Ai. To rid themselves of him, there was only one solution: invoke the old magics."

"Wasn't the use of magic in times of peace forbidden by the Aihi law at that time?" asked Las.

"It was punishable by death," said Imen. "This did not cause the enemies of the Great High Priest to hesitate in their actions. They were afraid of Aio nonetheless, and made sure that nothing of their deeds became known.

"Many attempts were made to kill him through various magical and scientific methods, all quite unsuccessful. In desperation, the renegade priests made the decision that almost destroyed the Five Islands: through a meticulous search, they were able to locate and summon the reincarnated spirit of Orlek."

At this, Las looked a bit puzzled. "This is one part that I have not yet fully grasped. In one section of the histories, it says that he was thrown out of the Council building window, that the cracking of his bones was heard. At the point in history where you have arrived in your retelling, he is alive and reincarnated?"

Imen nodded. "No one to this day has delved as deep into the magic as had Orlek. All that we have been able to decide is that during his experiments with magic, he found a way to detach his spirit from his body at the last possible moment, and then find another body in which he could abide. How he was able to do it, no one can say.

"The rest of the history you know in detail. I shall recite it briefly. Orlek had come into power, eventually becoming ruler of a land far to the north, populated chiefly by Orcs and sorcerer men. When he was summoned, one could expect that he was more than delighted at an invitation to destroy not only the Great High Priest, but also the incarnation of his greatest foe, Lord Aio, the personification of the Ai. He stretched out his spirit into the Five Islands, telling the conspirators that he would come immediately. He neglected to tell them of the great force of Orcs that he would send to precede him, or of his plans to take control over the Five Islands from them. At the beginning of the fortieth year of the Lord Aio, the first of his forces landed on this Island.

"The war that ensued continued for almost four years. Everyone on the Islands that had conspired against the Lord Aio either changed his mind or had been killed in battle after joining the Orc army. At the end of those four years, it seemed that neither side would gain any advantage. Both Orlek and the Five Islands had poured the blood of their armies like water. The valley floor became black with the bodies of Orcs, our rivers ran red with our own blood. It was then that Orlek decided to show his strength in full."

Las nodded. "It took all the magic of the High Priests just to repel this last attack. A dragon was released into Oakvalor and Talvaard, and even the body of the Great Lord Aio was destroyed in this battle."

"Along with Orlek's. It has been said that the two departed to battle in the spiritual realm. As Orlek's physical body was robbed of life, so was he lost to the Five Islands. He is but a distant memory, if that, in the minds of the people.

"He has, however, remained quite alive in the minds of the High Priests. In the mind of the Great High Priest Dazu, especially. As you know well, he was one of the greatest prophets our history has ever known. It was said that he was, when prophecy came to him, able to leave his body and go to the places and times where the prophecies would take place. He knew that whatever battle fought by Aio and Orlek in the spiritual realm would not finish itself out there. It would have to end here, on the Five Islands, where it started almost six centuries ago. On his deathbed, he asked for a pen and parchment. He began to sing the song which I sang to you as he drew the symbol from which I have drawn. He prophesied of the coming of Orlek to retake the Five Islands, an admonition to the Aihi."

For a moment, neither of them spoke. Imen was content to sit watching the valley beneath him, not waiting for a response. Las sat doing the same thing, wishing she could say something. Anything.

She sighed. "One can never fully appreciate what one has until one has it no more. Everything about the Lord Aio and his early years as a priest was known to me. I realize now, especially with what is supposed to happen, that I have taken all of my advantages for granted."

Imen looked at her, smiling in response. "It might not be that your labors here were quite as useless as I had thought. One of the messengers, along with another, approaches as we speak."

A few seconds later Erasen and another figure cloaked in brown turned the corner. One could see the glint of white armor, the color of the Island of Ban, in the last rays of sunlight. Yet it was not Lady Melar that came with Erasen but the eldest of her pupils, Lord Arum, who had also been considered for the High Priesthood over the Red Island. It was not the coming of Lord Arum that set the Priest and Priestess sitting on the stones ill at ease, but the absence of the Lady Melar. The ceremonies were to be performed the next day. Although it was most likely that Arum would be chosen as High Priest of the Red Island, Lady Melar would also have been present.

None of this, however, was enough to prepare Imen for what was to come. Lord Arum came and knelt at the High Priest's feet, saying, "Hail Lord Imen called Aio, Great High Priest of the Aihi!"

Imen stood, facing the bowing Priest. "Greetings to you, Lord Arum. You seem to be a bit mistaken. I am merely the lowest of the High Priests. Where is the Lady Melar?"

Arum got up, his long, bony frame a few inches taller than Imen's. "There is no mistake, my lord. As for the Lady Melar, her end was much the same as that of the Lord Aio and the other three."

"The others?" asked Imen, choking on the words.

"The entire Council, save for yourself, murdered in their own huts, the symbol cut into their backs."

"The Order is respected and feared. Wizards can control the elements, summon powerful creatures, and even control other's minds. The Divines help us if they can't."

- Artivolian,
current Abbot

CHAPTER 12

Shortly after arriving back at the abbey, Velkyn and Calderon were both summoned to the Abbot's chamber. They walked together through the stone halls quietly, each absorbed in their own thoughts. Calderon kept replaying the terrifying events of that morning in his mind, desperately trying to figure out why Prince Ranaan would have murdered his own brother.

Perhaps what Velkyn said earlier about a coup was the truth. Maybe the younger prince was not happy with being second in line for the throne and murdered his brother out of anger and jealousy? Yet from all that he had heard, both princes were respected and mature, never having any real dispute with one another. It didn't add up.

"The world feels ... darker somehow," Velkyn

whispered to Calderon. "I feel it in my spirit. It is as though some unseen force blankets the land." Calderon didn't respond. He considered his friend's words. While he didn't feel what Velkyn spoke of, it did make sense to him. Perhaps the darkness that Velkyn felt was behind the actions of the young prince.

They reached the door to the abbot's chamber and paused, glancing at each other. "What do you think he wants?" Calderon asked softly. Velkyn shrugged in response. "Only one way to find out."

Velkyn knocked on the door, but there was no answer from within. He waited a moment and then knocked again, louder this time. The door swung open silently and they were greeted by Donovan. The former Musician said nothing as he walked out in what Calderon thought was quite a hurry. The Abbot sat behind his desk writing. Without looking up he told them to shut the door and have a seat.

They sat down and waited for the Abbot to speak. The old leader of the monastery finished writing and folded the parchment in three creases. Lifting the burning candle that rested on his desk, he poured the hot wax onto the paper. He removed one of the rings that adorned his fingers and pressed it into the quickly cooling wax, leaving an imprint of a flag with a water drop in the center, the official seal of the church. He set the letter to the side and looked at the young monks.

It seemed to Calderon that their leader had grown older since that morning. The lines of age creased his face and his eyes seemed dimmer. "We are in danger." Calderon and Velkyn exchanged looks. Velkyn turned his gaze back to the Abbot. "The sphere is safe," he managed to say before he was silenced by the Abbot's upraised hand.

"That may not true," the Abbot said. He ran his hands through his thinning white hair and sighed aloud.

"We fear that the dragon may have escaped the sphere somehow."

"How?" Both monks echoed in unison.

The Abbot shook his head hopelessly. "Donovan thinks the enchantment has failed, perhaps the magic was too old to be strengthened by the music. We can only speculate. He has gone to see if our fears prove to be true." Velkyn realized then why he had been summoned with no one left to protect the sphere. His protection may no longer be required.

"How can he know if the creature is no longer bound within the sphere?" Calderon spoke up.

"Donovan has been the Musician longer than any other before him. He has been in the position since he was barely eighteen and he is now ninety. He has studied the sphere longer than anyone of our brotherhood. If anyone could know, it would be him."

Calderon felt fear welling up in his stomach, threatening to overwhelm him. He cracked open his mouth to speak, but nothing came out. His life was over. He had messed up and there was nothing anyone could do to help him. He decided then to confess hiding his condition and express his fear that he had fallen asleep when he was supposed to play the music.

Velkyn sat forward in his chair, staring intently at the abbot. "What if it is true? What if the dragon has escaped … what does that mean?"

"Absolute destruction," Donovan's voice answered. Neither Calderon nor Velkyn heard him enter. "That is what is upon us," his tone was grave and ominous. Donovan walked up to them slowly. "The sphere's magic has failed."

All three men turned to look at Donovan, alarm evident on their faces. The Abbot rose from his chair. "And so it begins."

"What begins?" Calderon looked questioningly

from Donovan to the Abbot. He had the feeling that they knew something he didn't.

"It is written that the dragon, before it was captured in the sphere, wreaked havoc across the land. It burned entire cities to the ground with its very breath. The only reason it was stopped was because of Oakvalor. The people there do not fear wizards as the people of Talvaard do. What begins, Calderon, is the quest to save our world. In order to recapture the dragon's spirit, we must first know where it is. The wizards of Oakvalor are our only option."

Velkyn sputtered in disbelief. "Our kingdoms have no love for each other, everyone knows that." The Abbot smiled at him. "True, but the church's loyalty lies to the Divines, not to the crown. We have allies there that will aid us. And the wizards, though they have helped their king in the past, do not concern themselves with politics. They will know the importance of this task."

"We have lost enough time already." Donovan added. He and the Abbot shared a knowing look. "Make the preparations." Donovan nodded and left the room. Velkyn and Calderon stared at their leader, waiting for further explanation. "Neither of you are ready for this, but you will not be alone. Donovan is going with you."

"Going with us? Where are we going?" Velkyn wasn't sure he fully understood the Abbot's meaning.

The Abbot stared at him, the old man's eyes drilling straight into his soul. He slumped into his chair dejectedly. "To Oakvalor, my son. You are both going to Oakvalor."

● ∞ ● ∞ ●

Calderon sat upon the edge of his bed, trying to prepare himself mentally for the journey he was about to take. He should have been getting some rest, but his mind was racing. Truth be told, he was a little curious and a lot afraid. Curious about the world outside the abbey, yet afraid of the unknown all at the same time. He had to travel light and only bring the things he absolutely needed. They would travel by horseback until they reached the mountains, but then they would have to pass through on foot.

The Abbot had shown them to a room full of miscellaneous items that the monks did not have any need for. He had taken a thick brown traveling cloak trimmed in black silk and some leather boots. They would be leaving under the cover of night so as not to draw any unwanted attention and there was only a few hours of daylight left. He was glad that Donovan was going with them, despite the fact that he was so aged. He trusted him and found comfort in the fact that he was so knowledgeable.

He extinguished the candle on his desk then laid down and tried unsuccessfully to fall asleep. Not far from Calderon's room, Velkyn too sat pondering what lay ahead. Unlike his friend, however, he was not afraid. He was pleased to be leaving the abbey. Adventure was calling his name. He had written a note to Nydel and would leave it for her in the event she didn't visit him tonight. He couldn't leave her behind. He was confident that she would find some way to come with him. Velkyn smiled as he thought about her.

She usually wore her hair down and the long black strands reminded him of the ravens that often flew into the fields around the abbey, always trying to eat the crops. Her eyes were bright green and shined like her free-spirited soul. Every detail of her face was etched into his memory, every moment spent with her locked into his remembrance. He loved her with every fiber of his being. Velkyn stretched out across his bed and stared at the smooth stone ceiling, running their last encounter back through his mind.

He drifted off to sleep peacefully.

● ∞ ● ∞ ●

Calderon was awakened in the middle of a pleasant dream. Velkyn stood over him, shaking his shoulder. "Time to leave," he said softly, as if fearing his voice might be heard throughout the abbey. Calderon pushed himself into a seated position, hanging his feet off the edge of his small bed. Donovan appeared in the doorway. "Grab your things and meet me in the courtyard by the main gate. And make haste," he added, almost as an afterthought. Then he was gone.

"I'm not sure about this," Calderon said quietly. Velkyn's excitement showed in his demeanor. "What do you mean? We will finally get to see what lies beyond these walls, probably farther than any brother before us has traveled. What are you unsure of?"

Calderon couldn't quite put his finger on it, but there was something at the edge of his mind that gave him the uneasy feeling that life would not be the same after this journey. "There isn't anything specific," he said, "but I have the feeling we will soon learn things that will change our lives. It's as if there is a veil, and something—whether good or ill—is waiting behind it to be revealed. And I am not sure that I am ready for it."

Velkyn stood in silence listening, taking in the words of his friend. "If what you feel does come about, do you think that though you are not ready now, you will be when it happens? The Divines will work everything out as it should be. Now come on, we need to leave."

Calderon wasn't sure why, but he didn't think Velkyn's last statement was true. He decided there was nothing that could be done about it and got up off his bed. He had slept in his new leather boots and grabbed his cloak off the chair by his desk before following his friend out of the room. He looked back one more time, staring into his room. He wondered how long it would be before he saw it again. They made their way down the halls and to the courtyard. They found Donovan waiting for them at the main entrance. "Don't we need a couple more of our brothers in order to open this gate?" asked Velkyn as they approached Donovan.

"We would if we were leaving through it," Donovan replied. He smiled at their look of confusion and motioned them to follow him. The old man led them along the east wall. Stopping abruptly, Donovan felt along the stone until he found one that felt loose. He grunted as he pulled on it and was rewarded when a grinding sound revealed a hidden doorway. "We are going this way," he told them, "to avoid being seen leaving. We don't need to draw any unwanted attention to our departure."

They pulled the stone door open enough to fit through. On the other side of the door was a steel handle attached to the door. They used it to pull the hidden door closed behind them. Calderon heard the soft nickering of horses before he saw them. Three horses were tied to one of the many wooden posts along the side of the abbey that were used for the delivery carriages. Calderon eyed them warily, having never ridden one before. "Are they safe?" he asked.

Donovan untied the reigns of each horse and handed one of the reigns to each of the monks, keeping hold of one for himself. "They are safe. Don't be afraid, Musician. They will speed our journey considerably." Donovan placed his foot into the stirrups and climbed atop his mount with a practiced ease. Calderon and Velkyn, having never ridden before, looked from their mounts to Donovan, and then back to their horses. Shrugging, they mimicked the old man and attempted unsuccessfully several times to climb onto their own horses before finally finding success.

Calderon gripped the horse with his knees tightly, afraid of falling off. Velkyn seemed to have better balance and merely held onto the reigns for stability. "You seem to be comfortable riding for someone who's lived in the abbey their entire life," Calderon remarked to Donovan, still trying to find a comfortable way to ride his mount.

"There are many things about me that may surprise you. With such a long journey ahead of us, I am sure you will learn a lot more about me before the end." With that, he pulled the reigns of his horse and turned eastward. It took both young monks a few minutes to get their mounts to follow their commands as Donovan did not give them any help. "You said the end …" murmured Calderon, "… the end of what?" Donovan looked over his shoulder at his pupil but offered no explanation. He urged his horse forward and turned his eyes back to the east.

The young monks were finding it much easier to get their horses to follow commands as they rode. "While time is something we don't have enough of, we must conserve the energy of our horses for now. We will stop to rest at an inn when the sun begins to set if the horses can make it that long." The horses trotted along at a leisurely pace. "What about food and water?" Velkyn asked.

Donovan reached behind him and patted a large sack tied to his saddle. "We each have enough to last us a couple days. We can buy whatever we need when we stop each night." Velkyn seemed pleased with the answer and merely nodded to himself. Calderon wondered how his mentor knew where they were headed and voiced as much. "I have been this way before, many years ago," answered the old man. Calderon looked to

Velkyn. "Do you think he's hiding something?" he whispered.

Velkyn nodded his head. "We all are hiding something. The better question would be what is he hiding. Only time will tell."

● ∞ ● ∞ ●

The day was long and uneventful. They had traveled without seeing much of anything or anyone except the occasional merchant caravan. Earlier in the day Donovan had pointed to their left as the road they traveled on forked that direction and continued straight, telling them that the castle they had visited the day before was that way. They had continued straight, the scenery nothing but tall grassland as far as they could see.

They didn't talk much as each of them were occupied with their owns thoughts. Velkyn thought about Nydel and wondered if she had snuck into the monastery and found his note yet. He looked behind him several times, hoping to see some sign of her trailing them, waiting for the opportune moment to meet with him. He was greeted by nothing except the empty road and the tall grass which swayed in the gentle breeze.

Calderon's thoughts were far different from his friend's. He missed the stone walls of the abbey the moment they were out of sight. As hard as he tried, he couldn't push the sense of foreboding from his spirit. There really wasn't anything to justify his fears other than the fact that everything outside of the abbey was unknown to him. There was also the new emotion of distrust he felt towards his mentor. He thought the man was no different than himself or Velkyn, that he had entered the brotherhood at a young age and had never ventured out. His assumptions didn't seem to line up with who the old man actually was. He also found himself wondering about the people of Oakvalor. The only thing most people knew was they were the enemy and nobody could remember why. Was the brotherhood there as devout in their faith as the men of his abbey? Was their king a believer in the Divines as well? He found that notion hard to fathom considering the ageless war both kingdoms were waging against one another. If they shared the same beliefs, whatever petty grievance they had with one another would be overlooked because if you shared the same values, you would be on the same page and fight for what mattered, not one another. All this and more swirled within the young man's mind.

Donovan was as unreadable as a blank page. He had learned many things during his long life, and if there was one thing that he knew was a mighty advantage, it was being able to conceal your emotions and intent. He hadn't survived this long by luck. The young monks traveling with him were clueless to the world outside the abbey, and though he mostly pitied them for it, he also envied them. To be oblivious to the things he knew and was burdened with, the things his hands had committed … he pushed the past out of his mind and thought about the journey that laid ahead. He wondered how much Oakvalor had changed since the last time he had seen it. He knew they would find help there, but he didn't know if they would find answers. The wizards there were not loyal to anyone but their craft, but he didn't know if the monks there held true to their faith over the king as those in Talvaard did. He had never seen the abbey in Oakvalor, but he had heard of its existence.

The sun had begun its descent behind the mountains and the sky slowly changed colors on the horizon. Deep oranges and reds lined the clouds and both young monks were awestruck by the beauty. "It's amazing," Calderon remarked in a hushed tone. "Indeed," Donovan said, "It is a sight that never gets old. Look there," he pointed.

"The first stop of our journey." They could see a small building in the distance, perhaps another half hour of riding left to reach it.

"We won't make it before dark," Velkyn stated. Donovan turned and looked at him. "Not at this pace," he agreed, grinning. He nudged his horse and the animal picked up speed, going from their slow pace to a fast run. Calderon and Velkyn followed the old man's lead, urging their horses in the same manner. They were thundering down the road, the gentle breeze seeming to gain strength and began to blow their hair around wildly. They made it to the inn with their quickened pace in half the time it would have taken. The horses were breathing heavily when they stopped.

Calderon had trouble getting off the horse and ended up slipping and falling face first into the ground. He pulled himself up, the embarrassment evident on his face as he spit dirt. Velkyn stifled his laughter. A young boy, possibly no older than twelve, came to collect their horses after they had pulled their belongings off and the boy led the horses into the stable that was located behind the inn.

Donovan turned to the young monks when he was sure no one would hear their conversation. "If anyone makes conversation with you, do not tell them where we are going or what we are doing. If knowledge of what has happened with the sphere were to become known, it could cause fear among the people that would result in chaos. As best as we can tell, there is almost no travel from Talvaard to Oakvalor. If people get the wrong idea, they might see us as traitors and we would be in no end of trouble." Calderon and Velkyn exchanged glances. "Is there food here?" Velkyn asked. They all laughed at the remark and Donovan nodded.

The interior of the inn was old and worn. Rough boards attached to the walls gave the place the appearance of a rustic wood cabin. From behind the badly scratched bar a woman took orders. Ten tables were arranged in a haphazard manner, each surrounded by three stools. Around those tables was a minimal crowd, although busy for this inn. The three monks made their way to an empty table and sat down. Calderon was relieved to be off the horse, but his backside was numb and his lower back was a bit sore. He couldn't wait to lay down. After a few minutes, the woman from behind the bar made her way to them.

"Evenin' gents. Welcom' ta the Sly Mare. What'll ye be havin'?" she asked. The monks found her lack of proper speech annoying. Donovan didn't give them the chance to speak and answered for them all. "We will take three orders of whatever the special is, and three mugs of water." The barmaid grinned at him and he noticed most of her teeth were missing. "Water? We ain't servin' no water 'ere 'cept ta 'orses. Ale er cider?" she asked him, still smiling. "Cider." She offered a mock curtsey and sauntered off behind the bar to place their order.

"Who doesn't have water?" Calderon asked, baffled. Donovan looked at his pupil and again found himself envious of his ignorance. "We probably will not find water at any of these types of establishments. They specialize in tasty alcoholic drinks." Calderon's eyebrow raised. "Why would people pay to lose their common sense?" Donovan shrugged. "Only the Divines know."

The barmaid returned several minutes later with the mugs of cider and made a second trip to bring their food. On each plate was a mound of chopped, skinless potatoes covered in butter and salt. She casually tossed three forks onto the table as she walked away. Velkyn, who had yet to speak, commented on her behavior. "She seems rude." Donovan merely nodded his head in assertion before closing his eyes. The two young monks lowered their heads and Donovan said a prayer over their meal. "Not everyone in our kingdom follows the precepts of the gods. Especially so as we get to the fringes of Talvaard. Our order has a rough history." None of them had eaten since midday and found themselves a lot hungrier than normal.

They ate in silence. Calderon mentioned the odd taste the cider had and Donovan knew it was not virgin. He didn't think one mug would hinder his companions and he let them drink it. Velkyn was busy watching the people in the inn. There was a man at the bar who appeared to be taking an interest in the conversation at a table near him. Velkyn shifted his attention to the table as well and took note of three men. He listened to their conversation and shook his head. All three of them were drunk.

● ∞ ● ∞ ●

Julian Brathenworth had misplaced eyes. He knew this fact for whenever he stared directly ahead at the beer in his glass, one eye thought it mostly empty; the other mostly full. What other explanation was there for this differentiation of opinionated eyesight than misplaced eyes? He held one unsteady hand before his face and closed his left eye. He concentrated upon the glass behind his hand as he opened his left eye and closed his right. His hand moved. He repeated. Yes, he was sure of it; his right eye made his hand appear higher than his left. Therefore his eyes were all wrong. "Crap!" he slurred.

"What's that gov?" A pale faced man with a lengthy mustache directed at him. Julian blinked several times and then turned his gaze upon his verbal aggressor. His puffy red lips pursed as he drew breath. He took an absent swipe at his straight shoulder length hair but

122

missed. "I think I said crap," Julian replied, making three attempts at his glass before his hand grasped it. While continuing to stare at the man, he raised the glass to his moist lips and swigged.

"Argh, that it is, but we drink the piss, eh?" The man chuckled, took a gulp of his own brew and then turned his attention back to his own table and his two companions. Julian sniffed hard as he again turned his back to the group. With nothing better to do, he began to eavesdrop.

"So Theo, what do you say?" One gruff voice asked. "What do I say governor what do I say?" replied the man who had addressed Julian. "Yes, what do you say?" asked a third.

"I say ... do you like beer nuts?" the familiar voice of Theo. That was followed by a series of humming and crunching, then some general noises of affirmation. "Now ... where was I?" said the gruff voice.

"You was talking about adventuring."

"Oh yes, I was. So what about it?"

"I don't know, you were the one discussing the topic. I was just listening politely," said Theo. "Of course I was doing the discussing. You would hardly talk about adventuring. You are not an adventurer. But you could be."

"Could I?"

"That is what this conversation is about."

"And what about beer nuts?" munched the third.

"Beer nuts ... what's the fascination with beer nuts?" said the gruff voice. "I guess they're delicious." Again more grunts and crunches. All was quiet for a short time. All except breathing and crunching.

"I'll do it!" Theo yelled, rising to his feet with one hand over his heart. "Good for you son, good for you," acknowledged the gruff voice, having finally received his answer. "Do what?" asked the third, spraying broken beer nuts from his mouth as he talked.

"Right. Now what's the plan?" asked Theo.

"The plan … argh, the plan. The plan is simple. As adventurers, we need adventure."

"Oh that is true, very true," mumbled the third through a mouth full of beer nuts. "And the best source of adventure is Dillenger."

"Oh yes," burped the third, "Dillenger is full of adventure."

"So lets go get Dillenger!" Theo yelled. "We would, but …" At that moment, Julian decided to pitch a sale. He spun his stool gracefully on one leg so as to face the mob of adventurers. After rotating too far and too vertically, be picked himself up off the floor and presented himself to the crew.

"Gentlemen, I believe I can help you … for a price." The three stared at Julian for a moment, munching beer nuts. Julian averted his gaze, sought some inspiration and began afresh. "I am Julian Brathenworth, magician for hire."

"For hire … for hire," the gruff voiced man said with increasing zeal. "And what would we want to hire a magician for?"

"I believe you are adventurers," Julian said, proudly giving a knowing leer. "That we are gov, that we are," said Theo, stroking his mustache with a soggy finger. Silence.

"Well then, mayhap you could use a man of magic?"

Silence. Julian waited patiently.

"Why?" asked the third, whom Julian deduced looked a little like a weasel, with beady black eyes, greasy black hair, and a pointy nose. "To aid with your adventuring," Julian offered. All three stared at Julian, confusion on their faces. "I … do magic," Julian said tentatively.

"Oh," said the weaselish man, "magic. But I don't have any kids."

"What the hell are you talking about?" Julian warbled.

"You do party tricks, right? I don't have kids, but thanks anyway."

"No, no, no. I do proper magic. You hire me and I provide you with magical services so as to aid you in your adventuring."

"What adventuring?" inquired the third.

"You are adventurers, are you not?!" Julian screamed. "That we are gov, that we are," Theo smiled, stroking his mustache again. "Then you must need help on adventures?"

"So you can help us with magic on our adventures?" questioned the gruff voiced man, who had remained silent until now. "Yes," sighed Julian, relieved to be getting his pitch acknowledged. "How much?"

"Right. I demand an equal share of profits, nothing more."

"No, how much help?"

"What?"

"How much help can you give?"

"Oh. I … can give …"

"Do you like beer nuts?" asked the weasel man. "Yes … I guess …"

"Excellent. You're hired," winked the gruff voiced man. Julian looked from one man to the next, took a large swig of beer and then collapsed onto the floor. Either the alcohol had knocked him out, or the conversation had.

Velkyn snorted derisively and turned his attention back to his own table. He somehow felt less intelligent having heard that conversation. The barmaid came to collect the plates as soon as the three monks had finished eating. "Will ye be havin' anythin' else?" she asked

Donovan. "We would like a room for the night," he answered, finishing his cider and handing her the empty mug.

"With yer meal an' room, it'll be thirty silver." Donovan withdrew a small leather pouch from his robes and counted out the appropriate amount and handed it to the woman. She double counted it, smiling at him the entire time. Nodding in satisfaction, she left the table and came back a moment later with a key. "It be the door with a three on it," she said. Lowering her voice and leaning in close to the old man, she added, "Might want to keep an eye on your belongings. Things be comin' up missin' a lot lately." Donovan understood her meaning and smiled in thanks for the warning. He looked to the young monks after she had left.

"We should take turns watching our door," he said lowly. The two nodded and rose from their chairs the same time Donovan did. They followed him across the room to the left where a small flight of stair led them to the area of the inn that housed the rooms.

The beady eyes of the weaselish looking man followed them until they were out of sight. Looking to the man with the gruff voice, he smirked and nodded.

*"I have always thought the actions of men
the best interpreters of their thoughts."*

- Kelros

CHAPTER 13

"If I am forced to eat another one of these particularly disgusting cave creatures again, I shall …"

"Peace, Kelron," interrupted Kelros. "At least in the Tunnel's darkness, we do not have to look upon them too much. Besides, by looking at you with the light of one's fire, one could hardly say that your appetite has decreased significantly from this most undesirable fare."

Kelron looked down into the darkness in the direction of the large lump of flesh, blood, and scales, the like of which having been the sustenance for the two hundred Serpentauri during their residence in the Tunnel. He belched, a ball of flame erupting from between his fangs, his forked tongue flailing wildly about his open mouth. For a moment, the small segment of the Tunnel lit up by the almost blinding flash and then returned to its usual darkness. "Your skin does not draw so tightly over your bones either, Kelros. How can you stand to eat these things anyway?"

"What else is there to eat?" replied Kelros, somewhat irritated at his friend's constant complaining.

"It's a lot better than having to eat ourselves like the Cannibals of this Island. Did you know that if enough of these creatures band together, they could kill an unsuspecting Serpentaur and reduce him to pile of whitened bones within an hour? They even eat the scales and the coat. Quite a gruesome spectacle, from what Father Ean has told me. It is most important that we eat them before *they* eat us."

Kelron turned his head to the invisible stench in front of him. "Even so, I still do not understand why you do not leave the Tunnel—or at least allow the rest of us to do so—and eat an animal that makes its habitat *above* ground and lives off of something other than feces and rotting carcasses of its fellow cave creatures."

"Because," said Kelros, leaning his head down into the creature's body, ripping a limb off with his massive jaws, swallowing it whole. "Father Ean has ordered that we stay in the Tunnel, where we will be unseen by men who would destroy us or attempt to use us for ill purposes. I might also have you remember that both you and I fare much better than our brothers in the center point of the Tunnel where the five branches meet. Father Ean has let us come this close to the entrance on the Red Island. At least there is some small chance of getting some animal strayed from its home on the mountain."

"I would question the thinking behind his decision to keep us hidden. I feel no need for protection from men. As for stray creatures from the over-world, I have not yet seen one since we entered the Tunnel," said Kelron, reluctantly biting out a large piece of flesh from the mess in front of him, hardly taking the time to chew it as he forced the seemingly resistant food down his throat, trying his best—unsuccessfully—not to taste it.

"I haven't seen much of anything since we entered the Tunnel," stated Kelros.

"Indeed Kelros," said the young Serpentaur. "It has

been a long time since we have entered the Tunnel."

The elder Serpentaur took another bite from their meal, swallowing the rancid morsel. "It has been some eight or nine days we have lived here in hiding, I would imagine."

"Thank you so much, Kelros, for letting me know information that will make the rest of my eternal stay here much more bearable, being able to count the endless days we waste in here, while the Ai knows what is going on up there that might require our assistance," said Kelron sarcastically, stamping a hoof impatiently. "I am sure it will be of *such* great joy to the rest when we tell them that."

"I am sure it will," snapped the elder of the Serpentauri. "It certainly amazes me how much patience I never knew I had, having been stranded in this Tunnel for over a week with *you* as a test of it. Now, if you will shut your ever-opened jaw and stop complaining, Father Ean is coming. I would prefer to listen to some *new* news from *above* ground for a change."

Except for a smoke-filled snort in reply from Kelron, the two Serpentauri remained in silence as they heard the footsteps of Father Ean grow steadily in volume as he drew closer. "Greetings, cousins," said Father Ean, invisible in the absence of light. "How fare you in the darkness of this Tunnel?"

"If you could call it fare, we have plenty of these stomach-wrenching little ..." said Kelron, stopping himself so as not to offend Father Ean. "We do not seem to be dying of starvation, Father Ean," he finished.

Ignoring his friend's comments, Kelros lowered his head to what was left of their meal and set it ablaze. The smell of burning scales and flesh almost caused the Serpentauri to vomit.

"A light by which to see, and no great loss of good food to Kelron, although our stomachs do seem to agree on the matter of food. Tell us, Father Ean: what news today, or tonight for all it really matters, do you bring from the Red Island?"

Father Ean cupped his hand over the top of his staff, putting the weight of his body on it, resting his chin on his hands. A large sack lay by his feet.

"Just about sunset when I entered the Tunnel," he said. "As for news? Mostly ill news, yet maybe some might seem good to the two of you."

"I was afraid of that," muttered Kelron under his breath.

"Become familiar with it, my cousin," replied the old prophet. "You will hear much more such news, and most likely far worse in the near future. Both the Lady Moren and the Lord … the Lord … the Lord … I cannot seem to remember his name. The Priest and Priestess I told you earlier about have both returned from their journeys into the Island."

"How did they fare?" asked Kelros.

"The Lady Moren was somewhat successful in her task, and was able to push whatever body now governs the Five Islands into mobilizing the Priesthood's allotted five hundred men and any who wish to join, one hundred for each Island."

Kelron snorted into the fire, his flames disappearing into the burning carcass. "They mock the Lord Aio. Only five hundred?"

"Only five hundred," confirmed the aged man.

Kelros flicked his forked tongue about. "And of the Lord … the Lord … the other one. The Priest. What of him?" Father Ean looked about him, finding a large enough stone near the fire to his liking and sat on it.

"Much the same, only worse. Of all the Priests and Priestesses on this Island, one has promised his full and unconditional loyalty and aid. The rest have—in a more courteous manner—refused to even acknowledge the

Lord Imen his new position."

Kelros lowered his head. "Pity for the Aihi. It was not as hard for our race those five hundred years past. What precious few surviving priests lived on the Five Islands at the time of our ancestor's departure fought alongside us. This group of priests sounds to be the type that would fight against us."

"Yet by the Ai," said Kelron, "how are we expected to fight a host of Orcs in the thrall of Orlek—may he eternally rot in the Endless Depths—with five hundred fighting men, maybe two hundred Serpentauri, an ancient, though powerful, gardener, a handful of warrior priests newly ordained, and a tenth of the farmers and laborers on the Red Island?"

Father Ean sighed. "With only what we have, it cannot be done. It is impossible. I have faced many great difficulties in my all-too-long life. The empires have risen and fallen under my watchful eye. The world has undergone changes in such a manner and to such lengths that your language would not have words for it, and I was present. I have fought alongside the greatest of warriors, and have helped to defeat the greatest of foes. Even with my assistance, however, this trial that faces the Lord Imen has only been surpassed by one other, some ninety-five years ago. As with this battle, Orlek was the enemy."

"Yes," said Kelros, his serpent head nodding. "And this time, the Council of the High Priests is not aided by the Great Lord Aio being present among its members. If I recall your stories correctly, Father Ean."

"In the physical sense, no," said Father Ean. "However, this half-millennium old battle is between Orlek and the Ai, not between Orlek and the Aihi, though the Orc king would wish to destroy all men, Serpentauri, and his own people as well. We can rest assured that the Ai will enter the battle," he paused, "in his own time and manner."

The old prophet pulled the large sack in front of him, opening it up. "I have something for the two of you. It is not much, but even I make difficult of stomaching the provisions of the caves and tunnels, and I can sympathize with your plight. My innards turn at the *thought* of eating a creature of this Tunnel, or any tunnel, for that matter."

He proceeded to take out two objects, both somewhat round and covered with feathers with two thin, scaly legs limply hanging from one end of each. Both were a dark brown in color, covered in blood, sticking to both the sack and Father Ean's hands. "These used to be chickens, although the struggle which ensued obtaining them has changed that somewhat. I didn't want to use too much magic. The Priests would notice any excessive use of magic, and I wouldn't want to betray our presence for the wholeness of two dead birds."

Kelron stared at the two chickens. "After our rather distasteful diet these past days, it looks delicious. Not that I am saying it wouldn't be delicious otherwise. You will be partaking with us, Father Ean?"

Father Ean shook his head. "With your appetite, Kelron, I doubt there would be any left for Kelros, let alone myself. Besides that, I do not make it a practice to eat flesh, though I have had it in lieu of starvation at times. Before my return to the Tunnel, I overstuffed myself with the fruits of the laborers that tend the orchards. The Ai has blessed them with an excellent harvest this season. Most likely the last one for some time."

"That is too bad," said Kelron. "Fruits are usually too small for a Serpentauri to taste, unless eaten in large quantities. I am particularly fond of a good wheat … harvest, as I believe men call it. Where we come from, it grew wild in a small valley. Every autumn day when the harvest was good, I would venture to the edge of that field and help myself to some. Wheat is quite good when it is fresh."

"Some!" cried Kelros, half choking on his small meal, blackened and smoking feathers flying out of his mouth. "As if there would be any left for the rest of us."

Kelron appeared to glare at Kelros out of his serpent eyes, hissing. "At least you were given your fair portion when we would feast together.

Kelros reared his head. "If one could call it a portion compared to yours, yes. Although I do agree with you on one point: your daily trips to the wheat fields would definitely redefine the word 'feast'. Your eating habits are about as disgusting as our meal. You even eat the chaff."

"You should have tried it. It isn't that bad," said Kelron.

Kelros sighed in frustration, smoke and tiny flames coming out from between his jaws. The old man sitting on the rocks, almost forgotten in the exchange between the two Serpentauri, began laughing. "I shall certainly remember to bring some wheat to you, Kelron, the next time I leave, if that is even necessary."

The Serpentauri looked across the fire at Father Ean. "What is your meaning?" asked Kelros, cocking his head to one side. "You mean to turn these cave creatures into a field of wheat? At least it would put an end to my friend's incessant complaint."

Father Ean shook his head. "Not at all. Although I have never considered that idea in my thousands of years as the gardener of Oakvalor. It would make them more lovely to look upon. I meant that I intend for the two of you to come with me to watch the Ceremony of Ordination of the High Priest Council ..." he said, noticing the pleasantly surprised looks on the faces of the two Serpentauri, "… from a distance, but were a man to come near us, I am afraid that even my magic would not suffice were I hiding someone other than myself."

Kelron shrugged. "Magic, science, prophets, priests … all the same to me. I possess no magic, and do not mind it, as long as it does not harm me. I say that one's fire is as good a defense as any, at least for a Serpentaur."

Father Ean looked upon Kelron for a few seconds. "You do not believe in the importance of magic, do you good Serpentaur?"

The hungry one shook his head. "Not really. Don't worry yourself. I can see how it would have its function in certain lives. Otherwise I would be feasting upon wheat instead of being holed up in a tunnel, even if that tunnel happens to be *the* Tunnel."

Father Ean turned his eyes down, staring at his feet for a second. "You have much to learn, Kelron. The influence which magic has upon us as living beings is far greater than even I can imagine. How does the sun continue its daily trek, age upon age unending, giving light by which to see and a magic by which even the growth of wheat is aided? Or how does the moon and her children, the stars, do homage to their master and bestow the beauty of their light upon the people? What makes earth suitable for crops, or wheat to grow wild on a deserted, unknown land?

"There is a magic running deeply through everything that lives and does not live. The fact that the body of a man, Orc, or Serpentaur can live, that we think beyond the level of the two birds that have been devoured us a result of the magic. Even you have magic, Kelron, however limited it may be."

Father Ean stood up, stretched, and looked once more upon the two creatures in front of him. "Think on that, both of you, while I am gone. I must see to the other Serpentauri."

Kelros and Kelron both nodded as he stepped around the fire, heading for the deeper parts of the Tunnel. "*Ai'au c,*" they said in unison, using the ancient tongue of the Aihi. "May the favor of the Ai be upon you."

The aged man looked back at them, their massive figures but shadows framed by the firelight behind them. "*Ai'au cn,*" was his reply.

CHAPTER 14

"All five, murdered?" asked Imen, his face quickly losing its color. He shook his head. "Surely you jest, Lord Arum."

"As well as I might wish that I could, you of all people would know me better than to make light of such heavy matters, Lord Imen," said Arum. "Erasen and I arrived on the centermost Island at roughly the same time. We found the other three messengers waiting for us. It is they who have given us this tragic news."

"The other three messengers were sent back to summon those who are to succeed the deceased High Priests and Priestesses," Erasen added, "while we traveled here before them. The Ceremony of Ordination will take place the dawn following their arrival."

Imen sat back down on the stone, feeling the burden he was to bear settling upon his shoulders, slowly beginning to crush him. "Why must such a thing happen to me?" he prayed silently. "I am not ready. I cannot. Yet I must."

He looked upon the three people standing around him. Two of them were good friends, two of them fellow pupils of their deceased master. The death of the Lord Aio having repeated itself with the other High Priests and Priestesses on the other Islands, all three of them would look up to him almost as to the Ai Himself. They would follow his every word. In turn, it would be his word that would guide each follower to victory and safety, or to death and defeat. The correct command could save the lives of many, while the wrong command could be that which would lead all of his close friends to their deaths. Would he be forced to sacrifice these three and many others with them in loyalty to the Ai?

Every muscle in his body strained, all but forcing him to fling his body over the cliff face to certain death at the foot of the mountain. His mind battled with equal force to overcome his instincts. He sat upon that stone, his body tense, his mind fighting against his body and for control.

One more blade of grass. One more blade was all that was needed. All that was needed to break him. The troubles that were to come upon him by omen of the open Tunnel had already begun.

Las laid her hand upon his shoulder.

"It is difficult for us all, Lord Imen, when those who mentored us and guided us have departed, more so in the manner of this particular departure. Even more difficult it becomes when we must don their cloaks, seemingly too small to fill them."

At the voice of the soon-to-be High Priestess, Imen nodded, his muscles relaxing, his mind having temporarily won the battle. "It is difficult, however, for each of you. Lord Arum, you are to become a High Priest, and to sit at my right hand. You will have me to guide you. Fortunate is the Lady Las, who in becoming High Priestess of the Red Island will have not only myself, but also the rest of the Council to look to. To be envied are you, Erasen. You are yet a pupil, and will have all of us to hold your hand the entire way. Yours is but the responsibility to follow those who lead. As for me? Am I to be the one that stands in front, blindly leading everyone across the unknown parts of the future? The way is dark to my eyes. Who have I?"

"You have the Council of High Priests," said Arum, "as well as every Priest and pupil on each of the Five Islands."

"Perchance a mighty band of the Followers, or the military forces of the Five Islands," said Las, trying her best to sound hopeful.

Erasen cut in. "If I may be so bold as to speak to the Lord Aio, as you are soon to be called, Lord Imen. As well as to the soon-to-be High Priest and Priestess Arum and Las," he paused, "he has the Ai."

All conversations immediately came to a halt, everyone looking to Erasen in silence, allowing the weight of his words to beat down upon them. Imen turned and smiled at Erasen. "You have learned well, pupil, under the Lord Daio, called Aio, to remind Lord Imen of the most basic of the basics. I must now accept what I am to become. The way is still dark, but no longer does a *blind* man lead his sightless followers."

In saying this, he looked upward. The moon lived still, and the stars danced about her, beautifully decorating the blackness that dominated the sky. He still had one to follow. One unlike the Lord Daio called Aio that would never be found murdered in his hut. Not even one like himself, unconfident and afraid of leading everyone into the mouth of the giant Demon of Aihi legend. One far different.

He shifted his attention to the Lord Arum. "I mourn with you your loss, and grieve with you for your advancement in the hierarchy of the priesthood, yet still envy you your position as lower than mine. Of the two, yours is the smoother path, for the time being. Very well then. Hail, Lord Arum, High Priest of the Island of Ban."

Arum grinned. "Hail, my lord."

The white-clad High Priest turned to the Lady Las. "And hail the Lady Las, High Priestess of the Red Island."

Las giggled softly. "Hail, Lord Arum, Lord Aio. If we are done now with our greetings, might we best be in shelter? Darkness has already overtaken us, and the night's weather to the east bodes ill with me."

"A wise decision and great observance on your part. I am sure the Lord Arum is exhausted from the undoubtedly strenuous climb up the mountain. You will have him in your hut, Erasen?"

"As you wish, Lord Imen, called Aio."

Imen let loose a small laugh as he led the way farther up the mountain trail to the huts.

The next three days were spent working, preparing for the ceremony, moving the belongings of Imen and Las into their new huts, and each reviewing the business of the person whose position they were to take. During the afternoon of the first day, both the Lady Moren and the Lord Forgotten Man returned, bringing news of their journeys to Aicatan and to spreading the tragic news and warning to the Followers.

"Hail, Lord Imen!" panted the Lady Moren, nearly collapsing on one of the stones. "Hail!" came the unnoticed reply from the Lord Forgotten Man as he stood, half asleep, next to the Lady Moren. Immediately Las came to their sides, two pitchers of water in her hands.

"Hail, Lady Moren, Lord Forgotten Man," said Imen, slowly turning toward them, breaking his gaze from the valley. "What news do you bring from Aicatan, Lady?"

Drinking half the pitcher in one gulp, unceremoniously pouring the rest over her head, she caught her breath. "To call it either good or bad would be to look at it in the broadest sense," she said. "The Cabinet was, of course, skeptical. However, the opening of the Tunnel did give way to a general concern among them."

The Forgotten Man slowly gulped his water down, yawning. "What did they do, or have they yet to decide?" asked Las.

Moren laughed. "With a little help, I might be able to bring them to a quicker, more favorable decision. They do not know what to do about the main body of our armies, they being occupied with other matters, but according to ancient laws, one hundred men from each of the main Islands, along with any who of free will choose to aid us, are to be mobilized on demand and put in the command of the Great High Priest. The company from the Red Island should arrive at the foot of the mountain within a few days.

Imen shrugged. "That can be expected, although we shall need much more than five hundred if we expect to ward off the invasion."

"Invasion?" asked Moren. "*That* is why I was sent to Aicatan? Knowing that, I could have convinced the Cabinet to mobilize quite a few more from among the armies. Any idea on who is attacking?"

Imen shook his head, his face grim. "The worst has happened. Orlek is alive, and will most likely wish to return."

Moren's face turned white, her studies of history as a child coming back to her memory. "Orlek?" she asked, her voice shuddering. "Was he not killed, many years ago?"

Imen nodded. "That he was." He paused. "Twice." He then, with the help of Las and Arum, recounted what he had told Las the day before, as well as what happened on the other Islands. When they had finished, Moren pushed herself up off the stone. "It seems as though great tragedies have struck all of us, Lord Arum. However, I envy not your new position."

Arum solemnly nodded. "Indeed, tragedies strike all of us. Every Priest on the Five Islands by now grieves with you, feeling your loss as their own."

Moren pushed her long, dark brown hair back with her hands, squeezing the water out of it. "Such is my story," she said, "with one small hope. More discouraging is the account of the Lord Forgotten Man, if you wish to hear it."

All looked toward the Forgotten Man, who by this time was beginning to doze off. At the sound of his name, he groggily opened his eyes, yawning. He stared blankly at the rest of the group.

"My story," he droned in a low, monotone voice typical of a creature that has not slept well, "might be similar to that of the Lady Moren, yet much more disturbing. The Priests of this Island might be the youngest our history has seen, but must they be the weakest, the most skeptical and power hungry? Rejection. That is all I received for warning the Priests. Of course, they were courteous, as is customary to a priest of higher seniority, but their unbelief was tangible, even through the front of respect. Of the ten, only one I could discern actually believed my story and agreed to give us any help. He said he would warn the Followers under his care and have them make standard preparations."

"The others?" asked Imen, taking in what had been said, evaluating his next action.

The Forgotten Man yawned, sipping water once more. "They tried to sound as helpful as they could. Empty words. They agreed to talk to the Followers under them. The next time I come to them, a general consensus of the Followers' opinions on the matter will be given to me. They would promise me nothing more."

Imen solemnly nodded at the report of the Forgotten Man. Erasen gritted his teeth, suppressing his anger at the backslidden priests, a few of whom had been his best friends during his earlier years of studying for the Priesthood.

"'Tis grievous news you bring us, Lord Forgotten Man," said Imen. "It will make our task much harder. It might be too late for some people. I believe I shall meet with some of our 'Priests' soon."

"Who, pray tell, was that one good Priest?" inquired Las. "He might be of some help to us."

The Forgotten Man pinched himself, trying to keep awake. "Interesting that you of all people would ask, my Lady. He inquired into your well being. He was the youngest of the Priests. His name was Eroz."

Both Las and Imen nodded, smiling in spite of the ill news. "Eroz?" said Imen. "How could one forget a pupil such as Lord Eroz?"

"A pupil," explained Las, "studying for the Priesthood two years ago. As good a man and Priest as one could ever meet. After being ordained, he was sent to do work away from the mountain. I must have caught his eye. Never could stand looking at him, however. A likeable person, but he had such a horrid face." All six laughed, the Forgotten Man in his fatigue managing to chuckle somewhat.

"Although I have seen naught of him in my last year here as a pupil," said the Forgotten Man, "then after my work on the Island, as a Priest, I still saw nothing of him."

Las, having finally regained her breath, leaned against the rock wall. "You may tell him, then, when you return that I still think his face to be quite ugly."

More laughter ensued. When the laughter died down, all present fell silent for a few minutes, each deep in their own thoughts. It was Moren who decided to break the silence.

"The dawn after the ceremonies have been completed, I will leave to prod the Cabinet to make a quicker decision." Imen shook his head. "No. I shall go. I am to be the Lord Aio. Not only is it my right and duty, my presence in my new position might just offer them more incentive to act."

"Nay, lord," said Arum. "If anyone is to go, it is I. It is not customary for the Great High Priest to serve the function of his own messenger, except in time when the positional influence or use of magic is completely necessary."

"Neither is it customary for a messenger, regardless of his level in the Priesthood, to serve such a function on the Island of another High Priest. To report of happenings on the Red Island would not only be highly improper, but would no doubt push us farther back then where we started. If I am not to go, a messenger from this Island will be sent."

Las cut in with her opinion. "If we are to follow the customs of the Priesthood to the letter, I would be the one to go. As the new High Priestess of this Island, my word is to be honored as having come from the Great High Priest and the Ai Himself, and might be enough to sway the opinions of more than a few members of the Cabinet. Your place, Lord Imen called Aio, is where you are, sitting on that stone. My work is to this Island. Your responsibility is to the entire Five Islands, and mine to just this one."

"She is right, Lord Aio," said Erasen somewhat timidly. "If I may be so bold as to speak, my Lord, you will be needed for the managing of the affairs of the Five Islands combined. The affairs of this Island might need close attention as well, but that would be the duty of the High Priestess and Priests of this Island."

"Very well then," said Imen, a bit cross at having been corrected by his soon-to-be pupils. "It shall be the Lady Las." He got up from his seat on the stone. "I have yet more moving of materials from my hut to my new hut to finish before the day is out." He looked over at the Forgotten Man. "If I were that poor Priest," he said, loud enough to wake the sleeping priest, "I would wake up for a time long enough so that I could be accompanied by the new Great High Priest to my hut where sleep would be slightly more comfortable than on such a cold, hard stone."

Imen achieved more than the desired effect. The Forgotten Man, having been shocked awake at the loud voice of the new Great High Priest, immediately jumped, his cloak falling out of place. He quickly bowed to Imen, causing his cloak to fall completely over his head. While struggling to get it off, he tripped, falling face first on the ground, entangled even more in the folds of his cloak.

The others laughed, helping him to his feet and removing the cloak from him. The exhausted—and embarrassed—priest quickly grabbed his cloak from them, folded it over his arm, and red-faced walked up the trail to the huts with Imen.

- The Book of Faith

CHAPTER 15

Calderon woke with a start. Sunlight was beginning to filter through the patched material over the window that was considered a curtain. He sat up quickly and looked to see if Velkyn or Donovan were up. He could tell by their rhythmic breathing they were still sleeping. It had been his turn to watch the door. It seemed that his disorder had reared its ugly head again.

Calderon went to stand up and almost screamed out. A horrible burning pain shot through his legs and lower back. He gave up trying to move and realized this was most likely caused by gripping the horse with his legs the day before. He grit his teeth and tried hard not to move at all, hoping vainly that if his legs were still he wouldn't feel the pain.

"Mother of Faith!" Velkyn swore loudly. Calderon realized his friend must be experiencing the same feeling of pain. "I can't move!" He didn't bother to respond. He noticed Donovan was awake now as well. "What's going on?" the old man asked as he rolled out of bed, seeming unbothered by any pain himself.

"My legs are on fire!" Calderon yelped. Donovan chuckled knowingly. "I forgot you two have never ridden before. Unless the inn has any salve, we may lose a day to let you two recuperate. I'll ask when we …" he paused mid sentence as he looked around the room. "Where are our bags?" he asked suddenly. Calderon and Velkyn forced themselves out of bed against their bodies' protest. Their bags, which they had set on the floor next to the single chair in the room were missing.

Velkyn met Calderon's eyes and knew immediately what happened. "I … I must have fallen asleep," Calderon muttered sheepishly. Donovan sighed. Calderon waited for the verbal lashing, but it never came. "We can buy more supplies," Velkyn said, attempting to be of some help and come to his friend's aid. "All the money we had was in my leather pouch. And it was in my bag," Donovan replied. "Don't worry about it," he added, sensing Calderon was beating himself up over it.

"Perhaps there is someone who saw something, saw who took our things and where they went." Donovan tried to make his tone sound hopeful, but he knew better. Things were likely to get more difficult than they already were. They were going to have to track them down. "Get dressed and meet me downstairs," the old man instructed. He looked into the mirror that hung on the wall next to the chair, patted his hair down, and walked out of the door.

Calderon looked to Velkyn. "I think my disorder is going to get us in a lot of trouble. Maybe I should just go back to the abbey." Velkyn slowly walked over to him. "Calderon, I don't think you understand. This isn't about you. This isn't even about me, or Donovan. It's about something bigger than that, something bigger than us." He forced himself to walk over to the window, ignoring the pain in his legs. Velkyn pulled the curtain aside and stared out at the mountains in the distance. "This is about the kingdom. Maybe even the world. The task set before us is going to require much. It may even demand our lives ..." he trailed off, pausing as if thinking about something. He turned from the window and looked at his friend. "Are you ready to make that sacrifice, if it comes? To give your life for others?"

Calderon didn't answer. He didn't have to. If his friend didn't know the answer, he obviously didn't know him that well. He didn't want to die. Especially not for people he would probably never know. It was selfish, but he didn't care. He wasn't like Velkyn, willing to do whatever it takes for the good of the kingdom. They left the room in silence and limped down the stairs to where they had eaten the previous night. They found Donovan at one of the tables with two plates of food waiting. The only other patron in the room was the man Velkyn had seen the night before, the one who had passed out on the floor. He was holding something against his head, apparently nursing some sort of bump.

The two young monks sat at the table and looked questioningly at Donovan. "I thought we didn't have any money?" Calderon asked quietly, looking around warily even though they were essentially the only ones in the room. Donovan smiled and nodded toward the barmaid behind the counter. It was the same woman from the night before. "It's already been paid for. No one saw anything. She said that this has been a problem only recently. Guests stay and then their things go missing. No one ever sees anything or anyone. It is not going to be easy, but we have to find them. We won't make it through the mountains without supplies. We have to retrieve our things."

"We could turn back," Calderon said. "We only traveled one day." Donovan was shaking his head as the young monk spoke. "We can't afford to lose any more time. The creature," he lowered his voice, "if it finds a way to restore its body, will be almost impossible to stop."

Calderon looked at his plate which had scrambled eggs and some hard biscuits on it. It didn't look very appealing, but he decided to eat it anyway. He chewed a mouthful of eggs and thought about what Donovan said. Velkyn was devouring his food with a vengeance. Calderon looked back at Donovan. "The dragon was stopped before. Why would it be impossible to stop it now if it was stopped before?"

Donovan bit his lip. "The kind of magic that was used then … doesn't exist now." Calderon looked confused. "What do you mean?" Donovan tried to explain. "Each wizard specializes in a specific type of magic. They can cast any kind of magic, but the type they are most adept at is much more powerful. Each wizard explores their powers on their own to learn their capabilities and limits. Wizards create their own spells once they progress in their knowledge. The spell that was used to capture the dragon was made specifically by the wizard who cast it. That is why I said that kind of magic doesn't exist. If the wizards in Oakvalor can find the dragon's spirit, they can reactivate the magic in the sphere. Spells like that can be reactivated, but never recreated. At least, not the way it worked originally."

"You know a lot about magic," Calderon said. Donovan shrugged. "I have studied many books. With knowledge comes strength." They finished their meal and were talking with the barmaid about possible places where they might find who stole their things. Velkyn noticed the man from last night was looking their way and listening to their conversation. "He's a wizard," Velkyn said to Donovan. "I think his name is Julian. He was trying to find work last night." The old man looked at Julian. He stared at him for a moment before looking back to Velkyn. "No, he's not."

"How do you know?" Velkyn questioned. Donovan sighed. "We're still in Talvaard. If he were a real wizard, he certainly wouldn't be parading that knowledge about. The Massacre might be a thing of the past, but people still don't trust those who practice magic." As they rose from their chairs, so did Julian. They thanked the barmaid for the food and the information and left the inn, making their way around the back to collect their horses.

"Gentlemen," a voice rang out. Donovan turned to see Julian stumbling toward them. "I believe I can help you," he said, brushing off his pants and straightening his shirt. "I am Julian Brathenworth, magician for hire."

Donovan snorted in response. "You are not a wizard." Julian's face scrunched up in a look of indignation. "I most certainly am," he shot back. "I can do magic." This last sentence was laced with smugness. "Even if you were a wizard," Donovan said, "we don't need one. We've got enough to deal with right now. And if I were you, I wouldn't be telling people I was a wizard, even if I was. The people here aren't so accommodating to wizards." Turning back toward the stables, the three monks collected their horses and thanked the young boy who had made sure they were taken care of. As they came out, they found Julian waiting for them.

"Let me demonstrate," he offered. He put his two index fingers to his head and began mumbling something under his breath. Seeming to discover something, he looked back at them and smiled. "You're looking for something!" Donovan urged his horse forward and rode past the man without a second glance. Velkyn followed suit, but Calderon held back.

"What are we looking for?" he asked Julian, wondering if the man really did have some magical powers. Julian glanced about as if he were going to reveal some sort of secret. "You're looking for … something that belongs to you." Calderon frowned at Julian. "Some magic," he said. He urged his horse to move, feeling the burning pain in his legs starting to feel like a thousand tiny ants biting him. The man wasn't as useful as Calderon thought.

"I know where they went," Julian added, almost as an afterthought. This stopped all three of the monks. Donovan looked at Julian from over his shoulder. "You know where who went?"

Julian realized that he might have found his in. "The people you are looking for. I know where they went. But you will have to take me with you." Donovan looked at the two young monks, then back to Julian. His conscience told him it was a bad idea. The man was obviously a schemer, but if he did know something about their missing belongings …

"Do you have a horse?" Donovan questioned. Julian shook his head. "No. I have something better." He disappeared into the stable and returned a moment later with an odd looking creature. It was much shorter than their mounts and covered in grey fur. A dark brown stripe ran the length of its body, beginning at its nose and continuing to its tail. A similar stripe ran from one shoulder to the other, forming what looked like a cross shape.

It was an odd sight to the three of them, and Julian riding the creature made it look even more ridiculous. "Where are we headed?" Donovan asked, eyeing Julian dubiously. "South," Julian answered, "to Dillenger."

"Dillenger? Why Dillenger? I hear it's full of nothing but cut-throats and thieves." Julian nodded. "That it is. It's also a place full of adventure. We will certainly find them there."

"How do you know we will find who we are

looking for there?" Velkyn chimed in. "How do we know you didn't take our things and you are leading us off to be killed?" Julian looked shocked that someone would accuse him of such things. He forced his animal to stop and looked at Velkyn. "Because I can do magic," he said with a wink.

● ∞ ● ∞ ●

Dillenger was a dilapidated town. The entire place was once protected by an enormous stone wall that rose at least twelve feet high. Here and there, entire sections of the wall lay crumbled upon itself or entirely missing. The three monks and Julian entered the town through a large archway that used to be a guard house. The massive iron gate was useless now and lay rusted on the ground.

Calderon looked warily at the various buildings that were abandoned, or at least appeared to be. Where many of the doors and windows should have been, boards and soiled sheets covered the openings. He half expected an army of thieves to jump out from the shadows of each alleyway. He looked to Velkyn, whose face was as stoic as if it were made of the same stone as the walls around the city. Donovan was keeping his gaze straight ahead, and Julian was babbling on about the history of the place. None of them were listening to him though. They didn't see anyone—not even in the shadows—as they made their way deeper into the city.

As they headed toward the center of the city, the buildings became more maintained, some of them even painted and operational by their outside appearance. As they rounded a corner they could hear the faint sound of music. It got louder as they approached a two story brick building. A sign hung over the front entrance that was weather worn and unreadable. "Maybe we can find some answers in there?" Velkyn said, pointing. They all exchanged glances and decided it was a good place to start. A long wooden rail ran the length of the front of the building and they used it to tie their horses up.

Julian pushed the doors open and noted the well-oiled hinges that allowed it to open silently. That was evidence that the place was used often and seeing it as a good tiding, he led the monks inside the building. The walls were adorned with all sorts of paintings and the floors were polished to a clear shine. The elegance of the interior belied the room full of customers, all of whom appeared to be criminals. There were several people working behind the bar.

All but one of the tables were taken, and as Julian looked about at all the patrons, he recognized three men, the same three men from the previous night. "There," he muttered to Donovan, nodding his head in their general direction. "I am about sure they are the men you are looking for."

Donovan led them to the empty table and they all took a seat. Donovan leaned into the middle of the table, motioning for the two younger monks to do the same. "This is a dangerous place. I suspect if we accuse those men of taking our things, the whole inn might attack us. We need to figure out if these men really do have our things before we accuse them. Any ideas?"

"We could find out where they are staying and search their room," Calderon suggested. Velkyn smiled and looked at Julian. "We could send him over there. Let them take him in on their 'adventuring' and find out for us." Donovan considered both options and honestly didn't have any ideas himself. The quicker they retrieved their stuff, the quicker they could get back on the road to Oakvalor. Donovan glanced at Julian, and though he still didn't trust the man, he knew their options were limited and they were short on time. "Go work your 'magic'," he said sardonically.

Julian pushed his chair out and stood up, pausing a moment to smooth out his clothes, and then walked over to the table where the three men were sitting. "'Ello," he greeted them. "I am Julian Brathenworth, magician for hire."

● ∞ ● ∞ ●

"Stay close and keep quiet," Donovan bade the younger monks. After a considerable amount of time, and ale, Julian had convinced the three men (again) that he was a magician who could help them. The men had left the inn with Julian in tow, and the three monks followed them from a safe distance.

They made their way down several streets, seeming to travel deeper into the city. The buildings all looked similar in design to those near the nameless inn they had just left. "I still don't trust this Julian," muttered Velkyn, casting wary glances every few steps. "That makes two of us," Donovan replied. "But he is the only lead we have." They watched as Julian and the other men stopped at one of the buildings. One of the men produced a key and unlocked the door. They entered the building and the sound of the door closing echoed off the neighboring buildings throughout the street.

"Let's get a closer look," Donovan suggested. They moved quickly but quietly down the cobblestone street and bent low under the windowsill. Donovan pressed his ear against the wood. He could hear voices, but nothing distinguishable. He was startled suddenly when a loud thump sounded, followed by what sounded like laughter.

"What do you hear?" Velkyn asked, continually scrutinizing their surroundings. "Not much," Donovan admitted. "Let us go in and demand our belongings," Velkyn said, pointing at the door. "Our time grows shorter the longer we spend here."

Donovan considered the young man's words. It was true that time was slipping away, but he didn't feel comfortable barging into the Divines knew what—and possibly getting them all killed. Their mission was bigger than some highway thieves. "You are the only one skilled in the art of fighting," Donovan finally said, looking to Velkyn and Calderon. "Then I'll lead the way," Velkyn answered simply. Donovan sat silent for long moments, unsure what to do. Finally he shrugged and pressed his ear back to the wall. He didn't hear anything now. "I leave the decision to you two," Donovan said.

Velkyn and Calderon looked to each other and nodded in silent agreement. "We can't leave him here," Calderon finally spoke. "Not in good conscience." Velkyn took that as his sign and nimbly leapt over to the door. He centered his concentration and focus. In a blur of movement, he spun in a complete circle, lifting his leg as he came full turn and slammed his foot into the door. Whether it was locked or not, Velkyn couldn't tell. It probably wouldn't have mattered either way, as the old wood splintered under the force of his kick. The door flung open and he charged in immediately, Calderon and Donovan running in behind him. Pain flooded the left side of Velkyn's head and he crumbled to the ground. He could hear shouting and assumed it was his companions, but didn't have time to sort out the sounds as darkness overtook him.

Calderon saw the man hit Velkyn with a wooden pole and watched as his friend hit the floor. It happened too fast for him to yell a warning or intervene, but he quickly ducked as he ran through the doorway, narrowly missing a similar strike from his right. He dropped down beside Velkyn and could see a large welt across his face. He looked behind him as he heard a grunt and saw two men wrestling with Donovan. Julian lay crumpled in a heap in the corner of the room. He saw the third man, possibly the same man who knocked Velkyn out, calmly walking toward the struggling men. He lifted the wooden pole up as if to strike the old monk, and Calderon jumped up and threw himself bodily at the man.

The unexpected force dropped the man to the ground and Calderon desperately tried to wrest the makeshift weapon from him. The man was much stronger than Calderon expected and he was quickly overwhelmed. The man punched Calderon in the mouth several times, causing the monk to lose his grip on the pole. The man untangled himself and kicked Calderon hard in the ribs. Calderon gasped audibly as the air in his lungs rushed out painfully and watched helplessly as the man dropped Donovan with a bash to the head.

It was all he could do to try and force air into his body. The three men drug Velkyn and Donovan beside Calderon and tied them all together with their backs facing each other. Apparently thinking them immobile, they went into another room. Calderon was able to find his breath after much effort and heard a groan. He looked over in Julian's direction and saw him stirring. "Julian!" he whispered as loud as he dared. "Julian! Are you all right?" Another groan was all he received.

Velkyn and Donovan began moving and he struggled to face them. The ropes didn't have much slack and so he wasn't able to see their faces. "What happened?" he heard Velkyn's familiar voice say. "Shh," Calderon replied. "Keep your voice down. We were ambushed. They must have seen us following them."

"What'ev we got 'ere?" a voice interrupted. Calderon didn't even notice the three men had reentered the room. One of them, the one who had spoke, reminded Calderon of a weasel. The one holding the wooden pole, judging from his demeanor, seemed to be the leader. He was tall and broad shouldered with a bald head and a black beard that was thick and bushy. The third man was taller than the weaselish man, but shorter than the leader. His face was pale and he sported a lengthy mustache that used to be popular among the men of Talvaard.

Julian groaned again and the pale faced man walked over and helped him to his feet. "Seems we have some thieves looking to steal from us," the big man with the beard said. His voice was deep and gravelly. "What should we do with them, Theo?" the big man asked, looking to the man who had helped Julian. The pale faced man, Theo, stroked his mustache as if in thought. "I never seen a man killed by magic," he said with a smirk.

The leader looked at Julian. "Well magician, it seems you're services are needed. Give us a show." Julian's face paled and he looked feebly to the three monks. Theo pushed Julian forward. "We are not thieves," Donovan said.

"No?" the big man questioned. "Then why were you sneaking around outside my house?" Donovan was moving his hands behind him, trying to loosen the rope that bound Velkyn's hands. "Someone stole from us. Took everything we owned. We came here hoping to find our stuff." The leader frowned. "Are you calling us thieves?" The man that resembled a weasel snickered.

"I don't believe I made that accusation," Donovan replied. "We are just looking for information." He was having a hard time loosening the rope. The big man didn't seemed convinced. "Continue," he bade Julian.

"Wait," Donovan pleaded. He could feel the binding giving way and worked his hands furiously. "Let me fully explain." Julian began weaving his hands in the air, forming odd looking shapes and whispering something unintelligible. Donovan slid the rope off Velkyn's wrist and shouted "Now!"

Velkyn quickly sprung into action. He pushed himself onto his feet and turned to his assailants. He somersaulted over his companions and landed in front of the leader, knifing his hands into the throats of weasel and Theo. Without pausing, he slammed his head into the big man's face and was rewarded with the crunch of cartilage. Julian quickly fled into the other room. Donovan and Calderon helped each other to their feet and worked together to untie the rest of the rope. Theo and weasel were making choking noises and grasping at their throats. The big man's nose was bleeding, but he wouldn't be as easy to take out. He grabbed Velkyn by his robes and pulled him in close and returned the monk's head butt.

Velkyn's head snapped backward and he felt his own nose running with blood. He brought his arms up, palms together, between the big man's arms and pushed them outward, breaking the leader's hold on his robes. He struck out with his fist, attempting to punch the man in the throat. The big man merely slapped his hand away and tried to grab the monk again. Velkyn ducked under his reach and snapped his foot up and forward, connecting with the man's kneecap.

The big man fell back with a pained roar and crashed to the floor. Julian came running back into the room with three bags that Donovan recognized. "I told you they had your stuff!" Julian shouted as he continued across the room and out the door. Donovan and Calderon followed quickly behind him, and Velkyn brought up the rear ensuring they wouldn't be followed. The day was nearing an end and the three monks were lost. Julian was waiting for them at the end of the street waving his arms excitedly. "Come gentlemen! Hurry!"

They reached him and each grabbed their own bags.

"Thank you," Calderon said sincerely. "You didn't have to help us." Julian waved his hand. "I doubted you," Donovan chimed in, "and I apologize for judging you unjustly. We are indebted to you." Velkyn kept his eyes on the house they escaped for any sign the men would come running after them. "You hired me, remember?" Julian winked at them. "And maybe you can pay that debt … some other time. I'm afraid I must take my leave of you gentlemen now. Safety and such," he smiled. "Follow this street and turn left, go to the end of that street, and turn left again. That will put you on the street with the inn. Can you find your way out of the city from there?"

Donovan nodded. "I'm certain we can. Thank you again, Julian." Velkyn clasped Julian's hand. "Until next time," he said. Julian smiled and off he went, disappearing down another street and out of their view. "Make haste," Donovan said as he glanced down the way they had come. "I want to be long gone from here."

The two young monks nodded their ascent and followed Donovan's quick pace. They were leaving the city's crumbled walls almost an hour later, headed back toward the mountains.

"The responsibilities and privileges that come with the role of being the Lord Aio are many and great. The greatest of both is to serve others. I live selflessly and serve others, and in that I find my privilege, and my responsibility. To those ends do I dedicate my life."
-Lord Imen,
called Aio

CHAPTER 16

The sun peered over the southern hills of the Red Island with a seeming reluctance, hesitating slightly before continuing its journey upward into the sky, greeting that portion of Oakvalor in its full brightness. The moon had already deserted the expanse, leaving it full of the trailing stars until the time when the sun should blot out their trek over the horizon with its glorious presence.

Not a cloud, gray, black or otherwise was to be seen on that day. On all areas of the Island not shaded by some larger body, such as the mountains or trees, the morning dew glittered with the beauty of diamonds, countless as the grains of earth of which Oakvalor was composed.

The side of the mountain facing the valley was by no means covered in shadow, allowing the three watchers at the peak to see what transpired below them with perfect clarity. For any ceremony, this was a more than perfect morning. One almost would have felt that such a ceremony could not be done with a greeting less worthy than the one given it by the sun. "Fortunate, for the moment, is this young Council," thought Father Ean. "Even the appearance of the Great Lord Aio was not hailed with such splendor."

Father Ean had been watching as the pupils from the other four Islands began their trek up the mountain's trail the evening before, and he had run into the Tunnel to wake up the two sleeping Serpentauri. After having passed by the Tunnel's guard unnoticed, they found a perch at the top of the mountain, just close enough to see, yet just far enough not to be seen.

They had spent the remainder of the night on the top of the mountain, waiting for the ceremony to begin. Except for a few words about the absence of any morning meal from Kelron, the hours of waiting were spent in complete silence. For the first in almost two weeks, the Serpentauri were able to hear the sounds of life outside the Tunnel. Even to Kelron, whose mind was preoccupied with food, it felt like a dream to be able to see the stars, hear the chirping of the crickets, and to experience being under the sky again.

Father Ean motioned the two Serpentauri to watch closely as the Lady Moren and the pupil Erasen quickly walked down the trail in the brisk dawn air, readying the Ceremony of the Clearing of the Five Stones for the ceremony. Cloaks of all colors were spread out at the foot of each stone, a sword thrust into the ground next to each cloak. A ring was placed upon each stone.

Once this task had been completed, the Lady Moren and Erasen walked to the edge of the cliff overlooking the valley below, preparing to call all Priests on the mountain to arise and to take their part in the ceremony that was about to be started.

Erasen pulled a small, hallowed out wooden rod

from the folds of his pupil's cloak, examining closely the holes that had been put into it. "What is the reason for hesitation?" asked Moren, impatient for the ceremony to begin.

Erasen looked up from the instrument. "I am sorry, Lady Moren," he said. "I just hope that Lord Imen will not mind us using *his* flute for waking everyone up." Moren slowly shook her head. "Have you not been studying the histories, specifically where they speak of such events?"

"From my recollection, there is really only one example to look upon. When the Great Lord …"

"I know, I know," said Moren impatiently. "It cannot be helped. You now hold the only musical instrument on the mountain at this time, and are the only person on this mountain other than Lord Imen who can intelligently breathe through that thing and make sounds to become music. The ceremony requires music for the waking of the new Council or Council members, and would it be proper for Lord Imen to wake himself up with the music when he is to be given the Red Sword?"

"I would suppose not," said the young pupil. "Very well, Lady Moren. The sun has risen, and so must the rest of the mountain." He lifted the flute to his lips, playing the same melody that had been played the night the Lord Aio was murdered. At first—to the disapproval and impatience of the Lady Moren—the sound was weak, his breath barely making any music come out at all. Gradually, however, Erasen gained more confidence in his playing, the sound becoming stronger, sweeter. Life seemed to surge anew through everything that could be seen at the music played by the pupil. The sun, its lower part finally escaping the bonds of the horizon, seemed to shout for joy in all its splendor in thankfulness for its very existence.

Erasen turned around after finishing the song,

finding most of the group already standing behind him, listening to the music. The Lord Arum, the Lady Elaran, the Lady An, and the Lord Irn stood in their places beside the stones respective to their Islands, a sword in front and a cloak to the left of each of the soon-to-be Council members. Lady Las had positioned herself in the middle-front of the stones, kneeling. A suit of armor lay in front of her. The Lord Forgotten Man stood guard at the part of the trail leading to the valley, while the Lady Moren had moved to the part of the trail leading toward the huts. Imen was not present.

Erasen bowed to the group of his superiors. The Lord Arum nodded in reply. The Lady Las smiled. All attention was quickly turned to the sound of the footsteps on the trail, coming down to the Clearing of the Five Stones.

All the Priests and pupils present knelt down on their right knees as Imen appeared from the bend in the trail. He bowed quickly, acknowledged Erasen, and slowly walked to the center of the Five Stones, facing the valley.

"Fellow Priests and pupils," he said, addressing the entire group. "We gather here now to ordain a new Council of High Priests, an event such as has not been seen in the past century. The histories concerning this ceremony are quite vague, and not much applicable to the situation we find ourselves in. We have, by studying deeply of the histories, found what we need to know in the carrying out of this ceremony but for one thing: Who is to ordain the Great High Priest? There has been only one in the history of this Council worthy of self-ordination. In other cases, there were other High Priests who could very well perform the task. We have neither this morning, aside from myself. Who shall ordain the Great High Priest? The question ran through my mind a thousand times as I slept and as I walked to this

Clearing, and I have only one method in mind that I would think proper for such an occasion in the situation we find ourselves."

The Priests held their breath, waiting for him to finish. Erasen trembled slightly, mostly out of nervousness at the importance of what he was witnessing and participating in.

"The Ai shall ordain, and the Ai shall revoke ordination. Erasen," he said, looking directly at the young man facing him. "My lord," said Erasen, standing up from the kneeling position. Imen smiled. "Take the red cloak off of the ground, and help me put it on. If I be not the man ordained by the Ai, than may this cloak be drenched with water, and may I be soaked through my armor and my undergarments."

Erasen slowly dropped his flute on the ground. He solemnly walked over to the centermost of the Stones, picked up the cloak in front of it, and spread it open behind Lord Imen, allowing the High Priest to put his arms through the armholes. When the cloak rested on Imen's shoulders, the pupil stepped back a few paces, waiting in silence for whatever would happen next. All the Priests watched in silence for something, anything, to happen. After what seemed an eternity, Imen cleared his throat.

"Erasen, feel the cloak. How wet is it?"

Erasen stepped back up to Imen, taking a part of the cloak in his hands, feeling it for any bit of moisture. "It is completely dry, my lord," he said. Imen smiled, nodding at the pupil. "Remove the Red Sword from the ground," he ordered, pointing at the Sword. Erasen promptly obeyed.

The High Priest continued. "Should I be unworthy of this holy position which I bestow upon myself, then may this sword turn to lead as my hands close over the hilt, and may I not be able to hold it above the ground."

Erasen handed the sword to Lord Imen, waiting for the worst to happen. Imen held the Red Sword for a few seconds, then in one quick motion causing Erasen to lose balance and fall on his back, he swung the sword high into the air. The early morning sunlight penetrated and reflected off the rubies that studded its hilt, casting a wondrous red aura over the Circle. The sword itself seemed to shimmer without the aid of the sun. The Priests, Priestesses, and Erasen looked up in awe at the wonder they were witnessing.

As quickly as the miracle had started, it ended, the sword losing its magical light. Imen lowered it to the ground, holding it out to his side. His breath was quick and heavy, as if he had climbed the mountain trail again. The rest of the Priests and Priestesses looked at him worriedly, yet said nothing as he continued.

"Lord Arum, a Priest of the Island of Ban, come forward."

The tall, thin young man arose, a breeze blowing his back-length black hair behind his shoulders, leaving a few loose strands near his face. When the Lord Arum was not a pace's distance from the Great High Priest, Imen raised the Red Sword between them, broadside out.

"Do you, Lord Arum, warrior and Priest of the Island of Ban, pledge your life and blood in service to the Great High Priest, the Red Sword, and the Ai?"

"I so pledge," said the Lord Arum, his face stern and solemn. "Raise your right hand," said Imen, turning the blade of the Red Sword out.

Arum obediently raised his right hand, bringing it close to the blade of the sword. Imen immediately touched the blade to the Priest's hand, pulling it back quickly. A dark, red ribbon of blood was left where the Red Sword had touched. A corresponding red liquid dripped from the blade.

Imen smiled, motioning for Arum to turn around,

facing the rest of the clearing, and below that, the valley. Erasen, without having to be told, picked up the white cloak, handing it to the new Great High Priest.

"Of this cloak cometh knowledge and the wisdom to use it. Should you be unworthy of the blood oath which you have taken, and of the cloak which shall be placed upon you, may you babble like the foolish child when this cloak rests upon your shoulders." Imen then proceeded to open the cloak, placing it upon the Priest. Arum immediately smiled, looking up to the sky, saying nothing.

As Imen looked to the Stone to his right, Erasen, on one knee, held the White Sword out to him. Imen nodded at the pupil, taking the sword. Arum turned around, again facing Imen. "As it has been said in the prophecy of the Lord Dazu called Aio, 'From the White Sword cometh wisdom, and many great tasks for you to do.'" Imen paused a moment. "The test of worthiness by wisdom has been passed. Should you be unworthy of this sword, may you be unable to perform the next task I give you, no matter how its simplicity."

He handed Arum the sword, saying, "Raise the sword above your head, Lord Arum, Priest of the Island of Ban." As if by itself, the sword was lifted high above Arum's head, the diamonds glittering in the sunlight. Again, it seemed for a brief moment that the sword itself produced light.

As the Lord Arum lowered the White Sword, Imen nodded at Erasen yet another time, and this time, the pupil bringing to him a large ring, cut from a single diamond, the ancient Aihi symbol for the Island of Ban cut into its intricate design at the top. "Although this object has no known value where magic and science are concerned, it is the symbol of the High Priest's position. Honor this symbol with a service equal to the honor that this ring gives you."

He then took the ring from Erasen and placed it on Arum's finger. "By the ceremonial powers vested in me of the Ai, and according to the customs of the ancient Aihi, I hereby ordain you, Lord Arum, now High Priest of the Island of Ban, next in the line to bear the Red Sword."

Arum knelt again, before returning to the stone closest to Imen's right, only to bend the knee again. The Lady Elaran, kneeling, stood up next, her tall, strong heavyset frame solemnly lumbering toward Imen, coming to a halt in front of him. Although she did not look so tall from a distance, anyone could tell that she was at least a head taller than Imen.

"Do you, Lady Elaran, warrior and Priestess of the Island of Carn, pledge your life and blood in service to the Great High Priest, the Red Sword, and to the Ai?" said Imen again, holding his sword in between the two in the same manner as with Arum. "I so pledge," said the young Priestess, raising her right hand without waiting for instruction to do so.

The blood pledge was repeated, the stain more visible on the Red Sword. Imen took the black cloak from Erasen, who had been holding it, waiting for the chance to give it to Imen. He motioned Elaran to turn around, facing the growing Council.

"This cloak shall be more a protection to you then will the shield you carry with your armor, for while wearing it, you can neither be wounded nor become ill. Should you be unworthy of this cloak, may your face break out in boils, and may you die of painful sickness at my feet in the presence of those gathered here."

The group gasped at hearing the consequences of unworthiness. Elaran became tense, knowing the type of death she faced if she were not meant to wear the cloak. "Into the will of the Ai I place my life and my body," she murmured.

Imen spread the cloak open, standing on his toes and stretching his arms in order to rest it on Elaran's shoulders. The Priests and Priestesses held their breath, waiting to see what would happen to the giantess of a Priestess. Elaran closed her eyes, expecting the worst. Elaran waited for a few seconds after the cloak had come to rest on her shoulders, Imen having drawn back. Eyes still closed, she reached her hand to her face, feeling around for any deformities that had not been there earlier. Breathing a sigh of relief, she turned around, facing the new Lord Aio again.

Imen took the Black Sword from the waiting Erasen, holding the hilt toward the large Priestess. "From the Black Sword cometh healing for those wounded and without rest," he said. "Should you be worthy to wield the healing power of this sword, may its hilt heal your hand from the wound inflicted by the blood pledge."

She grasped the sword in her right hand, immediately dropping it to the ground. Not only had the sword cut on her hand disappeared, so had all the other scars and scratches that hand had obtained through the various activities of a Priestess.

Imen next took a ring from Erasen, cut from a single piece of onyx. As with the White Ring, the symbol of the Island of Carn carved into the plain smoothness of the stone. "This ring which I now give you, although it has no magical or scientific powers, is a symbol of healing, to be worn only by the greatest healer of the Five Islands." Imen placed the ring on her finger, surprised at how smooth the ring slid onto Elaran's thick, strong finger. "By the ceremonial powers vested in me by the Ai, and according to the customs of the ancient Aihi, I hereby ordain you, Lady Elaran, now High Priestess of the Island of Carn." The High Priestess bowed on one knee to Imen, returning to her place at the stone to the left of Imen, then bowed again, facing Imen.

The Lady An hesitated a few seconds before standing up. Although very small and quite thin even while wearing her blue armor, she was not the frail Priestess that the sight of her figure led many to believe. A very young Priestess, yet already a veteran of war, her small size and peculiar skills with the sword had kept her from death many times, and had been the downfall of many seasoned warriors.

She stood before Imen, repeating the blood oath as had Arum and Elaran. The Great High Priest had to bend down a bit to complete this task, the part of the Red Sword that had performed the blood pledge covered and dripping with blood. Imen then spread the cloak, preparing to place it on the young warrior-priestess. "You, Lady An, who have fought well with the sword and have lived because of it and by it, may your body fall backward onto the Red Sword should you be unworthy of this cloak, that by the sword you may die."

Imen placed the cloak on An's shoulders, making sure the size would not cause it to slip off. He then quickly knelt, holding the Red Sword that she should fall on it if not one of the chosen by the Ai. The Lady An suddenly doubled over, away from the Red Sword, as if having been struck in the stomach. She immediately came back to an upright standing position, not having fallen onto the Red Sword.

By the time she had turned around to face Imen, the new Great High Priest was holding out the hilt of the Blue Sword to her. "From the Blue Sword many wonders that only the Ai can best," he said. "Should you be worthy to wield this great sword, may you with it perform a wonder for us."

The Lady An grabbed the Blue Sword, immediately thrusting it into the ground. The ground began to shake slightly, the quake growing in intensity the longer the sword was in the ground. A shocked look came over An as she tried to pull the sword out. The shaking of the ground, however, had become so violent by that time that she could barely hold onto it. She was shaken off her balance, landing on the ground, her body swinging with the shaking of the mountain as her hands kept a hold on the Blue Sword. Imen attempted to stumble over to help her, but fell hard on his back, feeling a sharp pain, his breath becoming short.

In an effort to push herself off the ground and to try to yank the Blue Sword free while standing, An took her hands off the Blue Sword. The shaking immediately stopped. Imen raised his eyebrows, immediately closing his eyes tightly in a wince as he got up, his back unable to completely straighten, having been injured by his fall during the short, violent tremor. "I suppose that we have our wonder, although I would have preferred a thunderstorm or a fire show in the sky to *that*," he said.

The rest of the Council, ordained or no, began returning to their kneeling positions, each grimacing at the pain from some hurt caused by the 'wonder' of the Blue Sword.

The Great High Priest took a blue ring, cut from a single piece of sapphire. Its design was simple, being no more than a couple straight lines crossing each other at certain irregular places on the ring. The symbol of the Island of Sares—the Island from which she came—was carved onto a flat part of the ring. It too, like the ring's design, was quite simple.

"This ring, Lady An," said Imen, "is the symbol of your High Priestess-hood, stained through the centuries by blood, sweat, flesh, goodness, and honor, not by disgrace, cowardice, or evil. Let not so much as a speck of dust mar its future." The ring was then placed on her finger. "By the ceremonial powers vested in me of the Ai, and according to the customs of the ancient Aihi, I hereby ordain you, Lady An, now High Priestess of the Island of Sares."

The High Priestess bowed to Imen, returning to the outermost stone to the right of Imen. A tall young man, his skin drawn tightly over his face as if nothing but skin and bone composed his body, rose from a kneeling position, approaching the Lord Imen. He had no hair on his head, but instead proudly wore the scars of many wounds and injuries to his head in place of the hair.

Imen looked up, the Lord Irn seeming even taller now that his back was bent. They went through the blood oath quickly, the blood dripping down the hilt of the Red Sword. As the blood oath was finished, Imen motioned the tall man to stand up. "Lord Irn, of all the members of this Council gathered here, you alone have shown no deceit, even as a child so young to not know the better. Within you is honesty and integrity without flaw or blemish. Should your blood oath have had the smallest part of any deceit, may the weight of this cloak bear you to the ground."

He took the green cloak from Erasen, putting it over the tall, thin body of the new High Priest.

"Put me down! Put me down!" shouted Irn angrily in a high pitched nasal voice. "If it won't stop I'll have it burned when I get to the ground," trying to remove the too large, yet too short cloak as he began floating up into the air. The cloak immediately set him down, as if to say that it did *not* wish to be burned. Those of the new High Council not in too much pain to laugh did so. Irn frowned, walking up to Imen, brushing off the cloak.

Imen took the Green Sword from Erasen and held it out, hilt forward, to Irn. "The Green Sword shall bring back the past in the form of the Great Serpentaur. This, Lord Irn, is the prophecy which all High Priests of the Island of Cerel dream every night to come within their time, yet dread it with the passing of every day. With this sword comes not a test of worthiness, but a blessing: that you might be the worthy bearer of this sword in the fulfilling of this prophecy." He handed the Green Sword to Irn, who solemnly bowing, accepted it.

A green ring was then handed to Imen, cut from a single piece of emerald, the symbol of the Island of Cerel carved into it. "This ring, Lord Irn," he said, "is the symbol of your high Priesthood. No finger that has worn this ring has ever belonged to one of the false tongue. Do not let your finger be the first." Irn held out his hand allowing Imen to put it on his finger. "By the ceremonial powers vested in me of the Ai, and according to the customs of the ancient Aihi, I hereby ordain you, Lord Irn, now High Priest of the Island of Cerel."

Cerel's new High Priest walked back to his stone, the outermost to Imen's left. Las timidly walked forward, her red armor shining in the rising sun. She bowed to Imen as she neared him, standing up again and repeating the blood oath as those who had gone before her. "Lady Las, Priestess of the Red Island," Imen addressed her. "The high Priestesshood of the Red Island offers no magic cloak to the one who claims this title. No powerful sword is given. No perilous test of worthiness is taken. There is only this ..." he said, motioning to Erasen, who promptly placed the ring, cut from a single ruby, into his hand.

"This ring is the symbol of your high Priestesshood. It has but one power: while you remain worthy and the rightful bearer of it, it will never slip off your hand. Should you ever commit an act that would prove you less than worthy to bear this ring, it would burn your finger as fire, until you would cast it away from you. Bear this ring well, and do not give yourself reason to remove it." He then placed the ring on her finger. "By the ceremonial powers vested in me of the Ai, and according to the customs of the ancient Aihi, I hereby ordain you, Lady Las, now High Priestess of the Red Island."

Las bowed, returning to her place directly across from Imen.

Imen, still bent over from his injury, motioned for the new Council to rise. "May the Ai grant this Council the wisdom with which to lead our people in these ever perilous times, and may we be granted the power with which to carry out wise decisions. I hereby, as spokesperson for the Ai, ordain this High Priest Council, to lead and serve the Five Islands of the Aihi in the name of the Ai."

He walked past the other five members of the Council, motioning to Erasen to follow him. He motioned for the other two priests to come near to him as well. "Have preparations made for a meal in my hut. Prepare also a resting place for the Lords Arum and Irn, and Ladies Elaran and An. When you are done, do as thorough a search as you can of this mountain. Magic is in use here on this mountain, apart from the wonders of the ceremony. Faint traces, but there is definitely some magic. I can feel it. Erasen, I have a task for you when these are finished."

Father Ean got up, stretching. "Took them long enough," he said, watching the sun near its zenith. "I suppose the two of you are hungry?" The two Serpentauri nodded. "I can smell the ripe wheat from here," said Kelron, stamping a hoof.

"We had best wait a bit longer," said Father Ean. "The Priests and Priestesses must travel to their huts, rest, eat, feast and whatever else civilized men do. We must wait until such a time as they are all inside their huts, engrossed in whatever activity they happen to partake in."

Kelron raised his head. "You speak of civilized men, Father Ean. Do you not consider yourself to be civilized?"

Father Ean laughed. "I once considered myself civilized, although I cannot speak for the other men of my time who knew me. Now, that is the last word that be used to describe the gardener of Oakvalor."

Kelros nodded. "How long shall we wait, Father Ean?"

Father Ean looked down upon the deserted Council Circle. "A short time. Your feasting shall be worth whatever longer wait you must suffer."

"Upon this road, at this time, the only
certainty is that nothing is certain."

- Calderon

CHAPTER 17

They lost almost two full days, but they had finally passed the Sly Mare. They didn't stop at the inn again, choosing instead to put more distance between themselves and the three men who might have killed them. At the base of the Vish Mountains rested the last sign of life until one crossed over the mountains. The monstrous line of rugged terrain stretched from the Ocean hundreds of miles north straight to the Deadland. The mountains were the official boundary between Talvaard and Oakvalor. Once they traveled into Oakvalor, they would have to rely on help from their enemies to find their way to the monastery of their brothers.

They set up a makeshift camp in a small clearing of trees close to the stables of the small town that named itself after the mountain range. The population of the town had steadily declined over the years as most of the youth had gone off to join the king's army. Vish's only inn was more a shack than any actual accommodations, and none of the few rooms it had were available. The monks made the best of it, tying the flimsy limbs of the small trees to each other, which helped to make a sort of roof covering. The sky showed no signs of rain, but one could never be too prepared.

"The trail through the mountains is not well worn. People do not cross the borders enough, for obvious reasons," Donovan said later that evening, as the sky turned black except for a few visible stars. Calderon stretched out on the ground and used his sack as a pillow. "I suppose the people there will not be so inclined to help us," Calderon remarked aloud. Donovan and Velkyn made themselves as comfortable as possible on the hard ground as well. "Don't be quick to assume," Donovan replied. "There is not much difference between the people of our respective kingdoms. They will not know we are from Talvaard unless we share that information."

They remained in silence for long moments before Velkyn broke the peaceful hush. "Do you think we will succeed?" That simple question, asked with such honesty, seemed to weigh them all down heavily. "We must have faith in the Divines that we will," answered the old monk. "Without faith, we are nothing."

Calderon wondered, not for the first time, if their faith might be misplaced. "Have you ever …" he started to say but instead fell silent. "Speak honestly," Donovan bade quietly. "Have you ever wondered if, maybe, our belief in the Divines is … wrong?" Neither monk responded and so he continued. "Not that our faith in the higher powers is wrong, but that the ones we place our trust in is? I have lived in the monastery walls most of my life, and yet I have never once heard my prayers answered. Am I alone in this?"

In the far distance they could hear the howling of wolves. Calderon noticed then that the moon was full this night. "I suppose we have all questioned ourselves, and our faith, at some point in our lives. But the Divines do not just speak to us through prayer. They speak to us through other people, and through the holy Scriptures." Silence fell over the three, and yet again it was Velkyn who broke it. "I have never heard my prayers answered either."

No one spoke after that, and eventually they all fell asleep. As Calderon's eyes got heavy and he began to slip away into sleep, he vaguely heard "Neither have I."

● ∞ ● ∞ ●

Daylight brought the chirping of birds and the sounds of the small town coming to life. Calderon opened his eyes and sat up to find Velkyn and Donovan missing. Their packs were still there, but he didn't see either of them. His neck was stiff and he rubbed it for a moment before getting to his feet. He assumed they must have went into the inn to get some breakfast and started that way when he saw them coming back towards their camp. "Sleep long enough?" Velkyn asked, smiling to show he was jesting with his friend.

"Perhaps too much," he smiled back, rubbing his neck again. "Where did you two go?" In answer, Velkyn produced an apple and a small chunk of bread. "For you. Eat quickly though. Donovan says it will take us most of the day to reach the other side of the mountains. He wants to be in Oakvalor before dark."

Calderon nodded and ate, consuming the food as hurriedly as he could while still enjoying it. They strapped their packs on and untied the tree branches that had given them shelter. Donovan was right that the path was not worn, they almost missed it entirely. Once they got going, they found the trail was straight and the climb easy enough. It seemed they would make good time, until the trail began winding in wide circles and became steeper. An hour into their journey, Calderon and Donovan began to feel burning in their legs. Velkyn, being much more physically fit, was having less trouble.

The sun crested the top of the mountain peaks and the air warmed considerably, making the three monks uncomfortable in their thick brown robes. They began to sweat profusely and eventually had to stop to rest and to eat. They didn't talk much but focused their energy on simply making the climb. When they finally reached the peak of the trail hours later, they stopped to admire the scenery.

They found the air was thin this high, and the clouds seemed to rest upon the surrounding peaks. It was quiet. Too quiet. It unsettled Calderon, who expected to hear the many sounds of wild animals. Calderon looked down into an enormous valley that swept from the base of the mountain and out as far as he could see. Off in the distance he could see small tendrils of smoke rising lazily into the air. "Palindrom," Donovan said, seeing the direction where Calderon was looking. "I have heard it is a city of unrivaled beauty, where one can find the answers to almost any question."

"How?" Calderon asked, not taking his eyes off the distant city. "The Hall of Mirrors," Donovan answered. "It is said that the wizards created it in the early days of discovery, when no forms of magic were prohibited. It is a hallway that contains magical mirrors that show the future. It is for that reason we go to Oakvalor. If we can get the wizards to allow us use of the Hall, it is likely we will find the dragon's spirit."

"How do we get them to even hear our request?" Velkyn asked, coming to stand beside the old monk. "That is why we seek out our brothers. They will be the ones to help us."

The rest of the journey was much easier as they now traveled downhill. They saw the occasional signs of what appeared to be animal crossings. At one point, Calderon thought he saw someone in his peripheral view. He stopped and searched his surroundings, but saw nothing. Shrugging, he continued down the trail. It was well past midday when they were a few hundred feet away from the valley. They still had a few hours worth of daylight left. As they came around a bend in the trail, they could hear voices.

Donovan held his hand up, motioning for the two younger monks to stop. He crouched down behind a large boulder and peered down the trail. He saw a number of soldiers wearing the customary bronze armor of Oakvalor's military. The old man looked around and knew this was the only way down. Heaving a sigh of resignation, he stood and beckoned the two young monks to follow him. They stepped into the open and continued down the trail.

If the soldiers noticed the three monks, they didn't act like it. When they were a stone's throw away, one of the soldiers stepped forward. His hands were wrapped around the shaft of a spear and he placed the butt end into the dirt and leaned against it. "What is your business here?" he questioned.

"We are on a pilgrimage," Donovan answered, meeting the soldier's gaze. "We have been traveling to the holy sites of the Divines." The soldier's eyebrows raised in curiosity, or was it confusion? "Divines?"

The soldier drew closer to the old monk. "What is your name? And where do you hail from?"

"My name is Donovan and I hail from a distant land," the monk answered cryptically. "As I said, we are traveling to the holy sites of our faith, the Divines. Is that not allowed?"

The soldier didn't answer for long moments. "I'm afraid I don't know what you are talking about. Who are the Divines?" That question set Donovan back on his heels. How did this soldier not know about the Divines? Even the most remote villages knew of the Divines. "We are seeking our brethren in the chapel of Hermiston."

"The ruins?" the soldier still seemed confused. "I am not sure what faith you follow, but here in Oakvalor we follow the Lord Aio of the Five Islands."

This was a surprising turn of events to Donovan. What did the soldier mean by 'ruins'? And who was Lord Aio? "I have been gone from my home a long while," Donovan said, lowering his voice so that Calderon and Velkyn could not hear him. "What do you mean the ruins? Has the chapel at Hermiston been destroyed?"

The soldier shook his head. "No, not destroyed. Abandoned." Donovan's face turned incredulous. "What did you say your name was again?" the soldier asked.

"Donovan."

The soldier scratched his beard. "Donovan … Donovan …" his face lit up with recognition. "… *the* Donovan?" The old monk hushed the soldier and glanced over his shoulder at his two young counterparts. "The same. I am on a mission of the utmost importance and I need to get to Hermiston." The soldier bowed low and stepped aside, allowing the three monks to pass. Donovan shook his head in confusion. Why would the chapel be abandoned? That thought haunted him the rest of the way.

● ∞ ● ∞ ●

The Chapel of Hermiston was a tall structure of salt-and-pepper colored granite. The walls soared up roughly twenty feet high, with a taller tower at each of the four corners of the chapel. In the center of the front wall was an archway that served as the entrance. As with most of the chapels, they were constructed without gates to allow anyone entrance. The three monks made their way into the courtyard and found it eerily empty.

"Where is everyone?" Calderon questioned aloud. Donovan didn't have an answer. How could he know what happened? "Look around … see if you can find anyone or any sign of what might have happened," the old monk instructed. They separated and went through the various rooms within the structure, searching everywhere. An hour later they met back in the courtyard. Velkyn shrugged his shoulders. "No signs of any kind of battle," he said. "It doesn't appear they left in a hurry either," Calderon added. "Everything is intact and nothing appears to be missing."

Donovan considered their words but did not say anything. "This is going to hinder us getting an audience with the wizards," Donovan finally said. "The question is, where are all the people? They couldn't have just left."

"Or could they have?" Calderon responded. "There is nothing to support an attack or the threat of one. What if they all simply left? When was the last time the Abbot heard from this chapel?"

Donovan cleared his throat. "He hasn't."

Velkyn and Calderon's eyes widened in surprise. "What do you mean he hasn't?" Velkyn demanded. Donovan held his hands up to calm them. "The Abbot has not heard anything from this chapel since he was ordained," the old man paused, "and neither had his predecessor." The two young monks stood silently. "We never thought anything ill had happened, we merely assumed they were not in need of anything from our central abbey. But this," he swept his hand out, motioning toward the chapel, "this is disturbing to say the least."

"What do we do now?" Velkyn asked. Donovan gave a cursory glance about the courtyard. "We don't have time to investigate these new revelations. We must find a way to meet with the wizards on our own." His tone did not inspire confidence in the young monks.

A loud clatter sounded then, and all three monks spun about quickly. A man, wearing robes and a cloak that looked similar to their own, stood staring at them. "Who are you?" Donovan questioned. "Are you a brother of this chapel?" The man shook his head but offered no explanation. "Are you following us?" Calderon asked, thinking back to the mountain path and how he thought he saw someone. Again the man shook his head. They watched him warily, for he carried a sword across his back and they were unarmed.

Finally, the man spoke. "I am Erasen, servant to the Lord Aio." Donovan immediately recognized the name Aio, the same name the guard had mentioned. Who was this Aio, he wondered. "I am Donovan, and these—" he waved to the young monks "—are Calderon and Velkyn. We are brothers from the Abbey of the Divines in Talvaard."

"What brings you here?" Erasen asked. "Do you not know this place is forbidden?" The monks looked at each other uncertainly. "We did not know that," Donovan answered honestly. "We have not heard from this chapel in a very long time. Why is it forbidden? Do you know what happened here?"

Erasen laughed at them. "Truly you do not know," he said, more of a statement than a question. "This place is forbidden for it is a place of idol worship. The Great Lord Aio taught that there is only one, and that it is he." Seeing confusion, and possibly alarm, on the faces of the three men, Erasen grew distrustful. "Why are you here?" he asked again.

"We could ask the same of you," Velkyn answered. "If this place is forbidden, why do you stand in its midst?"

That put Erasen back a step. "I am here at the behest of the Lord Aio." Donovan raised his hand to silence what Velkyn was about to say. "We are here because this place is under the jurisdiction of the Church of the Divines," he said. "It is not forbidden to us, it is a holy place. Your clothes are like ours, with little major differences. Do you know what happened here? We have no time to spare and we are on an important task."

Erasen walked over to them, his steps slow and measured at first, then bold and quick. "I do know what happened here," he answered. "And I will tell you, but you must tell me some things as well."

"Very well," said Donovan, seeing no other way to get any answers. Erasen pointed to the south. "I am from the Five Islands, where the Great Lord Aio was born one hundred and forty-three years ago. This forbidden place at one time had many people living in its walls. But they left."

"Left?" Donovan asked, confused. "Why would they leave? Did they build a new chapel elsewhere?" Erasen shook his head. "They left this place and the beliefs it held them to. This place represents what some see as truth, but what we know as false," he said. "There is only one, and that is the Great Lord Aio."

"Where did they go?"

"They left to follow the Ai. Word of him and his deeds spread even to this place," Erasen said. Donovan couldn't believe it. How could anyone abandon their faith for another? Something didn't add up. Something sinister was going on here, something far more dangerous than a dragon loose upon the land. They had already run into delays, but perhaps this Erasen would have some answers that might give them direction on their next step.

"Let me tell you why we are here," Donovan said. "This may take some time."

● ∞ ● ∞ ●

She swung her sword, a deadly looking weapon, with such ease that anyone who had seen her wield it knew without doubt she was well versed with it. Her body was lithe and agile, stepping this way and that, her sword like an extension of her physical body, striking this way and that. She fought no foes this day, but instead was practicing, ensuring her body was in peak condition. She had too many enemies to count, which left her overly cautious. She dipped low, sliding her foot across the ground in a sweeping motion that would have taken the feet out from under any opponent. Without any hesitation or pause, she leapt up and spun about, kicking the same foot outward and landing back down on her feet with perfect balance.

"Jovanna!" she heard him shout her name.

Jovanna turned to face him, twirling a strand of her black hair with her finger and pulling it behind her ear and away from her face. "I trust you come with good news," she said as he approached her. "M'lady," Julian said, kneeling down before her. "Rise," she said, motioning him to stand.

Julian rose to his feet and brushed the dirt off his pant legs. "Well?" she demanded impatiently. He smiled at her and produced a large silver ball. There was nothing remarkable about it. "You are sure?"

Julian nodded. "Yes. Three monks stayed at the inn I was at when I was trying to infiltrate a group of thugs from Dillenger. The closest chapel is the Abbey of the Divines, so they must be from there."

Jovanna took the sphere from him and turned it over in her hands, studying its surface. "It seems to match his description," she said finally. It was smaller than she expected, fitting in the palm of her hand and being slightly larger than an egg. She opened a small pouch on her belt and slid it inside, pulling the drawstrings tight. "You did well. Where are they now?"

Julian shrugged. "I know only that they left quickly after our run in with the thugs. They headed back towards the east as far as I can tell." Jovanna pondered her options. "Perhaps they will realize it is missing and come looking for Julian?" she hinted, turning her blue eyes to meet his gaze. "It's possible," he conceded. "Though I think they will have much trouble indeed if they try to find me."

"Did you use the guise I told you to?"

Again Julian nodded. "I told everyone I spoke with I was a magician, as you instructed." Jovanna grinned, she liked his obedience. "And?" she asked.

"No one seemed to care, or believe, that I was a wizard," he answered. "Though I was also at the edge of the kingdom, where many probably turn a blind eye."

"Go farther," Jovanna instructed. "Go to the city of Talvaarin itself and do the same. We shall see how long the memory of its people are. Return to me in two weeks time." She turned and began to walk towards the small shack she currently used as home.

"M'lady," Julian called after her. She stopped but did not turn around. "My payment?" he asked. Jovanna turned her head to look at him. "Your life is payment enough, don't you think?" The threatening look on her face was more than enough for him to know that no threat lurked behind that mask, but only promises of utter pain.

"Right," he said, hesitating only a moment before quickly leaving. She was beyond dangerous, he knew.

"That was the night my soul died."

\- Velkyn

CHAPTER 18

The three monks and Erasen made camp outside the ruined chapel of Hermiston, mostly due to the fact that Erasen refused to stay in the place, using the words 'accursed' and 'forbidden'. Erasen informed them that the area was safe and there was no need to set a watch. They each made their own makeshift beds and settled in.

Long after everyone else had fallen asleep, Velkyn lay awake staring at the night sky. He considered the last week and all that had transpired. He had traveled so far and seen so much, and yet he had barely entered the kingdom of Oakvalor. What other amazing sights would he see? What other knowledge would he gain? A sound nearby interrupted his thoughts. He sat up slowly, casting his gaze about and trying vainly to see what might have made the noise. Velkyn rose to his feet and made his way cautiously in the direction he heard the sound.

He paused, the shock evident on his face as he saw his beloved Nydel reveal herself from behind a small copse of trees. "Velkyn!" she whispered, a bit louder than she had intended. Velkyn took her into his arms and hugged her close. "I missed you," he said softly, giving her a gentle kiss. "And I missed you," she replied, returning his kiss. They held each other in silence for long moments before Velkyn pushed her back at arms length. "Why did you come here? And how did you get past the guards at the mountain? You know it isn't safe."

Nydel smiled reassuringly at him, trying to distill his fears. "I got here two days ago. I thought you'd be here, but this place was empty. I looked around some and decided to wait for you. Your letter said you were headed here for answers. I was afraid you had already come and gone." She leaned into his embrace, brushing her fingers along his jaw line and up through his hair. "Come," she said, leading him by the hand. "I found a place for us." He glanced back at his friends. Velkyn knew they shouldn't separate from the others, but he knew too what she wanted. His own body wanted it as well. He allowed her to lead him into the abandoned chapel. They went through the courtyard and into one of the rooms that once was used for prayer. Nydel pushed the wooden door closed.

Velkyn pulled his robes off and laid them on the cold stone floor. They began kissing and caressing each other, slowly moving to lay down atop his robes. She made sweet noises and he knew she was ready for him … had missed him as he had missed her. "I want to spend my life with you," he whispered to her. That seemed to make her even more wild with passion.

A loud bang echoed in the room and Velkyn quickly looked up. The door had been kicked open and three figures stood in the doorway. "I can explain—" Velkyn began.

"What'ev we got 'ere?" a familiar voice chimed. Velkyn felt his heart jump in his chest when he recognized the gruff voice of one of the thugs. He pushed himself to his feet and stood defensively in front of Nydel, who covered herself with his robes. "Leave," Velkyn warned, "or I will cause you much more pain than the last time we met."

The three thugs laughed. The weaselish man rushed into the room then, eagerly swinging a metal rod. Velkyn brought his hands up to block the rod while simultaneously angling his foot up to kick Theo, who followed behind the weasel. Theo grunted as Velkyn's foot slammed into his stomach. He staggered back, obviously struggling to breath. The weaselish man kicked out at Velkyn and swung his rod back and forth in an attempt to strike the monk. Velkyn was too quick though, and he dove into a roll, coming up behind the weasel and delivering a solid punch to the man's lower back, followed by another punch to the back of his neck. The weasel didn't fall, and so Velkyn kicked the back of the man's leg, which resulted in the weasel dropping to his knees.

An explosion of pain ripped through Velkyn's head and he fell forward, crashing hard into the wall. He looked up and through his blurred vision he saw the gruff voiced man, wielding a similar metal rod as the weasel. "Ye caused us a 'ho'lotta pain, monk. Now we're gonna cause ye some pain." Theo and the weasel had recovered and stood over him. "Get 'im on 'is feet," gruff said. The two thugs jerked the monk up roughly to his feet.

"See'in as how ye took somethin' from us, we're gonna take somethin' from ye." Gruff switched places with weasel. Velkyn's vision was beginning to clear and he saw the weaselish man unbuckle his pants. "She'll even the score, me thinks." Velkyn struggled against their grasp but he couldn't break free. "Get away from her!" he screamed. Gruff punched the monk in the mouth, causing blood to drip from his lips. "Ye shut yet mouth if ye know what's good for ye," gruff said. Nydel tried to fight the man as he ripped the robes off of her, so weasel punched her in the face, knocking her flat onto the floor. He invaded her body with his hand and turned to his fellow ruffians, but more specifically Velkyn.

"Oh she is ready, she is." He grinned wickedly and began to rape her. She screamed and struggled, but he was much stronger than her and kept her pinned down as he did his business. Velkyn fought with all his strength to get free, but the two men just punched him into submission. "Ye're gonna watch it," gruff said heavily. "Be quick about it," gruff yelled at weasel. "It's my turn next."

Velkyn watched helplessly as each of the thugs took turns raping his beloved Nydel. He could taste blood in his mouth and feel his left eye swelling up. When Theo had finished with her, she merely lay there feebly, her head twitching every so often, as if in some silent plea to stop. "I will kill you," Velkyn threatened weakly. Gruff held up his metal rod and looked Velkyn in the eyes. "Ye just try it." He lifted the rod up and swung it hard, bashing the monk in the left side of the face. Velkyn crumpled unconsciously to the floor. "What of 'is friends?" Weasel questioned.

"Who cares," gruff answered. "Leave 'em to die." Gruff looked down at Nydel and spat on her. "Tell yer monk we're even." The thugs left then, leaving Velkyn a bloody mess and Nydel laying naked and bruised.

Velkyn grunted as he opened his eyes. Or perhaps it was only one eye that was open, as his left seemed not to comply. He reached up and gingerly touched the skin around his eye; it was fat and puffy. And it hurt worse than his legs did when he rode the horse. Everything flooded back to him then, and he sat up quickly. Too quickly, for the room spun and he vomited. He spit the nastiness from his mouth and crawled over to Nydel. She lay very still but he could see that she was breathing.

"Nydel," he whispered softly. "Are you … are you okay?" He put her hand in his and she whimpered and pulled away. "It's okay, my love. It's just me." He tried to comfort her again, but this time she screamed and thrashed at him. Velkyn could feel the tears well up in his eyes. How could they have done this to her? How could people be so vicious to one another? He needed help. Calderon, he needed Calderon. Nydel was still lying on his robes. He stood up unsteadily, using the wall for support until he felt as though he might be able to walk. He moved over to the doorway and looked out, not sure if the thugs were gone.

It was still dark. There didn't seem to be any sign of the men, so he stepped out and made his way out of the courtyard and towards their camp. The air was warm but it felt cool to him with nothing but his loincloth on. He made his way slowly to where his companions were sleeping. Finding Calderon, he shook his friend gently. It didn't do anything, so he shook him harder. Calderon's eyes opened lazily. Seeing Velkyn's battered face, he immediately was wide awake. "What happened?" he asked, and Velkyn covered his friend's mouth. "Not here," Velkyn whispered and motioned toward the chapel.

Calderon got up and helped Velkyn walk. When they were a safe distance away, Velkyn told Calderon what happened. "How did they find us?" Calderon asked. Velkyn merely shook his head. "They must have followed us here," Calderon mused. Velkyn led his friend into the room they were assailed in to find Nydel in the same spot. "She won't let me touch her," Velkyn said brokenly. Calderon knelt beside Nydel and reached out to put his hand on her forehead. She jerked and moved her head away from him. Calderon bit his lip and looked to Velkyn. He had his back against the wall and was staring forlornly at Nydel. Tears flowed freely.

Calderon didn't know what to do. His knowledge of healing was almost nonexistent and he had never seen anyone who had gone through something so horrific. "We could take her to Donovan," he said, but immediately Velkyn was shaking his head. "If anyone finds out, I will be kicked out of the brotherhood. And what does the old man know about healing?" Calderon nodded in concession, but they couldn't just do nothing. "Maybe we can take her to a town somewhere and get her some help?" Velkyn considered the option. "We will have to wait until morning. We can't move her in the darkness. We don't even know where we are," Velkyn said.

"I agree," Calderon replied. "Do you want me to stay with you?" Velkyn shook his head. "No, I will be fine here with her." Calderon stood up and stared down at Nydel. He ignored the fact that she was completely nude, instead focusing on her bruised face and soul. He tried not to cry as he headed back to their camp, wondering how it was that such evil could exist in mankind. It was one of the many mysteries he could not unravel. He lay down but could not sleep. His mind was heavy and his soul was troubled. When the sun began to light up the sky, Calderon was still awake.

Velkyn opened his right eye. His left was still swollen shut. He looked to where Nydel was … only she wasn't there. Velkyn scrambled over to make sure he wasn't seeing things. She was indeed gone. He grabbed his robe and put it on, rushing out into the courtyard and calling her name. He didn't see her anywhere. He noticed Calderon making his way into the courtyard. "Nydel is gone! I can't find her!" Calderon started to respond but stopped mid-stride, his mouth dropping open in horror. Velkyn could feel a deep fear rise in his throat. He turned around to see what had so horrified his friend.

Nydel's body was hanging from the wall. Velkyn dropped to his knees and cried out. Calderon could only stand in horror. Her body was hanging from a rope that had been secured to a metal hook in the wall. Her lifeless form dangled from the other end of the rope. Erasen had called the place accursed. Cursed indeed.

"The destruction of the Five Islands remains a mystery. Who was behind the magical storm? What was the purpose of killing all those innocent people? One day the truth will prevail."

- Anton, Captain of the Guard

CHAPTER 19

"I'm leaving," Velkyn said quietly. He and Calderon walked several feet behind Donovan and Erasen. The old monk and the priest of Aio were talking about the differences between their faiths. "What do you mean?" Calderon looked to his friend. "What do you mean you are leaving? Leaving where?"

Velkyn met his gaze and Calderon could see the tears, barely being held back. He couldn't blame his friend for being so sorrowful. He had lost the woman he loved, and his secret was now known to Donovan. While Donovan had no authority to cast the young man out of the brotherhood, he didn't deny that the Abbot would do so. "I will not be welcomed back into the abbey. You know that."

Calderon shook his head. "I do not know that. And neither do you. Where would you go? You do not even know where you are." Velkyn stopped walking and turned to Calderon. "You know where I must go. There must be justice for this crime." Calderon's face turned to a horrified look. "Velkyn … there are proper ways to handle this … you can't just …" he trailed off as he looked at his defeated friend. He realized that nothing he said would dissuade him from this course. "How will you know where to find them?"

"I will go to the Sly Mare. If I do not find them there, I will go to Dillenger. I will not stop until I find them. I will travel as far as it takes. I will destroy anyone and everything in my way." Calderon noticed Velkyn had clenched his fists. The sheer rage, hatred, and sadness that his dear friend harbored was so intense, Calderon feared he might snap then and there. He tried his best to console Velkyn, but he knew that ultimately his friend would leave. "I don't know what to do without you," Calderon said sadly. "You have been my friend, my only friend, since we were young. I will not stop you, neither will I tell Donovan when you leave. Just do it when I am unaware. It will be easier that way."

Velkyn considered his friend's words and offered a smile. "I can do that." The two traveled in silence for hours afterward. Calderon took in the beautiful scenery. It was much different than what he was used to. The tall grassy plains around the abbey instilled a peacefulness that he had grown to love, but Oakvalor was like another world entirely. He could still see the mountains they had crossed over clearly in the distance. They walked along a well built cobblestone road which carved its way through the valley that stretched from the mountains to their west all the way to a massive forest to the east.

Velkyn kept his gaze at the ground, only occasionally looking up. He was lost in the swirling chaos that was his thoughts. He wanted to fulfill his obligation to recapture the dragon's spirit, but his love for Nydel compelled him to exact revenge on those thugs. He wasn't sure he could really abandon Calderon and Donovan after coming this far. He would sleep on it and decide the following morning.

Calderon learned from Erasen that one of the kings of Oakvalor had worked to pave all of the main roads to every major city. It made it easier for merchants to travel farther and faster, boosting the economy. It also made it easier to move armies faster, though which reason was really behind the upgrade of the roads was anyone's guess.

Erasen was an odd one, Calderon thought. The man called himself a priest of Aio. From what he had gathered, some divine figure named Aio came from the heavens and took on flesh, living among the people of the Five Islands. It was Orlek, a powerful Orc wizard turned evil who did battle with Aio and supposedly had resurrected himself more than once. It sounded more like folklore to Calderon, but the more he pondered it all, he had to wonder if there was at least some ounce of truth to what Erasen claimed. In all his years, Calderon had not once been given an answer to his prayers, or been shown a sign of the Divines' will for his life.

They had traveled nearly the entire day, stopping only a few times to eat and rest their feet, before finally they saw the tall gray walls of Palindrom. "The city of wizards," Donovan remarked. "Built long before the kingdom of Oakvalor was a united nation." Erasen looked at the old monk. "You know much about this land for one not from it."

Donovan didn't reply, but instead continued talking about the city. "Palindrom is the center of the world as far as the wizards are concerned. When men first began to realize their gifts in the magical arts, they banded together and traveled in small groups, living in tents. Not unlike the tribes of the Five Islands," this comment he directed to Erasen. "But one of the leaders, the man who would become the first head of the arts, Palin decided it would be easier for them to study magic in a central location that was open to all. The knowledge gained from the wizards would be shared with anyone who wanted to know the secrets. Thus Palindrom was conceived and then built. The city around the main structure built up over the years that followed. Many people do not know this, but Palindrom isn't really a part of Oakvalor. It is considered an autonomous state within the kingdom's boundaries."

As they neared the city, Calderon noticed several forms, probably guards, patrolling along the wall. As they neared the entrance to the city, they saw many people lined up waiting to enter the city. "This is different," Donovan muttered. Calderon looked to the old man with a raised eyebrow, but Donovan didn't notice.

At the gate were guards who were questioning the people seeking admittance. They didn't turn anyone away, but seemed to be asking a few questions and then motioning people in. "What's going on?" Calderon asked, but if Donovan or Erasen knew, they didn't answer. After nearly twenty minutes, the monks had reached the main gate. As Calderon looked at the guards, he noticed they were not dressed like the guards he had seen in Talvaard when they attended the coronation.

The men wore swords at their hips, but they did not wear any armor. They wore some sort of shiny clothing that looked like silver, yet it was obviously made of cloth. They also wore red capes that stretched from their shoulders down to within a few inches of the ground. One man, whom Calderon assumed was a captain of some sort, wore a blue cape. "Reason for entry?" one of the guards asked without looking at them. He was holding up what appeared to be a crystal. "We are looking for a place to stay the night," Donovan said, looking intently at the man wearing the blue cape. The crystal began to glow a light red. The guard holding it looked up at them. "He's lying," the man said.

The man wearing the blue cape stepped forward and surprised them all. "Donovan?" he questioned, tilting his head slightly. "I would recognize that face no matter how long I had not seen it. It's been too long, old friend!" Calderon and Erasen were greatly confused, and Velkyn seemed to be off in his own world. Donovan, however, knew that he would not be able to hide things much longer.

"Indeed it has, Anton. I come bearing some ill news, I fear." Anton held his hand up. "Not here. Come, we will set you up at the keep. Who are your friends?" Donovan pointed to Velkyn and Calderon. "These are my fellows from the abbey, and this man—" he pointed at Erasen, "—is Erasen, a priest from the Five Islands." His tone made the last part sound like a question more than a statement. Anton nodded and motioned them to follow him. "When the last of the people are in, close the gates," Anton ordered the two guards.

They followed Anton inside the walled city. "What is all this?" Donovan asked, nodding to indicate the guards. "These are dark days," Anton said ominously. "Many things have changed, most of them recently." Anton would say no more, even though Donovan prodded him the entire way. The city was massive in terms of size. It had grown to capacity within the protection of the walls, and so to continue building, they began adding second, and in some places, third stories to the existing buildings. As it was the end of the day, people had begun cooking and they could smell many different scents in the air, all of them mouth-watering.

Anton led them through the city until they finally reached an imposing structure. It was different than any of the other buildings they had passed, and it was definitely the largest in the city. There were no guards posted at the gates of this building. Anton led them inside. There was a small girl waiting in the antechamber that served as a waiting room. "Take our guests to the dining area. I will be there shortly." The girl bowed to Anton and began walking towards one of the doors. "Don't let her appearance fool you," Anton warned them. "She is not what she seems."

The girl turned back and smiled wickedly. Calderon could feel the hairs on his neck raise. "What is she?" he whispered aloud. Anton looked at the young monk and smiled. "A succubus." Calderon didn't recognize the term but it didn't sound good. They all reluctantly followed her anyway. Donovan hung back until they were gone and turned his attention back to Anton. "What is going on?" he demanded.

Anton's face took on a more somber look. "There are rumors of war," he said. Donovan shook his head. "Oakvalor and Talvaard have been at war for years." Anton looked around and lowered his voice, as if someone might hear him although no one was in the room. "I am not talking about *that* war. Although, we do have reports that the young prince of Talvaard killed his brother and the daughter of Elkanah, Oakvalor's king." Donovan nodded to confirm the story. "I was there. I saw the entire thing myself."

Anton shook his head. "The newest word is that Talvaard's armies march toward Oakvalor as we speak." Donovan seemed confused. "We traveled the main road to get here," Donovan said. "I saw no signs of any army." Anton nodded. "I hear they are slow moving. There is also rumor that they don't want to march, but the new king demands it. There is worse news still," he said, lowering his voice even lower. "Orlek has taken a new body." Donovan laughed at his old friend. "Don't tell me you believe that crazy priest's stories?" he said. Anton didn't laugh. "You have been to the Chapel of

Hermiston?" he asked. Donovan nodded. "Then I trust you see the truth of the word of Lord Aio. You have been gone a long time, Donovan. You left when we were young and adventurous, but many things have happened here since you left."

Donovan stared at Anton. The two of them had grown up together, studying the art of magic right here in Palindrom. Donovan saw his friend had aged better than he had. While Donovan had spent his years behind the walls of a monastery, Anton had spent his days training as a warrior-mage. Adept at wielding a sword just as much as magic, a warrior-mage trained for many years to attain the perfect balance between the two skills. Donovan had been sent by the leader of Palindrom to ensure the safety of the sphere. They had made many attempts to have the sphere brought into the care of the wizards, but the monks of the abbey had declined every time. Anton's hair was once brown but had been lightened considerably from his many days in the sun. His skin was a deep tan color, and his body was thin and muscular. Though they had studied together, Anton was ten years younger than Donovan.

"Erasen told me about this supposed Aio. Is there really truth to this?" Anton nodded his head. "There were whispers of this new faith when we were young, but that's all it was; whispers. Turns out there was much truth to the whispers."

The door of the front entrance flung open and a young man rushed inside. Both Anton and Donovan turned to see who was barging in. The man quickly bowed to Anton and held up a letter. "Jovanna?" Anton asked hopefully. The man shook his head. "No, Captain. Worse!" Anton held up his hand to silence the messenger. He turned to Donovan and smiled. "I'll meet you in the dining room shortly. I have some things to attend to. I won't be long." Donovan hesitated. "Who is

Jovanna?" he asked. Anton shook his head. "No one to concern yourself with," he answered curtly. They stood in silence for a moment before Donovan finally left. Anton took the letter from the messenger and read it. He lowered the missive and stared off, then reread it. "Has this been verified?" he asked.

"Yes, Captain. I came as soon as I could. Everything you read is true … all those people … what do we do?" Anton knew this was beyond anything he had experienced, beyond anything anyone here had experienced. Except for *him*. "Take this to Cygnus at once. He will know what to do."

The messenger took the letter back and rushed off. Anton had seen many things, and had heard many stranger things. This was not strange. It was pure evil, and he knew that Orlek's hand was behind it. When he felt he had composed himself, he joined the others in the dining room. They were all seated and eating quietly. All three monks and the priest regarded him with interest as he took his seat. The young girl set a plate of steaming food before him and moved off into the shadows. Several torches lined each wall every four feet, except for the corners of the room where darkness remained. Anton ate his food absently.

Donovan had had enough. "Anton, I know I have been gone for a very long time, but that does not excuse you from keeping me involved in the dealings of our order. What in the Abyss is going on?" he ended his shout by slamming his fist onto the table. Everyone looked at the old man, startled. Even Velkyn, who had been in some sort of trance looked up. Anton stared at him from across the table, but not in anger. "A storm has wiped out the Five Islands."

Erasen gasped, or would have had his mouth not been full of food, and he choked and began coughing.

Calderon and Velkyn didn't understand the implications of it, and Donovan fell back speechless in his chair. "The report tells of a strange storm that battered the Islands and destroyed everything. They don't think anyone could have survived. The ocean is littered with debris, but most of it is floating bodies …" Anton's words died as he imagined the horrific scene. "Something isn't right," Donovan said shakily. "Storms hit the Islands often. What do you mean a strange storm?"

Anton shrugged his shoulders. "I do not know. Witnesses on the coast said it was not like any storm they had ever seen. I suspect there was magic involved in this. Though whether it is Orlek or Jovanna, it is yet to be seen."

Donovan leaned forward. "Who is Jovanna?" he questioned Anton for the second time. Anton rubbed his hands over his face and he suddenly seemed much older. Heaving a great sigh, he answered the question. "Jovanna was an orphan that displayed obvious talent with magic. The people who took care of her brought her here to Palindrom to see if we could 'help' her." Donovan made an exasperated noise. "I know," said Anton, "I know. They didn't understand that this was not something that could, or needed to be, fixed. We offered to take her into our care and they did not protest much. She was only six and she had taught herself to cast a fireball."

Donovan raised his eyebrows, obviously impressed. "Six? That's incredible." Anton nodded. "Cygnus said that with training she would rival even the famed skills of Palin himself."

"Cygnus is still alive?" Donovan asked, surprised. Anton nodded. "And hasn't aged a day, it seems. Jovanna was an eager student, but she also had a dark side. There was an accident in the halls one night and several students were found dead, apparently burned alive. She was blamed and there was enough witnesses for Cygnus to pronounce punishment on her. She was given forty lashes minus one with the whip. That only seemed to fuel her anger."

"Burned alive with what?"

"Magical flames."

Donovan looked skeptical. "The halls of housing are protected by anti magic. How could she have cast magic so powerful that the anti magic would not stop it?"

"Exactly," Anton said. "Cygnus tried to figure that out as well, but he could find nothing conclusive."

"She sounds dangerous."

"Exactly," Anton said again. "We knew she was a liability waiting to happen. By the time we had enough evidence of her breaking the wizards code, she could not be found. She abandoned Palindrom and we have yet to find her. She is very powerful. Powerful enough to hide from scrying stones," he added, referring to the stones they used to see over vast distances.

"Perhaps it is a good thing she is gone?" Donovan suggested. Anton shook his head. "There is nothing good about that one. She craves power, and will do anything to have it. We fear she seeks the sphere."

Donovan looked down. "That is the ill news I bring. The creature has escaped." Anton sputtered. "What do you mean it escaped? How? You were ordered to protect it with life and limb!"

"I did!" Donovan shot back. "For most of my life I have kept it safe. But something happened. The magic must have weakened and failed. I believe it escaped during the coronation in Talvaarin."

Anton digested the words. "Where is the creature now? And where is the sphere?" Donovan pointed toward Calderon. "The sphere is safe in his bag. But as to the location of the creature, I do not know. That is why we are here. We need to use the Hall of Mirrors."

"Out of the question," Anton replied. "The danger is too great."

"I know it is dangerous, but that does not negate the fact that we must use it to find the creature. You must know this."

"You misunderstand me," Anton said. "Jovanna tampered with the magic of the mirrors. If she were to find out that the creature is not bound in the sphere, she would surely use that knowledge against us. She is a formidable foe, and we are already pressed with Talvaard threatening invasion at our door and Orlek with his orcish hordes preparing in the mountains. Oakvalor is surrounded by enemies and now the priests of Aio lie dead in the ocean. We cannot risk it."

Donovan knew Anton's words were not merely spoken in frustration. The embers of a war unlike any other were heating up, and soon a raging inferno would spread across the land. "We cannot afford the risk of the dragon gaining his body back. Where are his bones?"

"They decorate the king's war machines."

Donovan remained silent in thought. "Perhaps they are safe there. I need to use the mirrors," he said with a tone of finality.

"That is unlikely to happen," Anton responded. "Cygnus has forbade any use of them." Donovan felt helpless. He had to find a way to use the Hall of Mirrors. "Then what do we do?"

"That, gentlemen, is the question." Everyone at the table turned to see Cygnus standing in the doorway.

"One who cannot trust themselves can never truly trust anyone else."

- Jovanna

CHAPTER 20

Jovanna had learned long ago to trust no one. Her own parents had abandoned her when she was four, scared of what their daughter might be. She had scrounged in the trash heaps of the town, fighting with rats and other vermin to simply stay alive. When the local orphanage took her in, they soon began treating her like her parents did. Jovanna knew now that it was fear that caused people to act the way they did toward her. Fear of the unknown often caused people to treat others differently.

She knew she was different. Even when she was four, she knew she was not like other children. Not like anyone, regardless of age. But when she had been brought to Palindrom, she felt like she finally belonged. The people there were more like her than anyone she had encountered before. They could summon fire like she could, they could do things other people could not. And yet, as time went by, Jovanna realized even the wizards of Palindrom were not the same as her. She was different. She could 'see' the magic. No one, not even the half blood Cygnus, could do that. And so some of them treated her differently, just like everyone else in her life. She grit her teeth in anger at the memories.

They had given her knowledge to control the gift, true, but they could not wield the magic as she could. She had been laying in her bed trying to sleep one night when she realized something. There was nothing wrong with her. There was something wrong with everyone else. She was above them, had been given a gift that no one could fathom. She had learned when she was young that in order to get what you needed, you had to take it. No one was going to help you and certainly no one cared.

And with that thinking, she also decided that since she was above everyone, she needed to rule over them. Why have the power and not use it? But she was only one person. She could not defeat everyone single handedly, even she knew that. But if she had someone or something to help her achieve her rise to power … and that thinking had led her to the decision to steal the sphere. No, not steal it. To take it. She was not a thief, she was a taker. A doer. She had left Palindrom because she knew they were going to try to stop her. She knew they were searching for her too. She could feel the emanations of the crystal magic, could feel the eyes searching, ever searching.

If there was one thing she could do well, it was hide. She had to when she was younger. But soon, very soon, she would no longer have to hide. Jovanna smiled at that. Now that she had the sphere, she would release the dragon and use it as a tool to her ascension. The sun was rising and the sky was bathed in reds and oranges. She held the metal sphere up in the increasing sunlight and knew her time was at hand. She placed the sphere on the ground, using a few rocks to keep it from rolling around. Once she had bent both king and peasant to her will, she would seek out Orlek and destroy him as well.

He was the only one that could stand against her, she was confident of that. The wizards had grown soft in their teachings. They had ceased to study the old books, to learn the old magic. She was different.

She unsheathed her weapon, a light-weight, short-bladed sword. It was plain in decoration except for the hilt which was shaped like a dragon's body. The pommel was the dragon's head, its mouth stretched wide in a silent roar. The blade looked ordinary, yet it was anything but. She tilted her head to each side until it popped. Raising the sword, she brought it down hard onto the sphere's surface. The sound of clanging metal rang out, and then a heavy thud. Her blade had cleaved right down the middle of the sphere and into the ground.

She smirked. That was easier than she expected. She bent down to inspect the sphere and the smile left her face. The magic had all but faded from the sphere. And the dragon's spirit was not inside. She swore silently, sheathing her sword angrily. She had been so close—and now this!

She forced herself to calm down. Anger would get her nowhere, despite how good it felt to be angry. She picked up the two halves of the sphere and stalked back to the building she was currently staying at. The door banged shut behind her and she slung the pieces into a leather bag. "Never send a man to do a job right," she muttered. Julian had his uses though, she had to give him that. He was one of the first she had recruited into her cause. She had several spies in various places now, all of them reporting to her weekly.

She knew that Talvaard's armies were marching toward Oakvalor, but what she didn't know was why. The kingdoms had been at war for hundreds of years, but no actual fighting had happened in quite a long time. She pondered that, along with all the other information delivered to her of late. A knock at her door drew her from her contemplation. "What is it?" she demanded, expecting it to be the young man who had been following her around lately. He was infatuated with her but the feelings were one sided. She needed a man as much as she needed a dog; the upside being that a dog licked itself.

She was surprised to hear Julian's voice on the other side of the door. "Come in," she instructed. The door swung open and Julian sauntered in. "All goes well, my lady." He halted suddenly, her gaze cutting through him like a pair of daggers. "Where did you get the sphere?" she questioned.

"From the monks I told you about. They—" In one swift movement she pinned him against the wall, drew her sword, and had the sharp blade pressed against his throat. "I know *who* you got it from, I said *where*?"

Julian swallowed and a thin cut appeared on his neck. "The … uh, I found it in one of their b-bags in Dillenger. They seemed to be headed east before a couple of thugs robbed them. I don't know where they were going, they seemed to be very private men."

Jovanna glared at him, but she knew he was telling the truth. He was smart enough to know better than to lie to her. She released him and straightened his shirt. "I find it interesting that the sphere is supposed to be guarded within the Abbey of the Divines, and yet these monks were strolling along the countryside with it in their bags. Why do you think that would be, Julian?"

Julian wasn't sure where she was going with this. "I can't say I have a guess, my lady."

"Of course you don't. You are a man, and men don't seem to think much. The sphere is empty. The dragon is not bound within it anymore. Which means that it is roaming about somewhere. I need to find it." She paced the length of the room, turned on her heel, then paced back the other way. She did this several times before she looked up and saw Julian still standing there, apparently not sure what he should be doing. She was about to yell at him but remembered one of the tasks she had given him. "What was the reaction of the people when you told them you were a wizard?"

Julian smiled meekly. "They arrested me."

She raised an eyebrow. "Yet you stand here?" Julian nodded. "How?" she asked. "They realized that I was not really a wizard," he answered. She snorted derisively. "If they will not welcome their new ruler willingly, then they will bow to their new ruler at the end of my blade. Get out of my sight," she said scathingly. He bowed low and opened the door to leave. "Any new orders?" he asked hurriedly.

"Stay alive," she warned. Julian shut the door and scurried off. Jovanna continued her pacing. "Something happened," she reasoned aloud. "Perhaps the monks released the dragon ... no, that's not right. They had it with them and they were traveling east." She stopped her pacing. "East," she repeated. Her face lit up with realization as she began to put the pieces together. "They are headed to Palindrom!" She whirled about and grabbed the bag containing the halves of the sphere.

She would need to renew the magic and seal it back together, but it would work. "That's why he ordered the invasion," she breathed. "The creature wants its body back!" She would have to get close enough to the prince for the sphere to work its spell, but she was confident there would be many diversions to keep the beast occupied. She slung the bag over her shoulder and knelt down. She withdrew a small piece of chalk and traced a circle along the floorboards. She unsheathed her sword and ran her finger over the blade, cutting herself. Pressing her finger onto the top of the circle, she mixed her blood with the chalk, tracing over the chalk circle with her bleeding finger.

When she finished, she scrutinized her work, ensuring there was no gaps in the circle. She stood up and prepared herself for the magical journey. She would have to locate the prince quickly. If the wizards knew she was near, she would be just as much a target as the possessed prince. She grit her teeth. This part always sucked. The floor opened up and swallowed her.

*"The Deadlands is a hostile place filled with the vilest of creatures.
Most travelers have never returned."*

- Cygnus

CHAPTER 21

Donovan stared at the leader of Palindrom. Anton was
not lying when he said the man had not aged. Donovan
remembered the man clearly from his early days here.
Cygnus was tall, yet not overwhelmingly so. Standing
nearly six feet, his body was lithe and his movements
graceful. His hair reached midway down his back and
remained a golden blonde color. There was no sign of
wrinkles on his face and his eyes were as bright green as
they had been the first time Donovan saw them.

"It is good to see you again, Donovan. I did not
think I would see you so soon, though. It has been, what,
sixty years?" Donovan smiled. "At least," he replied.
"You haven't changed a bit in all that time."

Cygnus returned the old monk's smile. "I have
changed, just not on the outside." Calderon looked with
incredulity from Cygnus, to Velkyn, then to Donovan,
and finally to Anton and Erasen. Erasen seemed like
Velkyn now, as he was in a deep silence and tears ran
down his cheeks. Calderon had nearly forgotten that

Erasen was from the Five Islands, the same Islands wiped out by the storm. The priest didn't make eye contact and just stared blankly at the wall.

Anton looked to the young monk. "Who is that?" he asked Anton. "That is Cygnus, the head of the order of wizards and has been for nearly two hundred years."

"Two hundred years? The man looks barely into his twenties." Anton smiled at the ignorant monk. "Cygnus is a half blood. His mother was human, but his father was an elf from the Deadlands." Calderon still looked confused. "The Deadlands is the land north of us. It is a dangerous place. Elves and many other races call the place their home. Cygnus's mother was raped by an elf when her village was attacked by a raiding party. Cygnus is the product of that unfortunate union. It seems he favors more of the elf side, I think. Elves are long lived creatures, but they are evil. Cygnus is a credit to his race."

Calderon felt as though he had learned more about the world he lived in within the last couple of weeks than he had his entire life. Foreign lands, different races, the absolute evil that resided in mankind. It all seemed too much.

Cygnus took a seat at the table. "The devastation to the Islands is surely the work of magic. We have yet to locate Jovanna, but the signs of Orlek's impending invasion are obvious. The thing that baffles me is why Talvaard marches full force to our land." Cygnus drummed his fingers on the table. "The loss of the tribes of the Aihi surely puts us at a disadvantage." He looked to Erasen. The priest met his gaze. "I am truly sorry for your loss. If there is anything I can do, please do not hesitate. Our city is your home as long as you will it. From everything gathered, we suspect you are the only priest alive." Cygnus paused to let his words soak into the young priest.

"According to your customs, this would make you the new Lord Aio." Erasen's eyes widened. "I am not worthy," he whispered. "That is understandable, and I would not blame you, nor would anyone I suppose, if you chose not to take the calling. Think about it." Cygnus looked to Donovan. "Your mission was to keep the sphere safe. Is it with you?" The old monk nodded. "Yes, we have the sphere with us … but the creature is no longer bound within it."

If Cygnus was surprised, angry, or feeling any other emotion, it did not show. He merely nodded, his fingers continuously drumming on the table. "So then the beast roams the land in spirit …" his words trailed off and he rose slowly to his feet. "What is it?" Anton asked, noticing the difference in his superior's demeanor.

"It makes sense now. How I did not see it before …" he was shaking his head. Everyone at the table watched Cygnus, waiting for him to explain. When he didn't, Anton pushed him for one. "A dragon is a mighty beast, but it is limited to a physical form, just like any other creature. There is limited knowledge on them, as they are not originally from our world. What I do know is that, like Orlek, they have the ability to resurrect themselves. They only need their bones to do so. This is why Vallen decided to imprison it within the sphere. If they would have killed the dragon, it would simply have raised its own body from death. A dragon's soul is eternal, at least from what we know, and so it had to be confined inside something that could keep it there."

Everyone continued staring at him, still not understanding. "The dragon has to have a body to do anything … it must have possessed the prince of Talvaard!" Gasps filled the dining room. "That would explain why he murdered his brother," Donovan conceded. "By all accounts, he didn't want the throne. His body must be the pawn of the dragon."

"Then we must draw him out of Talvaard," Cygnus said. "Why would we do that?" Calderon asked. "Could the dragon not just as easily kill us in the body of a man?"

"Yes," Cygnus answered. "But since we have the sphere, we can still use it. The magic cannot be replicated, but it can be strengthened. With the enchantments reinforced, it can be used to recapture the beast."

"They have it here right now," Anton mentioned.

Cygnus seemed pleased with that. "Very good. Take the sphere to Antimodus. He will strengthen the enchantments. You four go and get some rest. I fear we may need all of you before the night is over."

They all stood up and Anton instructed the young girl to escort the monks to empty rooms for the night. Donovan waited until they had all left with the exception of Anton and Cygnus.

"I have a request," Donovan said to Cygnus. "I need to use the Hall of Mirrors." Anton was shaking his head. "You don't need to. We know where the dragon's spirit is now." Cygnus didn't answer, but listened to them both. Donovan sighed. "We are assuming that the dragon has taken the prince's body, but we do not know that for certain. We must be sure."

They both looked to Cygnus to settle the issue. "Your request is not an easy one to grant. A former student named Jovanna has messed with the magic that is in the mirrors. We are not sure what she has done to it. We do not know if it will kill the user, or if it will show them false images. As you are aware, the mirrors were crafted by Palin himself. Jovanna is a nuisance to be sure, but she is capable of anything dealing with magic. I fear what may happen if I let you use the Hall."

"I accept the risk," Donovan said. "I am an old man and I have lived my life. Let me use it and know that I accept willingly anything ill that may come of it. Your conscience can be clear."

Cygnus hesitated. The man knew the risks, to be sure. Yet Cygnus was keeper of the Hall, and if something happened, he could be blamed. Was it worth the risk? He couldn't know the answer to that question. "I approve your request. But use it now and quickly. You will need to be rested." Donovan bowed in thanks and made his way toward the Hall.

"Are you sure about this?" Anton questioned. Cygnus shrugged. "I am sure of nothing these days." And then he departed also, leaving Anton with his thoughts.

"The tattoo magic of the elves is as mysterious as they are. The power doesn't lie in the ink, but in the blood."

\- Anton

CHAPTER 22

Morning came all too quickly for Calderon. He felt as though he had barely fallen asleep when the sun began peeking through the small window of his room. A storm had arrived during the night and the incessant tapping of rain drops pelting the glass pane had kept him awake most of the night. Or at least he blamed the rain. If he was honest with himself, he would have to blame himself for his lack of sleep.

The news of a dangerous woman seeking the sphere and the armies of Talvaard marching on the city they were in troubled him deeply. He couldn't fight well and had never been trained with a blade. What good could he do in a battle that had nothing to do with him? That was a lie too. The truth of it was that he was responsible for the dragon. If he would never have fallen asleep, the beast would still be bound by the magic. He sighed as all of the thoughts and doubts from the night before reared their ugly heads in his mind again.

He had begun to wonder about this Aio and his priests. Calderon had somewhat decided to visit the Five

Islands if they survived the chaos to seek out his own answers. But now that hope lay in the bottom of the Ocean. He forced himself out of bed and stretched before making his way to the window. The rain had stopped early in the morning and the clouds were beginning to break. Shafts of sunlight slanted at an angle from the sky, coming to rest on the ground and bringing their warmth with them. His room was towards the back of the structure, and so he did not see the sprawling city. He saw the stretch of valley that met the forest in the east.

He wondered what lay within the woods. Considering everything he had seen recently, he assumed the forest could be home to any number of things. Calderon turned from the window and retrieved his brown robes. He had laid them across the desk, which happened to be the only thing in the room besides the bed. He sniffed them and scrunched up his nose. They were starting to smell like sweat. He was accustomed to washing his robes daily at the abbey. Numerous days on the road had caused the bottom of them to fray and stain with dirt. He made a note to find somewhere he could wash them.

He put the robes on and stepped out into the hallway. Velkyn had gotten the room across from his. His friend was an early riser, so he expected Velkyn to be up and ready for breakfast by now. He knocked on the door. After waiting a long moment, he knocked again.

Nothing. Calderon tried the handle and found it unlocked. He pushed the door open and walked in to find the room empty. As realization struck him, his heart sank. He would not find his friend; would probably not see him again. He shook his head at the futility of Velkyn's self made mission and went back to his room to collect the sphere. He was supposed to take it to someone named Antimodus. He rummaged through his bag but he couldn't find it.

He knew it was in there. He had packed it in his bag himself, and no one had touched it … he began to panic when he remembered the thugs who had stolen their bags back at the Sly Mare. Turning the bag over, he dumped all the contents onto the bed. It wasn't there. Terror gripped him. Without the sphere, they couldn't stop the dragon. A knock on his door startled him. He opened the door to find Donovan standing there.

"Where is Velkyn?" the old monk asked. "I'm not sure," Calderon answered. It wasn't really a lie. "We have a bigger problem." Donovan stepped inside the room. "What's the problem?" He looked over at the mess on the bed. "Where is the sphere?"

"That's the problem," Calderon said softly. "It must have fallen out or it was taken when we were robbed back in Oakvalor." Donovan's gaze narrowed on the young monk. "Velkyn and the sphere disappear at the same time, and you don't see anything odd about that?"

"Why would Velkyn take the sphere? He isn't a wizard and he has no use for it." Donovan considered the argument. Still, something wasn't right. Why would Velkyn suddenly disappear unless he was doing something he shouldn't. "Come with me, we need to inform Cygnus—"

The deep, long blare of a horn overpowered Donovan's words. A few seconds of silence, and then another identical blare sounded. "What is that noise?" Calderon asked.

"It's the city guard warning of danger."

Calderon ran to the window and looked out. "I don't see anything," he said over his shoulder. Donovan nodded. "You wouldn't from here. It's coming from the front of the city."

The sound of footsteps echoed in the hallway. The

two monks saw more than a few wizards hurriedly pass by. "Follow me. And stay close. We don't need anyone else to go missing," the old man remarked. Calderon respectfully adhered. They followed the wizards through the confusing maze of hallways until they reached the antechamber that led outside. The place had become organized chaos as groups of men and women dressed similar to the guards from the city gates the night before came and went.

"They are battle mages," Donovan explained. "They are trained in the art of magic and with weapons."

"Who are you?"

Donovan looked curiously at Calderon. "Who are you really?" the young monk asked again. "You know things about this place and you know some of the people here. You are hiding something, and I want to know what it is."

"That's not important right now," Donovan said, trying to avoid the conversation. "It is to me," Calderon replied testily. "I will not follow your lead anymore until you tell me what is going on. Who are you?" he reiterated. The old monk stared at Calderon, struggling with something internally. "I am not a monk," he finally said. "Before I tell you anything else, if we even have the time, you must promise not to tell anyone back at the abbey."

Calderon nodded silently. "I am not from Talvaard either. I was born here in Oakvalor, in this very city. I trained as a wizard within these halls."

"Why do you claim to be a brother of the Divines?"

"The leaders of Palindrom have long sought to bring the sphere out of the abbey and secure it here. Each time the request was issued, the abbot—regardless of who led it—refused. The monks have turned it into some sort of holy item of their faith. They do not understand that there is nothing sacred about it. It is merely a round piece of silver inscribed with magic. When the dragon was loosed by the hands of Orlek, no one could stop it. Talvaard and Oakvalor had been warring over dominion of the Five Islands for years, but both kings realized that unless they put their feud aside, everything would be destroyed by the beast.

"So the two kings united toward the common goal of stopping the dragon. Talvaard did not have wizards, but Oakvalor did. And Oakvalor did not have metal smiths because assassins from Talvaard had killed them all. Had either side have had both, there would surely have been no alliance. As the dragon was trapped in the sphere, the creature's body crushed the wizard who imbued the magic, leaving only the metal smith to protect it. Despite the protests of both kings, the smith took the sphere to the monks of the abbey. The king of Talvaard respected the monks enough not to try to take it by force. The wizards of Palindrom, in reward for their help in defeating the dragon, were given autonomy from the kingdom of Oakvalor and could not be convinced by the king to help take it. Nobody could forcefully take the sphere without causing either a civil war, or an all out blood bath between the two kingdoms. Since we could not bring it back here, we had to find other ways to safeguard it."

"By infiltrating the brotherhood?!" Calderon shouted in anger. "How could you make the vows with no intention of keeping them? They are sacred!"

Donovan tried to calm the young monk. "I kept an open mind to the teachings of the Divines. I even dared to believe they truly existed and guided the lives of men." Donovan shook his head. "But I am convinced now more than ever before that the Divines do not exist. I do, however, believe that there is some divine being who created our world and sustains it all. But I do not think we can really know that being."

The old man's honesty not only checked Calderon's anger, but it also left him without words. It was as if Donovan had looked into Calderon's own soul and put into words how he felt. Yes, he was angry that Donovan could take the vows of their brotherhood with no faith in them, but was he mad at Donovan specifically or at the possibility that all he claimed to believe could possibly be wrong? He didn't have time to delve any further into the conversation as Cygnus strode into the room, preceded by ten wizards. Two men followed behind that Calderon assumed were either bodyguards or more wizards.

"Donovan, I need you on the walls with me. Your companion should stay here and seek shelter in his room." Cygnus made a motion with his hand and five of the people with him rushed out of the door and into the city.

"What's happening?" Donovan asked. Cygnus paused as the horn sounded again. "The armies of Talvaard are before us. There is something … ominous … in the air," the half blood said. "Did you find the truth of our assumption last night?" he asked. Donovan didn't know how to answer the question. The mirrors had showed him many things, but he did not know what was real, and what was a possibility. "I am led to believe that the dragon has indeed possessed the prince of Talvaard."

Cygnus drummed his fingers in the air, something he did when he was thinking. "Did you have Antimodus strengthen the magic of the sphere?"

"We don't have it. It seems to be missing, possibly stolen by thieves while we were on the road traveling here."

Cygnus, despite the disappointing news, did not show any emotion or frustration. He continued drumming his fingers in the air. "This will make things difficult. If the dragon comes here in his borrowed body, we will not be able to capture him. You know as well as I do that we cannot replicate the magic of the sphere.”

“Could you not expel the creature from the man’s body?” Calderon chimed in. “Force the dragon out? Then the prince could call off his army. Is that possible?”

Donovan looked to Cygnus. The half blood stopped drumming his fingers. “It is possible, but I do not know that the cost is worth whatever the gain might be. And there is no guarantee that the creature will not simply take another body. It can possess anyone.”

“Anyone except you,” Donovan said.

“We don’t know that for certain.”

“What do you mean he can’t be possessed? Why not?” Calderon asked.

Cygnus pulled the sleeve of his robes up, revealing countless symbols tattooed into his skin. Calderon looked them over but could not read any of them. “The elves of the Deadlands have very unique practices,” Cygnus explained. “They tattoo spells into their skin with special ink. The flesh must heal before the spell can be used, and the spell is limited to only a few uses before the tattoo fades from the skin. The longer the tattoo stays in the skin without being used, the more powerful the spell. It is believed that there are spells that can keep one from being possessed as there are many dark creatures that walk the Deadlands with the elves who have that ability.” Cygnus paused. “But dragons are not from our world, thus there is no guarantee it will work.”

The horns sounded again, but instead of the two notes, it sounded three. “Our enemy nears,” Cygnus said. “We must decide on a course and act quickly.”

“I think we should take whatever measure necessary to expel the dragon from its host. It is a risk, true, but with the prince free to think on his own, he should cease the actions of his army,” Donovan decided.

Cygnus looked to Calderon. "You are not a wizard, but I find that there is much wisdom in the counsel of many. What say you?"

"I agree with Donovan's logic," the young monk replied. "Remove the leader."

"I will do what I can," Cygnus said. "Let us survey this army." Cygnus led the way out of the antechamber and out into the city. Calderon headed back to his room, hoping he could navigate the unfamiliar halls himself. There was no panic or discord in the streets. There really weren't many people out, and the ones that were seemed to be heading to safety. "We have seen many battles, and our walls have never been breached," Donovan heard someone say.

"We have never fought a dragon," Cygnus said in rebuke. "Do not let your pride affect your decisions." The man took the reproof in stride. They made their way through the empty streets and to the front of the city, then climbed the steps that led to the parapets.

"War machines," one of the guards reported as they looked over the wall. Tall structures jutted up from among the ranks of soldiers. The number of troops was incalculable, their line slowly stretching out around the walled city. As they marched closer, the defenders of the city could begin to make out formations. Most of them were ten men across and ten deep, with a captain leading each group.

"Steel your hearts," Cygnus bade them. "We slaughter innocent people driven by a fiend. If you have any hesitations, remember that you defend our own innocent people against the cruelty of a foul beast."

When the first rocks began to crash against the walls of Palindrom, all doubts of whether or not what they did was right quickly fled.

CHAPTER 23

The Abyss swirled past her. The clawed hands of demons reached out for her, wanting to tear her flesh off. She could feel the heat of the hellfire and hear the screams of the tortured. The faces of her attackers glared at her. Thankfully the magic kept them at bay. It was the fastest way to travel, but it was also the hardest. Jovanna feared very little, but every time she traveled this way, she felt like a small child scared by the unseen monsters under her bed. Only for Jovanna, they weren't unseen. They were very real, and if she were to make even the slightest mistake in the magic, there would be nothing separating her from the demons that desperately wanted to feast on her.

She felt a shudder as the magic ripped a hole in the ground above her and thrust her up ten feet into the air. Her arms and legs flapped about wildly as she attempted to right herself. She twisted her body and managed to land on her feet with a jarring thud. Several soldiers stood nearby, staring dumbly at her. She drew her sword and rushed forward. The sight of the ground spitting out a woman had momentarily distracted them, but they were trained men of war and quickly gained focus and drew their own weapons.

There were six men, all fitted with heavy armor and ready for battle. Jovanna knew she wouldn't be able to fight them all at the same time. She could use her magic, but that would alert the wizards in Palindrom and she couldn't risk it. That left fight or flee. She growled in frustration as she dodged past the soldiers. She sprinted as fast as her legs would carry her, trying to put some distance between them and herself. Luckily the magical tunnel had put her out toward the outer edge of the army and gave her a chance to hide. The wide valley would have left her out in the open, but since she was nearer to the forest, it offered her a chance to hide. She turned a corner and dove headfirst into a thicket.

The soldiers rushed by a few moments later. She waited to make sure they weren't coming back before she climbed out of the bushes. "Easy enough," she boasted, still breathless. She walked deeper into the forest, looking for a suitable spot for what she would need to do. Seeing a small clearing among the trees, she made her way toward it. As she neared it, she could hear what sounded like voices. Using the trees as cover, she stepped lightly, avoiding stepping on anything that would alert whoever was ahead. She stopped when she saw two men. They were talking, but she couldn't make out what was being said.

Jovanna reached into her leather bag and produced a small stone. It was a dull grey and polished to a smooth shine. On one side was a symbol that had been painted with some sort of ink. It was one of the trinkets she had taken from Cygnus before she left. She pressed her forehead to the stone until she felt it warm up. She looked to make sure the men were still there before she hurled the stone into the air. Her aim was true and it flew through the branches of the trees without hitting anything. It hovered in the air high above the men, but the magic was linked to Jovanna and she could now hear them talking.

"The creature has possessed Ranaan, the prince of Talvaard. And he walks among the troops now, commanding the assault against the city. The dragon is a mighty foe. The wizards will be hard pressed to win this battle," this from the taller of the two men. She couldn't make out their details as they were both wearing hooded robes. The shorter figure had a raspy voice that reminded Jovanna of an old man she once knew when she was young. "What of the sphere?"

"It has been taken from the monks that guarded it. They do not seem to know where it may be. Should we intervene?" The raspy voiced man didn't respond immediately. "Let us see how it plays out. If all seems lost, we will step in. But we mustn't be seen. We only keep the balance, nothing more."

"*He* didn't keep the balance," the tall man said. Jovanna wanted to try to see their faces, and she began slowly moving closer. She pressed her hand against a tree. Its bark was old and rotted and chunks of it fell off and noisily hit the forest floor. The two men whirled about and Jovanna almost gasped audibly. The taller man wasn't a man at all. He was an elf. The other man seemed more like a man, but his face was wrinkled beyond anything Jovanna had seen before. The elf drew up his sleeves revealing tattoos that covered the lengths of his arms and began to trace his finger along them. The smaller man slapped the elf's hand. He shook his head and in a burst of light, the men were gone.

She wasn't sure if they had actually seen her or not. She thought she was well hidden. Who were those people? And what were they talking about? The shorter man mentioned something about a balance. A balance of what? She stayed put for what seemed like an eternity before she was sure that she was alone.

Jovanna stepped out from the trees and retrieved the stone before moving to the clearing and pulling the halves of the sphere out of her bag. She laid them on the ground beside each other and produced a small pouch. She opened the flap and reached inside, dipping her finger into a thick, liquidy substance and coating the edge of each piece. She used a leaf to wipe her finger clean, then tossed it aside. She sat down cross-legged and closed her eyes. She concentrated on the symbols drawn on the inside of the piece to the left. She could see the symbols were dim, hardly glowing at all. The magic was very weak. Using her mind's eye, she could see the fragments of magic that floated about the world, and lifting her hands, began to sweep them toward the sphere.

When she had gathered numerous pieces of the fragments, she began to hum softly. The humming helped her to keep her concentration and had nothing to do with the magic. She began to touch the fragments, gently pressing them into the symbols. It was a time consuming process, as it was difficult to grab hold of the fragments. After roughly twenty minutes, the magical symbols began to glow brighter. Slowly at first, but as she added more fragments, it began to glow all the brighter. Once she was satisfied that the spell was strengthened sufficiently, she began work on the other piece. This was the skill that the other wizards didn't understand. They didn't believe that she could *see* the magic. When she was young, she believed the fragments of magic were fairies that wanted to speak to her.

Jovanna finished the task and placed the two halves together. She grabbed a few more fragments and used them to ignite the substance on the edges. The sphere flashed brightly and then went dark. She opened her eyes and lifted the sphere up. It was almost impossible to see the line where her sword had cut. She smiled, pleased with herself.

She would need a way to get close to the prince. That was her objective, but she couldn't help thinking about the elf and the man. Why were they here in the woods? She put everything back into her leather bag and stood up. She forced the thoughts of the men out of her mind. It was time.

"She has the sphere," the elf remarked. They were surrounded by an invisible barrier that kept them from sight and muted their words. The shorter man nodded, watching her with interest. "They say she can reconstruct spells created by other wizards," the man rasped. "What do you think she plans to do with it, Jerik?" the elf asked.

The shorter man, Jerik, shook his head. "That remains to be seen." He turned his gaze to Cahenrair the elf. "Be prepared," Jerik warned.

"For what?" Cahenrair asked.

"To set the balance, whatever must be done."

Jovanna stood at the edge of the forest. She could see stones flying through the air, flung from giant war machines. Thousands of soldiers were spread out before the city walls. "Fools," she said to herself. If they thought throwing rocks against the walls would knock them down, they would surely be disappointed. No army had breached those walls in the history of the city.

It would take much more than catapults to bring them down. She knew Cygnus would not offer a counter attack. He was too weak to use force. She was extremely surprised when, a moment later, a bolt of lightning blasted forth and struck one of the catapults, sending splintered wood everywhere. She fell back a step as the air reverberated with a resounding boom. It would be difficult enough to reach the prince with all the soldiers protecting him, and now the wizards were launching magic from their walls!

She growled in frustration. She didn't have any other choice. She would have to use magic to reach the prince. She pulled the sphere out and held it in one hand, and with the other she drew her sword. She was done hiding. She was done running. She was different.

She cast her magic quickly and furiously, weaving layer upon layer around herself, fashioning a thick shield of magic. She closed her eyes and waved her sword about, gathering fragments into her spell, causing it to fluctuate and tighten. Jovanna opened her eyes. She rushed across the valley, heading straight toward the army. The first few groups of soldiers had no idea what hit them. She hurled bolts of lightning from the tip of her blade, sent blasts of scorching fire from the other hand holding the sphere.

When they struck at her with their swords, they were flung back by her shield. She was unstoppable, a raging force of burning hatred. And she was headed straight for the prince.

"I will take what I please in any manner that pleases me."
- Jovanna

CHAPTER 24

"What in the Abyss is that?"

Cygnus looked to where one of the guards was pointing to see a form running through the soldiers on the field below, waving a sword and surrounded by blue pulsating light.

"Anton," Cygnus said, "She is here." Donovan and Anton looked down to see Jovanna dealing out death and destruction to everything in her path. "She looks angry," Donovan observed. "She's always angry," Cygnus replied. "We must stop her from whatever she is plotting. Send the guards." Anton looked at Cygnus warily. "Send them into *that*?" he said, motioning toward the army at their gates. "We will create a diversion," the half blood said. "She must be stopped. Send them now."

Anton bowed and rushed off to obey. Moments later, a handful of men were seen running from the gates out into the valley. Donovan moved over to where Cygnus stood. "What makes her so dangerous?" he asked.

"Many things, but specifically her lack of concern

for anyone or anything other than herself. She has passion, but it is not tempered with responsibility." The old monk nodded and looked back toward the building where Calderon was. He hoped the young man was okay.

Jovanna was laying low everyone that came against her. She was vaguely aware of her surroundings. Her sole focus was reaching that blasted creature. Her blade bit into the flesh of a soldier who got too close to her. Her shield was holding strong, but her strength was beginning to fail her. It was only adrenaline and anger driving her actions, causing her to move one foot in front of the other in a determined pace. She did take notice of the four guards of Palindrom moving to intercept her. She cursed silently, knowing she couldn't keep up her rampage.

She could see the prince, see him waving his men toward her. They didn't seem to want to obey, but their fear of him had them moving hesitantly toward her. The guards were also closing the distance. She was running out of options. She was tired of running. This was supposed to be her moment. She mustered her last bit of strength and hurled herself magically into the air, narrowly missing a rock launched from one of the few remaining catapults. Jovanna flew through the air, siphoning off some of the magic from her shield to give her the distance she needed. She landed a few feet away from the prince. His eyes widened when he saw what she held.

"Now I have you!" she shouted triumphantly. The possessed prince rushed her. She tossed the sphere onto the ground and watched as it began to glow. An unearthly growl issued from the man's mouth. Jovanna ducked as a spear was thrown at her from one of the nearby soldiers. The glowing sphere seemed to falter and change colors. "No!" she shouted, knowing the magic was not working properly. She came at the prince with her sword, slashing this way and that. Ranaan moved fast and dodged her attacks, sending his foot out to try and take out her knee. She managed to twist out of the way and avoid impaling herself on the sword of another soldier.

Lightning arced from the walls of the city, destroying the remaining war machines and blasting groups of soldiers aside. Blackened scorch marks littered the valley. Jovanna was trying to keep out of Ranaan's reach and get to the sphere to correct the magic.

Too late, she realized, as the sphere went dim. She rushed toward it only to be blown backward as the sphere erupted in a massive explosion. The blast leveled everything within a few hundred feet, blowing soldiers apart and scattering body parts. Ranaan barely seemed affected. Jovanna crashed to the ground and didn't move. All of time seemed to stand still as everyone slowly realized what happened. Cygnus was shouting orders, the generals of the army were dashing about madly, trying to organize the chaos that was their forces.

Cahenrair appeared on the battlefield not far from Jovanna's lifeless body. "Get back to the hellspawn you came here from," he said to Ranaan. The prince's face turned into a scowl and he glared at the elf. "Come, let me feast on your body," Ranaan said.

The elf pulled his sleeves up and began running his finger along the tattoos that covered his skin. Ranaan threw himself bodily into Cahenrair and the two crashed to the ground, punching each other and thrashing about. Cahenrair got to his feet, his robe twisted and caught from the struggle. He shrugged the robe off, revealing his tall slender body covered in nothing but a loincloth and many, many tattoos. The elf quickly traced his finger over several of the tattoos, enacting the magic.

A concussive blast of invisible force struck Ranaan as he was trying to get up. It knocked him backwards. As he closed the distance, the elf summoned more of his spells, one after another. Wicked looking green flames singed Ranaan's hair and face. Ranaan clawed at his skin, struggling to control the body of his host and keep the man's spirit at bay. "I can't do anything in this body!" he shouted.

Cahenrair quickly touched a couple of his tattoos, causing them all to come alive with a pale light. His body became wrapped in the same light and he wrapped his arms around Ranaan. "Let us see how you fare through this!"

His body exploded.

Jerik knelt beside Jovanna's body and felt for a pulse. Nothing. Everyone was distracted with the battle between Cahenrair and Ranaan. He placed his hand on her forehead and whispered a few words. He would take her body back with him. They both disappeared, just in time to miss the elf destroy himself and Ranaan. The explosion sent blood and bone flying in all directions. The beast that had possessed Ranaan could feel his spirit fading. No, fading wasn't right. His soul was … breaking. He silently cursed the elf and his magic until his last moment of his conscious existence. The creature's soul dissipated into the wind.

"Courage is not about knowing what your purpose is, but pursuing it."

- Calderon

CHAPTER 25

Calderon sat on the edge of the bed, feeling a slight tremor here and there as the rocks from the war machines slammed into the walls. He felt out of place. He was not a wizard, and certainly no soldier, yet here he was, in the middle of an important battle. And somehow he had managed to lose the sphere.

"At least things can't get much worse," he muttered to himself. He stood to stretch his legs and walked over to the window. He couldn't see the battle from his view, but he could hear it. He had never seen battle, but he had read books written by people who had. He could imagine the screams, visualize the bloody and wounded. It was enough to make him gag. He could never bring himself to kill another man. He heard something then, a slight rustling perhaps, that drew him from his contemplation. He turned to find a man in his room.

The man was of average height, pretty close to Calderon's. He wore robes like a monk, but they were black instead of brown. A hood was drawn over his face and he stood silently. "Yes?" Calderon asked. There came no reply. "Can I help you?"

The man reached up with thin, pale hands and pulled his hood back. Calderon almost gasped aloud. The man was bald, with a thin line of gray hair along his chin. His eyes were green and seemed slightly clouded. Calderon almost thought the man might be blind. Or at least not far from it. The thing that made him almost gasp was the jagged scar that covered the man's neck.

"Can you speak?" Calderon asked, his hands instinctively covering his own neck. The man nodded. "I can speak," he said, his voice a whisper. "Though not very well. I have come to bring you information that you may find valuable." Calderon was confused. Information? For what? "Would you like to sit down? The room is more for sleeping though." The man shook his head. "I do not have time," he replied. "You have heard of Orlek?"

Calderon nodded. "I have heard the name, and a little about him. To be honest, I don't know that I believe the stories. They seem like folklore to me." The man stared at him, his gaze like burning coals. Calderon shifted uncomfortably. "Stories? They are not mere stories," the man replied, stepping closer toward the monk. "They are realities. There is nothing that has been uttered about Orlek that is not true. And he lives still, even now, and plots the end of mankind."

Calderon backed up a step at the man drew near. "Who are you?" Calderon asked. Fear was beginning to make it hard to talk. The man waved a hand dismissively. "My name means nothing to you. Let me tell you my story, and then you can decide what you believe. This," he pointed at the scar on his neck, "is from a crossbow accident when I was a child. A hunter in our village accidentally shot me. I lived, but I had lost my voice. I studied magic in hopes of finding a way to heal myself. Unfortunately, magic does not heal as I found out later. Only Aio can heal, and I did not turn to him. I suppose I was talented, as the mysterious Guardians approached me with an offer to join them."

"The Guardians? Who are they?" Calderon asked. The man grunted. "Have you lived in a monastery your whole life? Everyone knows about the Guardians."

"I *have* lived in a monastery most of my life."

The man laughed then. It sounded more like wheezing to Calderon. "The Guardians are men, and some who are not men, who work to keep the balance of the world in order. They are few, but they are powerful, chosen by the leader of the Guardians for their talents, whether magical or otherwise. They cease to exist to the world, but are always behind the scenes, ensuring the balance. I was chosen to replace one who had died. I thought that if anyone could heal me, it would surely be the Guardians. Yet not even they could fix my voice," he seemed saddened suddenly, as if remembering it clearly. "I was upset and began to despair that I would never speak again."

"You speak now," Calderon said, pointing out the obvious. The man nodded. "One day, when I was in the mountains, I was approached by Orlek. I knew who he was and knew that he would bring nothing but trouble. I almost summoned the other Guardians so that we could defeat him, but he made me an offer that has become my biggest regret. He offered to give me my voice back."

"I thought magic cannot heal?"

"It can't. What Orlek did was beyond magic. It was … " his voice trailed off and his eyes shifted back and forth, as if seeing something. "It was something entirely different. I had only to gather some bones for him and he would give me my voice. It seemed simple enough, but I did not realize whose bones I was gathering."

"Bones?"

"Dragon bones," the man said. Realization struck

Calderon suddenly. "You gathered the bones of the dragon for this Orlek?" The man nodded. "I did not know then what I was doing. I simply wanted to speak again. Once I saw what the bones were for, and saw the terrible destruction the creature caused, I regretted my actions every day. Orlek did give me my voice back, but it was not what I expected. I am here in front of you, and you can barely hear me."

It was true. Calderon found himself leaning toward the man to hear what he said. "Why are you telling me this?" The man suddenly seemed very old. "I seek to make amends for what I helped unleash. I have lived longer than any man, but my time grows near. I want to give you the knowledge that I have, that Orlek might be stopped. Forever this time."

"Why tell me? What can I do? I am no wizard." Calderon didn't like where this was going. "That is exactly why I have come to you. You do not crave power as wizards do. And when you traveled through the mountains, Orlek did not sense you."

"How did you know—" Calderon paused. He remembered the trip down the mountain, when he thought he saw someone from the corner of his eye only to find no one there. "You were there, on the mountain?" Calderon asked.

The man nodded. "I was there. I could feel the power of the old man that traveled with you, as well as the spirit of the other monk. But I could not sense you, and neither could Orlek. I bring you this because I believe you can reach Orlek without him knowing you are there. And you can do what no one else has been able to do."

"What is that?"

"You will kill Orlek."

That put Calderon on his heels. "I have not killed anyone. I cannot kill anyone. I do not believe in murder."

The man laughed again. "Do you believe in justice? Do you believe in doing what is right? Orlek seeks the destruction of mankind. Ever since his first defeat he has sought to annihilate man. If the death of one could save many, why would you not kill the one?"

Calderon couldn't argue with the man's logic. He did believe in justice. But he did not believe he was strong enough to carry it out. He could not be trusted with such an important task, especially not with his sleeping disorder. And then it dawned on him. His disorder had not reared its head since his watch at the Sly Mare. Was it possible that his disorder was gone? He was at a loss. He had struggled his entire life with falling asleep at the most inappropriate times, yet he hadn't had any issues since the inn.

"I am not a soldier," Calderon said. "I have no skills, no talents. This is not something you should entrust to me." The man nodded. "That is why I know you will succeed. Orlek will never see you coming."

Calderon sat in silence. He had no more argument in him. He could not deny that if Orlek could not sense him, he might really be able to get close enough to strike him down. But what if Orlek did sense him? What if Orlek killed him? Velkyn's words echoed in his mind: *Are you ready to make that sacrifice, if it comes? To give your life for others?*

He sighed resignedly. "What must I do?"

"The most stupid things are always the result of the most noble motives."

- Cygnus

CHAPTER 26

The force of the blast that destroyed the body of the prince shook the earth. Most of the men of the Talvaard army were flung to the ground. Donovan and the men on the wall grabbed onto whatever they could to keep from falling.

"What just happened?" Donovan yelled, his ears ringing from the blast. Cygnus didn't answer. The half blood wasn't sure himself. The army would have gone into complete chaos if not for the generals. Cygnus motioned Donovan to come near. "We must parlay," he said. "With the prince gone, the army is in the hands of the generals. We must convince them we are no threat."

Donovan agreed. "Take my bodyguards," Cygnus said, pointing at the two tattooed elves that stood close to him. I'll raise the flag." Donovan took the stairs down to the courtyard and waited at the gates. Cygnus had the flag raised and waited for the sign to be returned. It was.

The gates opened and Donovan headed out, escorted by the elves. By the time he reached the tent that had the flag flying, several of the generals had already gathered. He bowed when he reached them, giving the proper respect as protocol demanded. The generals bowed back. "It is our desire to see you leave in peace," Donovan said. "Palindrom is a city of peace, not of war. We take no issue with you, and ask that you hold the same toward us."

One of the generals, an old veteran, took the lead. "We didn't want to march in the first place," he said. Donovan sighed in relief. "Our men just want to go home. We agree that there is no qualms between yours and ours. We honestly don't know what happened to the king. It seems he lost his mind in the end." The general seemed bitter. A horn sounded out from the army, startling everyone in the tent. A messenger came stumbling in, sweaty and breathing hard.

"Calm yourself," the general said. "Get him some water." Someone handed the messenger a water skin. He drank deeply and paused to catch his breath. "We have enemies approaching," he gasped. "Orcs! Thousands of them! They cut off our supply lines in the mountains and are marching this way now!" His legs gave out and he collapsed. Several men lifted him up and carried him out of the tent. The general looked to Donovan, troubled.

"Orcs?" he asked aloud, looking to his fellows, then back to Donovan. "I haven't heard of Orcs in the mountains." Donovan shook his head. "I have heard a lot of things lately. It wouldn't hurt to be prepared. I'll report to Cygnus and get word back to you. We can use our magic to confirm the report." The general seemed pleased with that and dismissed the monk.

He ran back to the gate, the elves following him without question. Donovan could hear the generals roaring out orders behind him. It seemed one battle had ended, only for another to begin. Cygnus was waiting for him in the courtyard. "They are leaving?" he asked Donovan.

"Not quite. We need someone to use the crystals. A man reported an army of Orcs marching from the mountains." Elves rarely ever showed emotion, and Cygnus, though he was a half blood, was no exception. So it surprised Donovan to see the color drain from his face. "Orlek makes his move," Cygnus said ominously. "So it is here, before the walls of Palindrom, that the fate of our world will be decided. Come, we must prepare." Cygnus turned and left. Donovan looked to some of the guards standing nearby. "Get someone to use the crystals, will you?" One of them nodded and left.

Donovan followed Cygnus back onto the walls. "The Talvaard army is between us and whatever is coming. What is there to prepare for?" Donovan asked, looking to Cygnus. The half blood stared out at the valley. "They cannot stop what is coming. The Orcs will overrun them and hit our walls with ease. Orlek is leading them, and he cannot be stopped. We can fight and hope to dwindle their numbers, or we can run. But I see no victory in either option."

Donovan started to respond but stopped short when he noticed Calderon making his way through the courtyard. The young monk made his way up the stairs to stand beside Donovan. "It isn't safe out here. You should go back inside."

Calderon shook his head. "There is something I must do. But I will need help."

Calderon stood at the entrance to the cave. They had flown him on the winds of magic to the mountains. It was the only way to get there quickly and safely. He only hoped the magic didn't give him away. The man had told him there were symbols etched into the walls that would help him find his way into the main chamber of the cave. He stared into the darkness. Taking a deep breath, he plunged into the darkness. The air was cooler inside the cave, an immediate difference from the outside. The robed man had warned him not to light a torch.

That was severely going to hinder him, but there was no way around it. Calderon put his hands on the walls and felt along the cool stone for the symbols. After traveling a few feet, he found the first symbol. The first step toward the chamber, the last step to his destiny.

Cygnus and Donovan watched the battle unfold in the valley below. The Orcs had come storming into the valley, hacking and slashing at the Talvaard army. The soldiers were holding their own, but they were steadily being pressed back. "Their line isn't going to hold," Cygnus remarked. "We may have to open the gates and let them into the city. What do you think?" he turned to Donovan.

"Do we have enough room? There are many men."

Cygnus nodded. "There are many, but a lot have fallen, and countless more will fall before it is over, I fear. We can only hope Calderon knows what he is doing." The Talvaard line of defense began to crumble. Chaos erupted and a retreat had been signaled. "Open the gates!" Cygnus yelled.

The guards obeyed and opened the massive gates. The soldiers began to run into the city. "What do we do now?" Donovan asked.

"We wait."

- Donovan

CHAPTER 27

The air smelled of mold. A few times, his hand had touched something wet and he would quickly jerk his hand away. Calderon was beginning to think he was lost within the tunnels of the cave. He didn't know which way went where, and he hadn't felt a symbol in any of the walls recently. He was about to turn around when he turned a corner and felt a horrible sensation in his stomach that made the hairs on his arm raise.

He could see nothing. He didn't hear anything either. Yet the feeling was there, as if something lurked around him, waiting to devour him. He breathed as quietly as he could and listened. Still nothing.

He slowly took a step. And another. His hand felt the wall curve away from him, out of his reach. He hoped he wasn't about to step off into a deep hole. He took a few more steps. And then he heard it. At first, he thought it was the echo from his breathing. But Calderon wasn't rasping. The sound could be coming from anywhere in the chamber, he realized. And he was blind in the darkness. How would he see what it was, and if it was Orlek, how would he see him to attack him?

A voice froze him in his tracks. "I hear you scurrying, rat. Come to me and let me feast on your flesh." The voice was weak. Calderon thought the voice was speaking to him, but discovered that thankfully it was not. The voice was talking to what it thought was a rat moving about the cave.

Could the weak voice be Orlek, the magic-wielding Orc? Judging by the voice, Calderon figured him to be weak and near death. How could something so weak pose such a threat to the people? He shrugged his doubts away. He had seen the army of Orcs marching into the valley. He steeled his nerves and forced himself in the direction he thought the voice came from.

He nearly tripped. He yelled at himself in his mind, listening. He could hear something shuffling around, coming nearer. His hands began to shake. Calderon didn't know what to do. He didn't want to risk injuring himself, but what if Orlek realized he wasn't a rat? He forced himself to calm down. Pulling the dagger that the robed man had given him out from his belt, he clenched the hilt tightly in his hand.

He heard the voice muttering something unintelligible. There was no other way around it. Calderon pulled out a flat stone that Cygnus had given him. The man told him not to use any light, but he couldn't see a blasted thing. He tossed the stone into the air and it lit up, momentarily blinding him. He heard a screech and gained his vision back enough in time to see something flying toward him. They crashed to the ground in a heap, and something was clawing at Calderon. The blade fell from his hand and he lashed out with his fists, pummeling with all his might.

He managed to push the thing away and scrambled to his feet. He saw the glint of metal in the dim light and quickly retrieved the blade. Whatever had attacked him was hiding in the corner, where the light didn't reach. Calderon cautiously made his way toward the shadows. The creature came hobbling out toward him. If this was Orlek, the creature was far from intimidating. It was thin and skinny. Its skin was reddish-brown and hung loosely from its frame. Scraggly long black hair covered its head. Two large teeth jutted up from its bottom jaw, protruding from its lips.

The creature was certainly ugly, but nothing frightening. Calderon held the blade out in front of him in an attempt to keep the thing at bay. It seemed to work as the creature paused, looking at the blade intently. "Where did you get that?" the creature rasped.

"From one you drew into your dark scheme," Calderon answered, using the phrase the robed man had told him. The creature laughed, a guttural, raucous noise. "I used him as I have used so many others," Orlek said. "I told that fool the magic was unpredictable at best. It was never meant for humans. Why have you come here?"

Calderon fought the feeling of despair. It was thick, palpable. "I have come to kill you," he said. Orlek laughed again. "I have died many times. You may kill me, and you may not. Though if you do, what good will it do? I will merely rise from the grave once again."

Calderon shook his head. "Not this time." He lunged forward, attempting to stab Orlek in the chest. Orlek was weak and his body was deteriorating, but he was not slow. The orc leaped out of the way, turned around, and slugged the monk in the shoulder. Calderon tumbled to the ground under the forceful blow, scraping his hands and knees on the rocky floor of the cave.

Orlek needed a new body. What kind of havoc could he create if he took the body of a man? The thought repulsed him. Maybe he would just kill the human and eat him. He shambled over to the man.

Calderon slashed Orlek across his foot. The orc cried out in pain but did not flee. Calderon got to his knees and rammed his shoulder into the creature, forcing Orlek to trip and fall backwards. Calderon was on him quickly, straddling the orc. Orlek moved his arms frantically, trying to push the man off of him. His strength was failing him.

Calderon forced his left arm under Orlek's arms and pushed them up, leaning forward and using his weight to hold them up. His brought his right hand in, still holding the dagger, and plunged the blade into the orc's chest. Orlek howled in anguish, and Calderon withdrew the blade and stabbed again and again. A rush of anger and emotions swirled within the young monk. Anger at this creature for causing so much evil, anger that he had lost his friend Velkyn to madness, anger at the men who raped Velkyn's woman and stole their belongings.

He stabbed Orlek again and again, losing himself in his anger. Orlek had long since stopped moving, his blood a massive pool around his body. By the time Calderon came to his senses, he had stabbed the orc more than a dozen times. He sat atop the dead orc, his breath coming in heaving gasps. When he had caught his breath, he pulled himself off Orlek's body and grabbed the dagger. There was one thing the man had told him was of extreme importance, otherwise Orlek could bring himself back to life. Calderon grabbed hold of the orc's hand and pressed the blade into the armpit, severing the arm. He began removing Orlek's limbs, one by one.

He had almost finished when the light of the magical stone began to sputter and crackle. Calderon looked at the stone, still hovering in the air. The light would start to dim and then flare up briefly dimming once again.

Calderon realized too late. That was no ordinary light. Calderon flung the limbs in different directions, grabbed Orlek's head by the hair, and ran toward the tunnel that brought him into the chamber. The light dimmed, then faded altogether. And then it exploded. Calderon crashed to the ground, smashing his head onto the rocks of the cave floor. Darkness, silent and comforting, took him.

Donovan watched the soldiers of Talvaard. They had snuck out of the back gate of the city and split into two groups, each group heading around the city and toward the front. They were going to try and route the orc army that had gathered at the front of the city. "They are outnumbered," Donovan remarked to Cygnus. "It was not my decision," the half blood said. "The generals decided it amongst themselves."

Donovan knew that. He just felt obligated to say something to try and stop them. It was a suicide mission. "Do you think Calderon will succeed?" he said aloud, not really asking anyone.

Cygnus didn't say anything. He hadn't taken his gaze off the mountains for the last twenty minutes. "They seem to be waiting," Donovan said. Cygnus nodded. "They await the right opportunity. Probably nightfall," the half blood answered. A rumbling sound like that of thunder filled the air. All eyes, including the orcs', went to the sky. The Vish mountain, it appeared, had exploded. Dust and debris filled the air and tremors shook the ground.

"Orlek is dead," Cygnus said incredulously. "He did it. Calderon slew Orlek!" Donovan was just as surprised. He noticed the Talvaard soldiers had taken the advantage of the disturbance to launch their attack against the orcs.

The creatures might have outnumbered them, but they didn't stand a chance. The route was working and the orcs began to scatter. "The four winds take them," Donovan cursed. He looked back to the mountain. "What of Calderon? Why did the mountain explode? Where is he?" his tone was frantic.

Cygnus laid his hand on Donovan's shoulder. "It is unlikely we will see him again. Take comfort in his sacrifice, my friend. Because of him, many will live." Donovan burst into tears. His eyes blurred. He could barely see the orcs fleeing the field in all directions. "It's over," he vaguely heard Cygnus say. "It's finally over."

Donovan was going to miss the young monk. He had really grown fond of him. He slumped down with his back against the wall. "What now?" he asked, his tone pleading. Cygnus knelt beside him. "Now?" The half blood paused and looked across the city. "Now, we work toward peace."

"Order is not pressure which is imposed on society from without, but an equilibrium which is set up from within."

- Jerik

EPILOGUE

Jovanna opened her eyes. Her body was throbbing with pain and she couldn't see from her left eye. She attempted to sit up but the pain was too much. She slumped back down. She lifted her left hand, excruciating pain lancing through the limb. Her skin was splotched black and red. It was slimy looking and appeared to be covered in some kind of salve. She reached over to feel it with her right hand.

"Don't touch it."

The voice startled her. She looked the other way and saw an old man standing there. "It's my arm. I'll touch it if I want." The old man smiled and shrugged. "I'm only trying to help."

He seemed familiar to her for some reason. "Where am I?" Jovanna asked. The old man drew near to her. "You are safe. Do you remember what happened?" She stared at him with her good eye. She tried to remember, but all she got was a swirling mass of fog in her brain. "I rescued you from a battlefield," he said.

A battlefield ... she tried to remember. "There was

an army," she said softly, trying to piece the fragments of memory together. "A city." It all came back to her. Her eyes widened. "The dragon in the prince! I had the sphere …" she went quiet, looking at the man distrustfully.

He nodded knowingly. "I know. I was there. Like I said, I rescued you from the battle. My name is Jerik. And I know you are Jovanna. I have heard many things about you and your unique gift. Perhaps when you feel better we can talk more about why you are here."

Jovanna rolled onto her side to better see the man. "Jerik," she whispered. She had seen him before. In the forest, talking with another man. "I saw you," she said. "In the woods with another …" she glanced about the room. Jerik smiled. "Yes. You are coming back better than I expected."

"Back? From where? Was I dead?" she asked, confused.

"Nearly," he answered. "Your soul was on the fringes of your body. I managed to coax your soul to come back."

"Why would you help me? No one has ever helped me," she said pitifully, a single tear sliding down her cheek.

"We will talk more about this when you are feeling better," he bade gently. "Get some rest, Jovanna. And welcome," he added. He turned to leave the room.

"Welcome to what?" she called out.

"To the Guardians," he answered. Then he turned and left.

ABOUT THE AUTHOR

Richard Fierce lives in Georgia with his wife and three step-daughters. He is the author of seven novels including Dragonsphere. Feel free to contact the author.

Email: Richard.Fierce@yahoo.com